CAPONE ISLAND

Murder Ink Press
Austin * New York * Boca Raton

ALSO BY STEPHEN G. YANOFF

FICTION:

The Graceland Gang

The Pirate Path

Devil's Cove

Ransom on the Rhone

A Run for the Money

NONFICTION:

The Second Mourning

Turbulent Times

Gone Before Glory

For more information, please visit:
www.stephengyanoff.com

CAPONE ISLAND

STEPHEN G. YANOFF

authorHOUSE®

AuthorHouse™
1663 Liberty Drive
Bloomington, IN 47403
www.authorhouse.com
Phone: 1 (800) 839-8640

Published by AuthorHouse 04/15/2019

ISBN: 978-1-7283-0829-6 (sc)
ISBN: 978-1-7283-0827-2 (hc)
ISBN: 978-1-7283-0828-9 (e)

Library of Congress Control Number: 2019904356

Print information available on the last page.

This book is printed on acid-free paper.

FOR

My Sweet Aunts,

Gladys Deatrick
and
Thelma Wilson

ABOUT THE FRONT COVER

The selection of this image was based upon a lovely watercolor painting by Elizabeth Bell Taylor, a prominent artist who lives in Hickory, North Carolina — in the foothills of the magnificent Blue Ridge Mountains.

Ms. Taylor is known for her bold and vibrant colors, her unique contrasts and textures, and her subjects... birds, flowers, and sunset landscapes.

Readers may view and/or purchase her artwork at the following website: lil-taylor.pixels.com

ACKNOWLEDGEMENTS

First and foremost, I would like to thank my dear mother, Hazel Yanoff, for allowing me to spend so much time in her beautiful Florida mansion — directly across the street from Capone Island. As they say, location is everything!

I would also like to thank my wonderful family for their continued love and support... My wife, Patty, my daughters, Rachel and Rebecca, their husbands, Adam and Peter, and my adorable grandchildren, Goldie and Fiona.

The founding members of my Austin fan club also deserve to be mentioned... Barbara and Max Talbott, Susan Marquess, and Helena and Lee Bomblatus.

I would also like to acknowledge the members of my Lakeway and Steiner Ranch fan clubs... Loyd and Shelley Smith, Sheila Niles, Gloria Crosthwait, Betsy Frost, Pat Hime, and Jimmy Deatrick.

I would also like to thank Glenn Yanoff for his invaluable insurance expertise.

Lest we forget, every good book has a good editor, and I had one of the best... Sarah M. Weber.

In addition, I would like to send a big hug and kiss to Elizabeth Bell Taylor and Gina Sigmon, two classy Carolinians.

Finally, in remembrance of my beloved Baker, this man's best friend.

CHAPTER ONE

When Fidel Castro died, the Cuban government cremated his body, which some Cubans believed was a foolish waste of money, considering his final destination. Ricardo Paz, one of Castro's bodyguards, felt this way, but he was smart enough to keep it to himself. Most of the time. One evening, after drinking a bottle of Havana Club rum, he made the mistake of sharing his true feelings with a voluptuous member of the *Policia Nacional Revolucionaria*. Unfortunately for Paz, the young lady was a firm believer in Article 64 of the Cuban Constitution, which clearly states that "Defense of the socialist motherland is every Cuban's greatest honor and highest duty."

Before Poor Richard could whistle *La Bayamesa*, he found himself under interrogation in Valle Grande prison, twenty-two miles south of the capital. The interrogator, a disagreeable fellow from the Department of the Interior, advised Comrade Paz to reconsider his imperialist opinion and suggested that he do so upon his arrival in *Norteamérica*.

Paz was tempted to lodge a protest, but then he remembered the old axiom, that a person could say anything he wanted in Cuba -- once. He also remembered *el paredón*, the wall, where thousands of "troublemakers" had faced the firing squad. A one-way ticket to Miami sealed the deal, and two weeks after Castro's ashes were buried in Santiago, Ricardo Paz became a proud, undocumented alien.

Three months later, he was caught in an INS raid, but then a very strange thing happened. Instead of detaining him indefinitely, ICE agents ushered him through the immigrant visa process and then hauled his butt before an immigration judge. The judge was pleasant and polite, and lo and behold, an affidavit of support was produced, signed by an anonymous sponsor.

Even stranger, Paz was promised that a green card would soon be on its way.

What a way to run a country, Paz thought. *They made it so easy to enter.*

On second thought, it was *too* easy.

Gringos were not known for their hospitality. So why the welcome mat?

After further consideration, Paz concluded that he was about to be recruited by the CIA. There was no other explanation. The cloak-and-dagger boys were going to pump him for information, hoping that he would spill the *frijoles* about the dearly departed dictator. A bodyguard could tell them plenty. He might even know where the bodies were buried, so to speak.

If this was the case, the *Yanquis* were in for a shock. Had the poor bastards done their homework, they would have discovered that their new recruit had been a bodyguard for less than a month, and during that time he was more of a nurse than a guard. Prior to babysitting *el presidente*, Paz had worked as a night watchman in a dormant sugar refinery in Camilo Cienfuegos, a small town on Cuba's northern coast. Before the revolution, the town was named Hershey in honor of the chocolate baron who owned and operated the refinery –– the most productive factory in the country, if not in all of Latin America.

In 1959, the refinery was nationalized, courtesy of the Castro brothers, renamed Camilo Cienfuegos –– after one of Fidel's commanders –– and placed under the control of socialist bureaucrats. The shift in ownership, along with the United State's embargo and the collapse of the Soviet Union, led to a shutdown and the end of the good life.

By coincidence, Fidel Castro's father, Angel Castro y Argiz, had become wealthy by growing sugarcane in Oriente Province, so the dictator had a warm spot in his heart for anybody connected to its production. Paz fell into that category, which is why he was brought to Havana and given an opportunity to better himself.

In a perfect world, Paz thought, sitting in the judge's chamber, he would tell the CIA what he knew and they would reward him with citizenship. Maybe that was the plan. Maybe, if he played his cards right, they would take care of him. A tiny smile appeared on his face. *Ay, caramba! This could be my ticket out of el barrio.*

A minute later, the door opened, and Paz turned around to see who was there. A man stood in the doorway, fanning himself with a manila folder and studying him with an appraising look. He was a large, heavily built man, well-dressed and reeking of cologne. A slick strand of black hair hung over his right ear and curled around the collar of a monogrammed shirt. He stepped inside, closed the door, and walked across the room to the judge's desk. He stood there for a few seconds before opening the folder and reading to himself. "My name is Nick Russo," he said matter-of-factly, without looking up. "I'm your sponsor. The guy that saved you from detention." He sighed deeply and turned his wrist a little so he could see his Rolex watch. Nine on the nose. "You speak English, right?"

Paz sat motionless for a moment, then said, "I speak four languages."

Russo dismissed this with a wave of his hand. "You're in America. Habla inglés."

Paz smiled mischievously. *"No problema."*

Russo slid the folder across the desk to him. As he turned over the photographs it contained, he recited from his notes. "Ricardo Paz. Former bodyguard. Thirty-two years old. Five foot seven, one hundred and fifty pounds. Brown hair. Brown eyes. No scars, no tattoos." He gave Paz a long and piercing look. A smile tickled the corners of his mouth, and then he closed the folder. "Did I miss anything?"

Paz thought of several sarcastic replies, but just said, "I've got a mole on my back."

Russo, not ruffled in the slightest, said, "Moles can be dangerous. You need to watch them closely. Remove the ones that cause problems." He smiled without a hint of humor. "I've had a few on my hands. I got rid of them right away."

Paz maintained a show of indifference, but inside he was worried, unable to shake the notion that somehow Russo was referring to him. "I'll try to remember that."

Russo stared at him, amusement in his wide, somewhat protuberant eyes. "So you got kicked out of Cuba, huh?"

Paz went silent while he considered this. "More or less," he said finally. "I was ready to leave."

"Yeah, I bet you were. Why'd you get the boot?"

"I pissed somebody off."

"Who?"

"Some *bastardo* from the government."

"What happened?"

"I said the wrong thing about the wrong person."

"Friggin' commies. They have no sense of humor." After fishing out a cigarette and lighting it, Russo exhaled a cloud of smoke and said, "Their loss is our gain. You know what I mean?"

"Not exactly."

"I'm your new patron. You're gonna work for me. I want you to be part of our agency. We could use a guy like you." He folded his arms across his chest and nodded. "You've got the right stuff."

"The right stuff for what?"

"A successful career."

"You think so?"

"I know so. I can spot a good recruit a mile away, and you're one of the best I've seen in a long time." A boyish grin crept across his face. "You can be a heavy hitter. All you need is some training."

"How much training?"

"Six months to a year. If you're a fast learner, you'll be handling your own contracts in three months."

"That soon?"

"Sure. In this business, the sky's the limit. If you target the right people you'll make a killing."

For a brief moment Russo and Paz locked eyes. It was Paz who looked away. "You make it sound so... easy."

"Nobody said it would be easy. You'll have to put in some long hours and do some studying. There's also a test at the end, but we can provide a tutor. Once you pass the test, you'll be on your way. The agency will supply most of your leads, but you can freelance on your own time." He tapped the cigarette gently on the side of an ashtray and then said very slowly, "I know it's a big commitment, but this is a once-in-a-lifetime opportunity."

For a moment Paz said nothing, just stroked his chin. Finally, a thin smile crossed his face, as if he found irony in Russo's statement. "What choice do I have?"

Russo's voice became tense, a mixture of anger and incredulity. "Hey, nobody's gonna force you to do anything you don't want to do. There are plenty of guys who would give their right arms for this opportunity. If you want to go back to the detention center, just say the word. You can file for asylum and spend the next few years waiting for a hearing." He shook his head and made a sympathetic face. "Your call, *amigo*."

Paz stared coldly at him, a sudden anger narrowing his eyes. And then his expression cleared. He looked at Russo and then at the floor. "You're right," he said matter-of-factly. "I'm being stupid. I should be grateful." He sat back. "When do we start?"

"Did you eat breakfast?"

"No."

"Me neither. I could use a cup of coffee." He jammed the cigarette into the ashtray. "Why don't we grab a bite?"

Paz gave him a cautious look. "Are you sure we can leave?"

"Yeah, I'm sure." He placed a hand on Paz's shoulder and squeezed lightly. "I went through a lot of trouble to make this right, but now you're a free man. You can go wherever you want."

"Sweet."

Russo smiled, showing most of his smoke-stained teeth. "I'll show you sweet. I know a place in West Miami that makes the best churros in Florida." He gestured toward the door. "Let's take a ride."

The distance between the Miami Immigration Court and La Palma Cuban Cafeteria was less than ten miles, but during peak tourism season -- November to April -- the trip often took over an hour. Today was no exception. Still, it was not an uneventful ride. When they turned onto State Road 836, Russo asked Paz to reach into the glovebox and find his sunglasses. Paz was happy to oblige, but when he opened the glovebox an automatic pistol fell onto his lap.

Paz muttered something, shifted position, and was still again. There was sweat standing out in beads on his forehead. *"Jesucristo,"* he whispered. "You expecting trouble?"

Russo looked at him wide-eyed, mildly startled. "Be careful with that thing. It's cocked locked and ready to rock."

Paz took a closer look at the weapon. "Nice *pistola*."

".45 Colt Automatic."

"Powerful gun."

Russo lit a cigarette, then shook the match out and looked at his passenger through the haze of drifting white smoke. "What did you carry in Cuba?"

"A Makarov. 9mm."

"Never heard of that one."

After gently placing the Colt in the glovebox, Paz told him that the Makarov was a Russian-made pistol, the standard sidearm of the Soviet Union's military and police from 1951 to 1991. After being replaced by the Yarygin pistol in 2003, functioning Makarovs were sent to Cuba, where they were still in use. "We get a lot of Russian hand-me-downs. I'd much rather have a Colt."

Russo leaned over, and with a suave smile said, "Your wish is my command."

"Huh?"

"The gun is yours."

"Qué?"

"A gift from me to you."

"Seriously?"

"Yeah, you can have it. I'll buy another one. Just make sure you keep it out of sight for a while. You won't be able to get a concealed weapon permit until you become a permanent resident alien or a citizen."

Paz shook his head as if trying to free a jumbled thought. "*Gracias, amigo.* You're very kind. I don't know what to say."

"Well, whatever you come up with, say it in English. You need to practice your language skills, and you need to lose that Ricky Ricardo accent as soon as possible." He glanced over at Paz briefly and cracked a small smile. "You catch my drift?"

Paz nodded, but he was actually thinking about his new toy. Back in Cuba, guns were strictly controlled, and if you were caught with one in your possession –– and you were not on active military duty, a policeman, or a member of the secret service –– you would go to prison for a very long time. The regime frowned upon private gun ownership, and there was no such thing as a simple hunting license or a gun collector.

On the other hand, gun crimes were virtually nonexistent in Cuba, and the murder rates well below those of most Latin America countries.

Paz had mixed feelings about gun control, but now that he was in Florida, he had nothing to worry about. The state currently had over 1.3 million concealed weapon permit holders –– nearly double that of the second state, which was Pennsylvania. He was amused by the fact that Florida had ten times more permit holders than Cuba had soldiers. No wonder his old employer was always so nervous.

Lost in thought, Paz didn't seem to notice –– or maybe he just didn't care –– that they were stuck in a traffic jam, surrounded by some of the world's most impatient drivers. Twenty minutes later, they turned onto SW 8th Street and pulled into the parking lot of

La Palma Cafeteria. Before they got out, Russo checked himself in the rearview mirror, running a hand through his slick, black hair.

"Today's your lucky day," Russo said cheerfully. "I've got a little surprise for you."

Another one? Paz thought. He was still dealing with the gun. He rubbed one hand across his forehead as if he were tired, or getting a headache. "What's up?"

"You're about to meet Morella Perez."

"Who's that?"

"The hottest waitress in Miami-Dade County."

"I don't understand."

"How'd you like to take her out?"

Paz could hardly believe his ears. Did "take her out" mean date her or kill her? He was afraid to ask. He looked out the window across the parking lot and the restaurant beyond. *I'm not ready for either*, he thought, hiding a frown. Wisely, he swallowed his words without speaking them. He took a long, slow breath and released it. "I think we're moving too fast."

There was a half-second pause, then Russo replied, "Don't underestimate yourself. You're a born ladykiller."

CHAPTER TWO

In his darker moments, much more frequent of late, Paz often found himself wondering why he had gotten kicked out of Cuba, what he'd done to deserve such a harsh punishment. After all, he never said that Castro was going to hell, only that he might –– that there was a distinct possibility. The announcers on Radio Marti had said the same thing for years. They used to say that Castro would go to hell when he died, but at least all his friends would be there, too. He assumed they were joking, and so was he.

One foolish comment and out he went, and now he was being recruited by the CIA! To kill a damn waitress! Life was not fair. Not fair at all.

When Paz saw Morella Perez, his heart did a little flip in his chest, and for him it was love at first sight. Not so much for her. She stood over their table, crossed her arms, and gave him a flat look. *"Que bola contigo?"*

"Nada," Paz said. *"No hay problema."*

"Why are you staring at me?"

Paz opened his mouth, then closed it again, opting to keep it simple. "Sorry."

She looked at Russo. "What's wrong with your friend?"

Russo grinned. "I think he's in love."

"Your friend have a name?"

"Ricardo."

"Why's he dressed like Tony Montana?"

"He just got off the boat."

"Does he speak English?"

"He's getting there."

"Let me know when he arrives."

Russo nudged Paz with his knee. "Say hello to Morella."

Heart racing, Paz said, "It's a pleasure to meet you."

She stared down at him, expressionless. "The pleasure's all yours."

Paz frowned, unsure how to take that. An uncomfortable silence fell between them. It was broken a few seconds later by the sound of rattling dishes. Another waitress walked by them, carrying a tray of coffee and pastries. Russo displayed the faintest trace of a smile and then placed his order -- two cups of coffee and a plate of churros. Chocolate sauce on the side.

When Perez walked away, Russo leaned in close and said, "How'd you like to get your hands on that papaya?"

Paz hesitated, at a loss for how to respond. He wondered if Russo knew that in Cuba the word papaya was slang for vagina. He made a show of deliberation, then said, "She's a very attractive woman."

Russo swiveled around in his chair, making a small, squeaking sound, and looked around the restaurant. Paz heard him mutter an obscenity under his breath, and he suspected it was aimed at him. *"Attractive?"* Russo whispered. "She's a total piece of ass. So what do you think? Would you like to take her out?"

Paz turned his head this way and that, trying to figure out what Russo meant by "take her out." He could see that Russo was serious and waiting for an answer. Jesus, the crazy bastard had a iron grin on his face, not a look of amusement or pleasure, but of something ominous. "Son of a bitch," he murmured. "I'm just not ready."

Russo frowned, confused. "You're not ready?"

"Not even close."

"Are you gay or something?"

"Huh?"

"What are you afraid of?"

Paz slumped in his chair. Time to confess. "I was just a bodyguard. I never fired my gun. I've never killed anyone. How can you expect me to do such a thing?"

Russo shot him a sharp look, a blend of confusion and irritation. "What the hell are you talking about?"

"Taking her out. I can't do it."

"Are you on drugs?"

"Look, I know what you're asking, but I can't do it. I just can't. I'm sorry." He forced himself to take a deep breath, and then another. The blood had drained from his face, and for a moment he looked like he was going to faint. "I'm not a murderer."

"No, just a babbling idiot. You better not be high." Russo fixed him with a flat disgusted look. "If you're wired, you're fired."

Paz laughed derisively. "Why don't we stop playing games? I know why you recruited me and what you want me to do, but

I'm no ladykiller. You'll have to find somebody else." He shifted uneasily in his chair. "There must be other jobs at the agency. Maybe I could be trained as a saboteur."

Russo gave him a withering look. "You're off to a good start. You're about to sabotage your whole career." He jerked upright in his chair and slammed his big fist down on the table. Paz almost jumped out of his chair. "Don't jerk me around, asshole. I won't put up with it. What the fuck do you think is going on here?"

Paz scanned the restaurant for several seconds before answering. When he looked back at Russo, he sighed. "I think I'm being recruited by the CIA."

"*The CIA?* You think I work for the Central Intelligence Agency?" He shook his head, smiling, as if Paz had said something funny. "Are you out of your mind? I don't work for nobody but me. Never have, never will."

Paz smiled an indulgent smile. "How did I get out of detention? How did I get a visa hearing? How did I get a friendly judge? You own a magic wand or something?"

"Jesus Christ," Russo growled. "If you had a brain you'd be dangerous. I paid for your TLC. I took care of the jailer, the judge, and a couple of clowns from INS. I bought your freedom. *Comprende?*"

Paz scrunched his face in concentration for a second. "You said that I was a good recruit and that you would train me. You also gave me a gun. You even asked me to take out a woman." He scratched his jaw with a spoon. "What was I supposed to think?"

"That's your problem," Russo said harshly. "You think too much."

Paz slumped back in his chair, leaning his head against the back and swiveling from side to side. He breathed deeply and felt a thick knot in his stomach. "When you mentioned the agency, I thought..."

With a wave of his hand, Russo cut him off. "Hold that thought." Their waitress placed two cups of steaming hot coffee on the table and said she'd be back with the churros. After she left, Russo said, "You were saying?"

"You kept talking about the agency."

"I never mentioned the CIA."

"No, but you told me that you were an agent."

"Idiot," Russo said, through gritted teeth. "I'm a realtor. I own a goddamn real estate agency."

In a fraction of a second everything changed. Paz was quiet a long moment, not sure how to respond. Frowning deeply, he said, "You're a real estate agent?"

"Sorry to disappoint you."

Paz straightened up, and his face abruptly drained of all color. "So the contracts you mentioned..."

"Residential properties."

"*Ay, Dios mio*. I don't know what to say."

"You're a piece of work, my friend."

"I feel so foolish."

Russo glanced down for a moment, shifting his hard gaze away from Paz and placing the palms of his big hands flat against the top of the table. "Well, what we've got here is a failure to communicate."

"All my fault."

"Don't worry, *amigo*. Your secret's safe with me. Nobody would believe this shit anyway. I can hardly believe it myself." His mouth grinned, but his eyes didn't. "Why the long face?"

"I hate going back."

"Back where?"

"Where you found me," Paz said, rubbing the back of his neck, the muscles tight with tension. "The thought makes me sick."

"Who said anything about going back?"

"No detention center?"

"Hey, you made a mistake. So what? Nobody's perfect. I say we let bygones be bygones. What do you think?"

"I think you're right," Paz blurted out. "I think you're a good man. I think America is the land of opportunity."

"There you go again," Russo said. "Too much thinking."

"Mind if I ask you something?"

"Fire away."

"Why are you so willing to forgive and forget?"

Russo told him it was a good question, and naturally, he had a good answer. Russo's firm, Sun Coast Realty, was a player in Miami-Dade County, but they were anxious to expand to Broward and Palm Beach counties. There were almost two million people in Broward County and over a million more in Palm Beach County. Twenty to twenty-five percent of those people were Hispanic, and in order to reach them, the firm needed more Spanish-speaking employees.

The Florida Constitution stated that "English is the official language of the State of Florida," but in reality, twenty percent of the population still spoke Spanish.

"I'm counting on you to improve our sales," Russo said. "You can't yell Bingo if you don't know the lingo."

Paz wasn't sure what that meant, but he reacted positively. "I won't let you down."

"I hope not."

A moment later, their waitress returned with a plate of churros and a bowl of chocolate sauce. She raised her index finger and touched the side of her jaw, as if demonstrating the act of thinking. She said, "So, let's see, would this be breakfast, brunch, or lunch?"

Paz looked up and studied her again, a smile edging across his face. Morella Perez was a striking young woman, tall with olive skin, gleaming black hair that was cut short, full red lips, and dark brown eyes beneath long black lashes. She dressed comfortably, as befitted her position, and showed just enough cleavage to arouse her customers. Paz studied her eyes, hoping to read them and be able to tell if she was interested in him. Unfortunately, there was nothing to read. No hint of anything.

Perez stared hard at Paz, then said, "Why don't you take a photograph?"

"Excuse me?"

"You're staring again."

"I'm sorry."

"Well, stop it. You're creeping me out."

"I was just admiring your... earrings."

"My *earrings?* Jesus, that's lame."

Paz gave a small, defeated laugh. "I didn't mean to offend you."

Perez snatched up her ringing cell phone, listened, mumbled something in Spanish, and listened some more. She turned off the phone and glanced over at Russo. "I have to run."

"What's wrong?"

"My kid is sick. Stomach virus. I have to pick her up at school."

Russo nodded glumly. "See you next time." When she was out of sight, he nudged the plate away from him. In a low, annoyed voice, he said, "I hope she washed her hands."

Paz ignored the comment. "She hates me."

"What?"

"Morella. She hates my guts."

Russo dismissed his concern with a wave of his hand. "You don't understand American chicks. She's just playing hard to get. A couple of months from now you'll be banging her brains out." He smiled, but there was no warmth in it. "I guarantee it."

CHAPTER THREE

In early May, Ricardo Paz became an American citizen, and shortly thereafter he obtained three valuable documents: a Florida driver's license, a Florida real estate license, and a Florida gun permit. He also managed to file his first insurance claim, and it was a real beauty. Russo had given him a congratulatory gift, a box of Cohiba Behike cigars from Cuba, valued at twenty thousand dollars. Russo also gave him some friendly advice, suggesting that it would be wise to insure the cigars in case they were damaged or destroyed. A local agent of the Anchor Insurance Company furnished a quote and bound coverage, and sure enough, there was a loss.

A total loss.

Twenty thousand smackeroos.

Due to the unusual circumstances of the loss, the claim ended up on the desk of Irene Kaminski, the president of the insurance company. Kaminski was a hard-nosed executive who did not suffer fools -- or frivolous claims -- gladly. Whenever she encountered one or the other, she'd release her frustration by breaking a few wooden boards with her hands or feet. Such were the advantages of having a large corner office and a black belt in Tae Kwon Do.

Three boards were the norm, but every once in a while a "five board claim" would rear its ugly head, and on those occasions, Kaminski would turn to her lead investigator. The man who held that position was Adam Gold, a world-weary claims expert who was about to find out that he had not yet heard or seen it all.

Not by a long shot.

When Gold walked into Kaminski's office and spotted the broken boards, he knew it was going to be a long day. A very long day. He tiptoed through the rubble and took a seat, pretending not to notice the mess. An awkward moment of silence ensued. Finally, he said, "You wanted to see me?"

Kaminski spoke in a low, defeated voice. "I'm not having a good day."

"Sorry to hear that."

"In fact, I'm having a lousy day."

Gold smiled humorlessly. "So it seems. Five boards?"

"I've lost count."

"What can I do to help?"

"You can give me your honest opinion." She leaned over her desk, resting her forearms on a manila folder. "On a scale of one to ten, one being the worst and ten being the best, how would you rate our underwriting department?"

Gold hesitated, but only for a moment. He began by reminding her that the Anchor Insurance Company had an A+ rating, which represented an independent opinion of the insurer's financial strength and ability to meet its policy obligations. He went on to say that there were almost three thousand property and casualty companies in the United States, but only a small portion of them were A+ rated. In Gold's view, that kind of success could only be obtained through sound underwriting.

Kaminski stared at him for thirty seconds without speaking. Finally, she nodded. "Investments help, too."

"Either way, we're standing in high cotton."

She bit her nails, an old childhood habit absently resurrected as she weighed that remark. *High cotton?* Nobody used that term in her native country of Austria. She guessed that it was one of those quaint Americanisms. "What does that mean?"

"What does what mean?"

"Standing in high cotton."

"It means we're doing well. Exceedingly well. You've never heard that term?"

"We don't grow much cotton in the Alps."

Gold managed a weak smile. "Well, to answer your original question, I'd give our underwriting department an eight or nine."

"Based upon?"

"The numbers they've posted."

"Which numbers?"

"If I remember correctly, our loss ratio is around 60 percent. I'd say that's pretty damn good."

Loss ratio is the ratio of paid and reserved claims, plus expenses, divided by total earned premium. For example, in the case of the Anchor Insurance Company, they paid $60 in claims for every $100 in collected premium, producing a loss ratio of 60 percent. Interestingly, as Kaminski had alluded to earlier, an insurer could still earn a profit even with a loss ratio in excess of 100 percent. This was done simply by earning investment income on the premium float –– the money that was invested in stocks, bonds, and other securities.

Kaminski sat back, folding her arms across her chest, considering Gold's answer. She gave him the cool, calculating, skeptical look that she had learned the hard way –– from climbing the corporate ladder in a pair of high heels. Keeping her voice under control, she faked a short-lived smile. "You've always been a team player. I admire your loyalty."

Gold didn't respond immediately. He stared at her for several moments, then glanced at the claim folder on her desk. "Loyalty has nothing to do with it. The numbers speak for themselves."

She smiled again. "You don't say."

Gold smiled back at her, wondering where all this was going. He drew a breath and let it out slowly. "Actuaries have a saying. Women lie, men lie, but numbers tell the truth."

"Well, you're half right. Men and women certainly stretch the truth, especially when it comes to money. Are you familiar with Samuel Butler?"

"Property or casualty?"

"He's not an underwriter. He was an English author. He wrote *The Way of All Flesh*."

"My wife won't let me read those kinds of books."

She cleared her throat and shifted her weight just a bit. "Butler was the one who said that any fool can tell the truth, but it requires a man of some sense to know how to lie well."

"Smart guy."

"He also said that the best liar is he who makes the smallest amount of lying go the longest way." She reached for the manila folder and passed it across to him. "Butler would have loved this claim. Take a look."

Gold glanced at the name of the claimant, printed on the edge of the folder. "Ricardo Paz?"

"Ever heard of him?"

"Nope."

"Cuban émigré. Real estate agent. Lives in South Florida."

"Lucky him."

"You know the area?"

"My mother lives in Boca Raton."

"Lucky her."

Gold opened the folder and read the claim report. A pained expression crossed his face. He made no attempt to conceal his dismay. "Jesus," he whispered under his breath. "We insured a box of cigars?"

Kaminski allowed herself a thin smile. "Cohiba cigars. They were worth twenty thousand dollars."

The blood drained from Gold's face. "How many cigars?"

"Twenty-five."

"Eight hundred each?"

"Sad but true."

"All gone?"

"Every last one."

After nearly a minute of silence during which they simply stared at each other, Gold said, "Eight hundred sounds high."

Kaminski swiveled her chair around to face the window. Through the sunlit blinds she could just make out the eastern shore of New Jersey. She wished she were there, heading for a rental cottage in Cape May. She held her hand up, signaling him not to interrupt. He didn't. He just listened. "I've done some homework. These were Cohiba Behike cigars, made at the El Laguito factory in 2007. The factory produced one hundred boxes that year, and since they were Fidel's favorite brand, they were difficult to come by. I don't know how our insured got a box, but he did, and one of our Florida agents obtained coverage for him." She spun around, scowling. "Which means that we've got some stupid underwriters –– and it's time to clean house."

Gold murmured, "Maybe so."

"So give me your best guess," Kaminski said, her eyes probing his face. "What type of person would submit such a ridiculous claim?"

Gold took a beat deciding whether or not he should laugh; he decided against it. "Good question," he said. "I was just wondering the same thing."

The claim, on its face, was not that unusual. The insured had purchased a basic dwelling policy, known as a DP-1, which provided very limited coverage. In fact, only "named perils" were covered, meaning that the insured causes of damage were limited to fire, hail, and lightning. This type of dwelling form was typically used to insure real property, primarily vacant buildings. But in this case, the insured had also purchased endorsement coverage C, extending coverage to personal property. As written, the policy covered the ACV –– actual cash value –– of the personal property: twenty thousand dollars.

The bizarre part was that the insured had *smoked* each and every one of the cigars and was now claiming that they had been destroyed by fire –– a peril that was clearly covered by the policy.

Gold shook his head, almost in admiration. "Very creative."

"So was Dr. Frankenstein."

"Well, you've got to hand it to the guy. He's thinking outside the box."

Kaminski stared at him, faintly annoyed. "You find this amusing?"

"I don't know whether to laugh or cry."

"The man's a con artist. He's looking for a quick score."

Gold nodded, as though he'd been thinking just that. "Yeah, you're right." He leaned back, placing his hands together, the fingertips of his index fingers resting on the bridge of his nose. "What are we going to do?"

"First, I'm going to fire someone."

"Then what?"

"What do you think we should do?"

Gold surprised her by saying, "Offer partial payment."

For a moment Kaminski stared unbelieving, trying to digest his answer. Then she asked a simple question. "You want me to pay the claim?"

"A portion of it. Five grand might do."

She snorted in disgust. "Surely you jest."

"Why look for trouble?"

"Why play the fool?"

Gold seemed to be wrestling with something. Finally, he came out with it. "Look, I know it's a hard pill to swallow, but the premium was paid, and we issued a policy. If we deny coverage we'll end up in court. And aside from the bad publicity, there are legal costs to consider." He reminded her that legal costs mounted quickly, even when in-house lawyers were used. The average annual salary of a corporate attorney was well over $100,000, and if the big guns of contract law were required, the costs could be exorbitant. He paused, his hand nervously massaging his chin. "A trial would be expensive, and in the end, the jury might rule against us. They could even impose punitive damages. Why take the risk?"

Kaminski laughed harshly, then leaned across the desk and answered in a firm voice. "Taking risk is what we do around here. Did you forget about that?"

"No, I didn't forget, but I still think we should settle."

She dismissed that with a characteristic curl of the lip. "As a matter of fact," she growled, slashing a hand at eyebrow level, "I'm up to here with these clowns. I'm running a business, not a charity. If we pay any part of this claim we'll be the laughingstock of the industry. I have no intention of becoming an ATM for conmen and crooks."

"I feel your pain."

"*Our* pain. We're on the same team." She stood up and began pacing in a small, tight circle. She was silent for a while, thinking long and hard about their predicament. "I've worked too hard for that A+ rating. I won't jeopardize it by looking weak."

Gold stayed quiet a moment, then said, "I understand."

She stopped pacing, looked up, and twirled her hair around her middle finger. "We go to the mat on this one."

Gold cleared his throat and drummed his fingers on the desk for a minute. Deep down he knew what was coming. Another fun assignment. Whenever Kaminski used a martial arts reference, it was time to start packing. Looking solemn, he said simply: "When do I leave for Florida?"

"Tomorrow morning. Bright and early."

"Swell."

Kaminski smiled to herself. She knew that Gold was not a morning person, but time was of the essence. Her expression remained impassive for a few moments, then she closed her eyes like she had a bad headache. "I want a thorough investigation."

"Understood."

"And something else..." She opened her eyes and glared at him. "I don't like this guy. He's too cunning. Find a reason to deny the claim. Something that will hold up in court."

Gold looked into her angry eyes for a long moment. Then he smiled weakly. "I might have to color outside the lines."

"Whatever it takes."

"I like the way you think."

"I'm flattered."

"Any chance of earning a bonus?"

In a more forceful and commanding voice than before, she said, "Give my regards to your mother."

CHAPTER FOUR

Strictly speaking, Gold should have read the Paz claim file more thoroughly, but as usual, he was anxious to get to the bottom line —– the amount of the loss. Now it was time to read the insured's statement from start to finish, looking for any tell-tale signs of fraud. Detecting deception in a claim report was not as difficult as the public thought, and from experience, Gold understood that a lot of lies connected to fraud were lies of omission rather than lies of commission. If the truth be told, it was common for a claimant to forget about pertinent details, especially when they had dollar signs in their eyes.

Step one in a typical investigation involved a careful examination of the insured's first interview or written statement. Gold used a method known as SCAN, Scientific Content Analysis, which had been developed by an Israeli polygraph examiner. After years of observation, Gold knew that liars and truth tellers used different types of language, different pronouns, gaps in time, and evasive answers that could help differentiate between true and fabricated statements.

To the layman, SCAN seemed complicated, but it was actually quite simple. Pronoun choices were always revealing, so if, for instance, an insured stated that, "I woke up, I got dressed, I had breakfast, and then *we* left..." Gold would know that somebody else had been present. The same insured might have stated that they had breakfast and then *later* on left for work. In that case, they would be asked to fill in the gaps.

Evasive answers also provided clues, and these usually involved answers that had nothing to do with the questions. This type of deception could be effective if the interviewer "zoned out" or the report was read by someone in a hurry.

Step two was a face-to-face meeting with the claimant, and this was where the rubber met the road. Many of these meetings incorporated elements of a criminal interrogation, and for good reason. Insurance fraud was a serious crime, and those who attempted to defraud a company were criminals. For this reason, step two often involved the Reid Technique of Investigation, one of the tricks of the trade that Gold liked to use. The technique, popular in law enforcement circles, employed a phony offer of friendship, a sympathetic ear, and a face-saving version of guilt, which a person could readily accept.

The Reid Technique was effective, but not without controversy. The main criticism was that it pressured people into making a false confession. Critics also claimed that its main assumption, that guilty people and con artists will act anxious, was simply not true. As Gold knew, scientific research had found little relationship between acting anxious and actual guilt. In fact, some folks could lie without anxiety, while others might be anxious because of the accusation, even if they were innocent. Of course, this was the same reason that polygraphs were unreliable, and seldom used in the insurance industry.

Gold had used the Reid Technique in a number of cases, but he actually preferred the PEACE Technique, which was more analytical. The letters stood for Preparation and Planning, Engage and Explain, Account, Closure and Evaluate. Popular throughout Europe, the technique involved questioning a subject without trying to manipulate him in order to obtain a confession. Critics claimed it was "old school," but the premise was sound. If an investigator kept circling back, asking for more details, a house of cards would eventually collapse.

After reviewing the file, Gold came to the conclusion that Ricardo Paz was more of a joker than a criminal mastermind. He probably thought he could take advantage of poor underwriting and a claims department that would be willing to cut its losses and settle out of court. The poor guy hadn't figured on someone like Irene Kaminski, and now his whole world was about to be turned upside down.

Halfway through the second reading of the file, Gold's cell phone vibrated in his coat pocket. He looked at it, jumped to his feet, and asked "Where are you?"

In a weak, dying voice, the reply came, "Right around the corner. I'm a little plastered, Gold. What's going on?"

"We need to talk."

The call was from Bill Burke, the underwriter who had insured the Cohiba Behike cigars. After a moment of silence, he said, "I'm at the Ketch."

"Stay put," Gold said. "I'm on my way."

The Captain's Ketch was on Platt Street, two blocks south of the Anchor Insurance Company. When Gold stepped inside, he spotted Burke at the bar, enjoying a liquid lunch with some of his buddies from A.I.G. "Bourbon Bill" was in his cups, laughing and joking, the life of the party. Gold nudged his way through the crowd and waved at the bartender. He ordered two fingers of bourbon, neat.

As expected, the order caught Burke's attention. "Blanton's Bourbon?" he said with a smile. "Damn, Gold, you're a man after my own heart."

"Don't get your hopes up," Gold quipped. "I'm only after a drink."

They shook hands, then Burke said, "I'm glad you could join the celebration."

"What are we celebrating?"

"My good fortune."

"Another Lotto win?"

"Nope, a long overdue raise."

Gold laughed nervously and, not knowing how to respond, said, "You got a raise?"

"Not yet, but I've got a three o'clock with Kaminski." He took a sip of his drink. "I don't know why else she would want to see me."

Now there's an idiot, Gold thought. After a short silence, he spoke softly, almost as if he were afraid of his own thoughts. "She might have another reason."

Burke scowled. "What other reason?"

"Maybe she's concerned about your underwriting."

Burke went on scowling at him for perhaps twenty seconds, then he snorted a little laugh. "Kaminski's a bean counter. Her only concern is the bottom line."

"I think they're connected -- profit and underwriting."

"They used to be. Nowadays it's all about investment income."

"Not all," Gold said. He took his drink from the bartender and mouthed *thanks*. "Let's sit down a minute."

"I'm with my friends."

"This won't take long."

They walked away from the bar and found a vacant table, a spot where they could talk in private. If Burke was worried, he hid it well. The moment they sat down, he told an off-color joke, then signaled for another round. "All right, you said we needed to talk. What's on your mind, Gold?"

Gold hesitated, reluctant to push too hard. But he had to push. "You're a senior underwriter. Thirty years of experience. What possessed you to insure a box of cigars?"

"Excuse me?"

"Ricardo Paz? The Cuban cigars? You were the underwriter."

Burke glared at him for a moment, then calmed. "Are you handling the claim?"

"Yep."

"I should have guessed."

Gold looked over with a pained expression on his face. "A total loss. Twenty grand. What happened, Bill?"

"You read the report. We had a fire claim."

"I'm not talking about the loss, I'm talking about your underwriting judgement. Why would you insure a box of cigars?"

Burke tilted his head, as if he found the question amusing. "Are you serious? Lloyds of London covers that type of shit all the time."

"We're not Lloyds," Gold shot back. "And we don't write high-risk policies."

"Well, it seemed like a good idea at the time."

Gold made a questioning expression. "I don't get it. You're a conservative guy. A solid underwriter. All of a sudden you get wild and crazy. Why? What happened? A senior moment? Temporary insanity? Too much booze?"

Burke swatted the words away. "I made a mistake. What can I say?"

"I don't know, but you'd better think of something. Kaminski's on the warpath, and she's after your scalp."

Burke sat in silence, fuming and biting his bottom lip, then suddenly bolted up and reached for Gold's wrist. "Jesus, is that why she wants to see me? Because I screwed up? I thought I was getting a raise."

"Try severance pay."

Burke's jaw dropped. "You gotta be kidding. She'd give me the boot for one bad decision?"

"You need to come up with a good excuse."

"I don't have a good excuse."

Gold leaned back with his arms folded nonchalantly against his chest. "You never answered my question. What possessed you to insure the cigars?"

"Who the hell knows? Maybe I was possessed by the devil." He shifted uncomfortably in his chair. "I don't know what I was thinking."

Gold gripped the arms of his chair, his features set in the concrete of having gone down this road before. This was precisely the sort of evasive nonsense he had come to expect from dishonest insureds. What troubled him most was not the evasiveness, but the realization that his colleague was no different than many of the bad actors he'd encountered. Burke might have thought he was being clever, but as usual, it was the small stuff that tripped people up.

Before their meeting at the Ketch, Gold had stopped by Burke's office, and since it was vacant, he had a look around. Among other things, he had spotted an ashtray and a couple of cigar rings.

A couple of Cohiba Behike rings.

When Gold mentioned the cigar rings, Burke looked away. "You're a nosy son of a bitch."

"One of my endearing qualities."

"You think so?"

"You don't find it endearing?"

"No, I find it annoying. You had no business snooping around my office."

Thinking out loud, Gold said, "Eight hundred for a smoke. Damn, that's a lot of money. More than I could afford."

"You're breaking my heart."

"How do you afford that on your salary?"

"You find a way."

"Scrimp and save?"

"Back off, Gold. The cigars were a gift."

Gold digested his answer for a moment, then shook his head in disgust. "Shit," he said. "You took a bribe."

Burke stared at him in icy silence, and Gold could feel his rage, his bottled-up anger about the situation. Abruptly Burke finished his drink, then slammed his glass on the table. "Spare me the holier-than-thou crap. I wasn't born yesterday. I know how you guys operate, and I know about the freebies you get. Dinners, drinks, entertainment. The whole nine yards. You have no problem being wined and dined by an insured, and you don't see that as a bribe, but that's exactly what it is. An inducement to look the other way."

Gold shot him a look. "For your information, I've got an expense account. I'm the one who picks up the tab."

"Who are you trying to kid? You never put your hand in your pocket. Investigators get treated like... gold."

"You've been watching too much television."

"I've got eyes and ears."

Gold grunted in a way that showed growing exasperation. For a long moment, he just glared, as if weighing his words, and in fact, that's exactly what he was doing. Finally, he reminded Burke that investigators were bound to a strict code of ethics. Crossing the line might be tempting, but a true professional had to avoid conflicts of interest, both real and perceived.

This was all well and good, but Burke wasn't buying the boy scout routine. He leaned forward and forced a smile. "Judge not, lest you be judged."

"Thanks for the tip, Matthew."

"You got anything else to say?"

Gold didn't say anything for a full minute, then he let out a deep breath, put his glass down, and stood. Now he looked directly at Burke. "Good luck, Bill."

Burke leaned back, obviously agitated. "Don't worry about the check. My treat."

CHAPTER FIVE

From time to time, Gold was required to up his game by purchasing surveillance equipment. Whenever that need arose, he turned to Victor Wong, a.k.a. *Inspector Gadget*, the owner of Jade Electronics in Chinatown. Wong, God bless him, was always able to provide the newest gizmo, and he was also a source of industry gossip and humor. When he spotted Gold, he ran to greet him, teacup in hand, anxious to welcome one of his best customers.

"Perfect timing," Wong said. "I just got back from a trade show."

"Lucky me."

"Three days in Vegas. Crazy town."

"Play any poker?"

"All work and no play makes Jack a dull boy."

"Confucius?"

Wong made a face. "I doubt it."

"Did you win?"

Silly question, Wong thought. He *always* won. Fact was, there were few players better at Texas Hold'em, and even fewer harder to beat in a cash game. But instead of bragging, Wong said, "The superior man is modest in his speech but exceeds in his actions."

He hesitated just a fraction of a second before adding, "Now we've come to Confucius."

Gold smiled. "I've missed your profundity."

Wong laughed so abruptly he choked on his tea. After recovering his breath, he wheezed, "A prophet is seldom appreciated in his own land."

"So they say."

"Speaking of profit... would you like to see my new inventory?"

"Some other time. I'm in a hurry."

"Nature does not hurry, yet everything is accomplished."

Gold glanced at his watch and saw it was nearly five-thirty; he had meant to be in Penn Station an hour ago. "I only need one item."

"One item?" Wong looked bewildered. "With so much to choose from?"

"No time to shop."

"I hate to see you miss the boat."

"I'm more concerned about missing a plane."

"Very well. What do you need?"

"A portable polygraph machine."

Wong stared at him, caught by surprise, as if he were unsure how to react to the request. "Why on earth would you want one of those?"

"Remember the plane I mentioned? Luggage restrictions."

Other restrictions as well, Wong thought. He felt obliged to remind Gold that polygraph results were inadmissible in most states. In fact, as far as he knew, only five states allowed the results to be used in a court of law: California, Arizona, Nevada, Georgia, and Florida. Even then, both parties had to agree to admit the test results as evidence.

Oddly enough, Florida was the only state that *required* some people to submit to a polygraph test, and those were previously convicted sex offenders. Even so, the results could not be used in court, but only within a course of therapy.

Gold listened politely, then asked about the cost. "How much does a good machine run?"

Wong swallowed the vulgarity that was on his tongue and shook his head. "Somewhere between four and five thousand. Half that if you want to buy a used one."

"Do you have any stock?"

"New or used?"

"New."

"Several models. Might I recommend the Stoelting CPS II?"

"I think you just did. Let's have a look."

Wong went down to the basement and returned with a small box containing a computerized polygraph system. He explained that it was a five-channel device that plugged into a USB port and was the very latest in state-of-the-art digital technology. The CPS model had channels that recorded thoracic respiration, abdominal respiration, blood pressure and pulse rate, electrodermal activity, and body movement. Software was also included.

"Easy to use," Wong said. "It comes with directions, but I'd be happy to give you a demonstration."

"That won't be necessary."

Wong gave him the eagle eye. "Are you sure?"

"Yeah, I'm sure."

"I don't remember you being the mechanical type."

"I'm not."

"I'd be happy to put it together."

"No thanks."

Wong was understandably annoyed and confused, but he still managed to smile. "Assembly is free."

"I appreciate the offer, but I have no intention of using the machine. In fact, I may not take it out of the box."

"I beg your pardon?"

"I've got a tough nut to crack. I thought I might intimidate him with a polygraph machine."

"You're going through all this trouble just to intimidate an insured?"

"Would you want to be hooked up to that contraption?"

Wong rubbed his forehead with the butt of his hand before responding. "Why not buy a used machine?"

"Less intimidating. I'm trying to make a bold statement. By the way, what's your policy on returns?"

"No money back. Store credit only."

"I can live with that."

Wong sat down, thinking, and scanned the showroom. His eyes eventually came down on the box containing the polygraph machine. "You still have a problem. How will you know if your insured is telling the truth?"

Gold smiled indulgently. "We employ certain techniques. Interview tricks. I know what to look for."

"You'd know more if you played poker."

"You don't say."

"How do you think I win all the time?"

"I assume you cheat."

Wong let that one pass. "Have you ever heard of a tell?"

"I've heard of William Tell."

"You've got much to learn."

"Make it quick, professor."

Wong jumped at the chance of educating his old friend, and without missing a beat, he reached under the counter and pulled out a deck of Bicycle Playing Cards. He shuffled the deck, then dealt five cards each to Gold and himself. Before they looked at their cards, he said, "We need to ante."

"How much?"

Wong gave it some thought. "Let's make it interesting. Ten dollars."

"Let's make it more interesting," Gold said. "Twenty dollars."

Wong shrugged. "A fool and his money are soon parted."

Gold looked at his watch, then studied his cards. "What are we playing?"

"Five-card draw."

"What are the rules?"

"You can stand pat or exchange any amount of cards."

"I thought you could only discard three."

"That's a home game rule. Pretend we're in a casino."

Gold laughed nervously. "How do I order a drink?"

Wong forced a polite smile. "Bet or check."

“I’ll bet twenty.”

“I’ll raise you twenty.”

Gold stared at him, tapping his fingers on the counter. His face was an absolute blank, but only for a second. With a confident tone, he said, “I’ll call.”

“How many cards?”

“I’ll play these.”

Wong smiled again. “I’ll take three.” He dealt himself three cards. “Your bet.”

“Another twenty.”

“You must have a good hand.”

“Fair.”

“I might have to raise.”

Gold frowned, more surprised than angry. He began to crack his knuckles, waiting for Wong to act. The old boy was taking his own sweet time. “Well?” he said impatiently. “What do you want to do?”

“Twenty on top.”

Gold looked away, trying to conceal his thoughts. After a moment of silence, he found his voice. “How much can I raise?”

“Whatever you wish.”

“Really?”

“We’re playing no-limit poker. You can bet any amount.”

Gold swallowed hard, and suddenly his left eye began to twitch. He fought to keep the emotion out of his voice. “How much was that polygraph machine?”

“Around four thousand.”

"All right, then that's the bet. Four thousand dollars."

Wong pushed out a loud yawn, trying not to show any concern. "I've got three aces, but I'm going to fold. Would you like to know why?"

"You think I have a better hand."

"I *know* you have a better hand. You see, my friend, you tipped your hand. Not literally, but figuratively. No offense, but you're a lousy actor."

"I can't sing either."

"I picked up six tells."

"Six?"

Wong rattled them off, one by one, reminding Gold that a poker tell was simply a change in a player's behavior or demeanor. Unconsciously, Gold had glanced at his watch, laughed nervously, tried to be funny, stared, cracked his knuckles impatiently, and twitched.

"Congratulations," Wong said. "You broke every rule in the book. Well, almost every rule. When you turned away, I couldn't see if your pupils dilated. Too bad. Pupillometry is a wonderful tool."

"Pupil what?"

"The study of pupil size as it relates to a wide range of psychological phenomena."

Gold inhaled heavily. "All right, professor. I'll bite. What the hell is pupillometry? In English, please."

Unperturbed, Wong continued. "The pupil response to cognitive and emotional events -- like being dealt a straight, a flush, or a full house in poker. The reaction is automatic and uncontrollable. If you're dealt a good hand –– as you were –– your pupils can dilate up to four times their normal size."

"So the eyes have it. Is that what you're trying to say?"

"More or less."

"I'll tell you a secret. Investigators look for tells during an interview. When insureds start to lie, they do a number of things. Little things, like coughing, licking their lips, playing with their hair, chewing their nails, and avoiding eye contact. If I see any of those, my antenna goes up, and it stays up until I'm proven wrong."

"Good thinking," Wong said. "Too bad you're not a poker player. If you played cards, you'd have all the bases covered."

"Did it ever dawn on you that I might have been bluffing?"

Wong made a sour face. "You weren't bluffing."

"How do you know?"

"Instinct. The best players –– myself included –– possess a sixth sense about cards. I can almost see what you're holding. Besides, you work with numbers, so you must know that the odds of beating a seasoned player with a bluff are not very good."

Gold shook his head. "You've got me all figured out."

"You're easy to read."

"You're forgetting that I've always been contrary to ordinary."

"What is that supposed to mean?"

Gold tucked the polygraph machine under his arm and started for the door. Looking back, he said, "Send the bill to my office."

When he was halfway out, he stopped in his tracks and looked back again. “By the way, thanks for the poker lesson.”

Wong didn’t like the way he said that, with a lighthearted tone and a smile on his face. After the door closed, it occurred to him that Gold had not shown his cards, and he wondered why. Since the game was over, Wong figured it would be all right to take a look at Gold’s cards, and when he did, his mouth dropped open and his eyes almost popped out of his head. Finally he threw the deck across the room, and said, “Son of a bitch.”

Gold had bluffed with a pair of deuces.

CHAPTER SIX

The flight from New York's JFK Airport to Fort Lauderdale International took three hours and fifteen minutes, a straight shot down the Eastern Seaboard, most of it over water. The aircraft was filled with the usual mix of passengers, business types and tourists, anxious to get the hell out of Dodge. Gold understood how they felt. After a cold, rainy spring he also yearned for some warmth and a dose of vitamin D.

Off-season, the terminal was easy to navigate, and there were no lines at any of the rental car companies. Thirty minutes after landing, Gold was behind the wheel of a Ford Expedition, driving north on I-95, arguably the most exasperating -- but essential -- highway in the nation. State troopers often referred to I-95 as "cocaine lane" because drug traffickers used it so frequently. Other stretches, mostly in the South, were called "iron road" because the highway was also a favorite route for the transport of illegal guns.

Not surprisingly, the 1,900-mile highway connecting Maine to Florida was also one of the most deadly roads in America. More than three thousand people had died on I-95 in the last ten years, and the state of Florida consistently produced the most fatalities. With this in mind, Gold was happy to reach Palm Beach

County in one piece. After taking the Hillsboro Boulevard exit, he turned left onto US-1 and then right into Royal Palm Yacht and Country Club. Home sweet home was a ten-thousand-square-foot mansion on Alexander Palm Drive, a mecca for a handful of lucky millionaires and billionaires.

Harriet Gold, the family matriarch, had lived in the lap of luxury for thirty years –– two-thirds of that time with her late husband, Arthur. She had never wanted such a grand residence, but her hubby had insisted on retiring in style. The house had been built as a "turnkey" home, which meant that it came fully furnished and decorated, stocked with food and wine, monogrammed sheets and towels, and enough champagne to choke a horse.

All the comforts of home –– especially if your home had been featured on *Lifestyles of the Rich and Famous.*

Luckily, the house had been purchased for half of its current value, so despite the taxes –– which could also choke a horse –– it turned out to be a good investment. Still, as Gold and his siblings knew, it was a bit much for a seventy-year-old widow who walked with a cane. Whenever one of the children broached the subject of moving, they were reminded that the house also contained an elevator, and that was the end of that conversation.

Of course, from time to time, Gold still felt guilty about living up north. He took comfort in having a brother in Delray Beach and a sister in Ft. Lauderdale, and they kept a close eye on their mother, but he still had qualms about doing his share. If the truth be told, Gold enjoyed coming to Florida, but there was no way he would leave New York for the land of silk and money. Florida was a fine place to visit, but it wasn't his style.

Too fancy-schmancy.

The heat and humidity were also problematic, and the moment that Gold stepped out of his car, he remembered why the snowbirds flew north during the summer months. Wiping the moisture from his face, he grabbed his luggage and made a beeline for the front door. Harriet was waiting for him in the foyer, a welcoming smile on her face. They shared a warm embrace, and then she led the way down the hallway into the kitchen.

Gold was surprised by how dark the house was, and he wondered why the lights were off and the blinds drawn shut. When he mentioned the lighting, his mother said, "We don't own shares in the electric company."

How many times have I heard that? Gold thought as he rolled his suitcase into a corner and placed a duffle bag between his legs. *At least a thousand times*, he thought. *Maybe more*. He chuckled to himself, then straddled a chair, putting his chin on his forearm and staring at his mother. "What's new, Mom?"

"Same old, same old."

"Nothing new to report?"

"We spoke yesterday."

"So we did."

"How was your flight?"

"Short and sweet."

"Are you hungry? Would you like some lunch?"

"No, I ate a big breakfast."

She looked disconsolate. "We could go to Flakowitz. Grab something light before dinner."

"There's nothing light at Flakowitz."

"Would you like to nosh on something healthy? I've got fruit."

"Are we doing the early bird thing?"

"Of course. We don't own shares in Bank of America."

Gold seemed to find that amusing. "I can wait a couple of hours."

She pulled her reading glasses out of her blouse pocket and then peered over the top of them. "What's in the duffle bag?"

"A lie detector."

"Be serious."

"I am being serious."

She gave him a doubtful look. "Let me save you some trouble. I don't have a favorite. I love all my children the same."

Gold looked crestfallen. "You do? Really? I always thought I was your favorite."

"You might move up a notch if you tell me what's really in the bag."

"A portable polygraph machine. Weighs next to nothing." He unzipped the bag and showed her the contents. "Would you like a demonstration?"

She made a sour face. "Why the hell did you bring that thing?"

"I've got some work to do."

"What kind of work?"

"I need to interview a claimant. Down in Fort Lauderdale. It won't take long."

Harriet chewed her lip a moment in thought. "All work and no play makes Jack a dull boy," she said at last. "I used to tell your father that."

"Dad was a workaholic. I know how to combine business and pleasure."

She was still eyeing him suspiciously, as if he were pulling her leg. "Tell me about the claim."

"You want to talk about insurance?"

"What do you want to talk about, the weather?"

So Gold told her all about Ricardo Paz, the Cuban cigars, the fire loss, and the purpose of bringing a lie detector. The only part he left out was how he planned to get out of the claim -- but only because he hadn't figured that part out.

But he was working on it.

Boy, was he working on it.

Harriet leaned across the table and patted him consolingly on the shoulder. "Don't worry," she said in a motherly tone, "You'll find a way. You always do." She stood up slowly, balancing herself with her cane, and walked over to the stove. "Would you like some coffee?"

Gold shook his head, noticing that his mother was moving slower than ever before. He also noticed something else. There was a pair of binoculars on the counter. That seemed odd to him. Even stranger, they were night vision binoculars. Bushnell. Dual lens. He rubbed his chin, heard the sandpaper scratch there, and smiled. "Have you been spying on the neighbors?"

"Excuse me?"

"What's with the binoculars?"

Harriet nervously adjusted her reading glasses and pretended not to hear, praying the subject would be dropped. "Are you sure you don't want coffee?"

Gold repeated the question. "What's the story, Mom? Why'd you buy a pair of binoculars?"

She answered hesitantly. "If you must know, I've got a new hobby."

"Snooping?"

"Bird watching."

"Bird watching?"

Straightaway, she knew she'd said the wrong thing. Harriet Gold was many things, but a bird watcher wasn't one of them. Nevertheless, that was her answer, and she was sticking to it. "Do you have a problem with birds?"

"No, I love birds. I never knew you cared for them."

"They're fascinating creatures."

Gold walked over to the window and opened the blinds. A flood of sunlight poured through the slats, illuminating the entire kitchen. "There, that's better."

"What are you doing?"

"Let there be light!"

She folded her arms across her chest and appeared sullen, saying nothing for a moment. Next, she made a gesture with her finger to say it was too bright. "You're hurting my eyes."

"You won't see any birds with the blinds closed."

"I don't watch midday. Too hot. There's not much activity." She gave him a penetrating stare. "If you lived here, you'd know that."

Touche, Gold thought. *She really knows how to hurt a guy. The old guilt trip. Works every time.* He looked outside, across a narrow strip of the Intracoastal Waterway toward Deerfield Island, a fifty-three-acre tract of swampland and mangrove forest. His voice remained unruffled, placid. "What's your favorite bird?"

"I beg your pardon?"

"Your favorite species."

She hesitated just a fraction of a second before saying, "I don't have a favorite."

Gold managed a hollow laugh, even as the sense of unease he felt grew stronger. "I don't know about you, mother. No favorite child, no favorite bird." He shook his head. "A foolish consistency is the hobgoblin of little minds."

Sounding a little frustrated, she said, "Don't be fresh."

He looked at her skeptically, and she looked back, forcing her face to be blank. She held his eyes and a certain worry took shape between them. He'd seen that look before, and he knew she was trying to hide something. But what? An alarm went off inside his head, triggered by the fact that his mother seldom hid anything. Finally, he said, "Have you ever spotted a Labrador Duck?"

She thought about it for a second, and with a tired sigh said, "I see a lot of ducks."

"Labrador Ducks?"

"Every now and then."

Gold reached for the binoculars and examined the focus ring, making a mental note of where it was set. He spoke quietly, without looking up. "You're a lucky woman," he said at last. "The Labrador Duck has been extinct for over a century."

The information caused her left eyebrow to rise a half inch. "I'm not a duck expert."

"Apparently not."

Her mouth tightened. "How do you know they're extinct?"

"I read a lot."

"Don't believe everything you read."

"What about my eyes? Should I believe them?"

"I don't know what you're talking about."

"These are night vision binoculars. Useless during the daytime." He turned toward the window and looked outside, scanning the island with the binoculars. "I couldn't spot a snowbird with these damn things." He returned to the table and sat down. "Why don't you tell me what's going on?"

"You'll laugh at me."

"I won't laugh."

"You might even think I'm crazy."

"I've always thought that."

She shot him a look of disdain. "Don't be fresh."

"What's going on, mom?"

"Is it too late to take the Fifth?"

"I'm afraid so."

Harriet, her mouth set tight, let a long, slow breath out through her nose. She took a sip of coffee and smiled a bit sheepishly. She said, "Do you believe in ghosts?"

Gold cocked his head slightly to the side, puzzled. "I'm not sure. Why do you ask?"

"I believe in them."

Gold sat still for a long moment, attempting to appear unfazed by the unusual conversation. Trying to maintain his composure, he asked the first question that came to mind. "Have you seen one?"

"Yep." Her face went a shade darker. "I know what you're thinking, but I'm not senile."

"When did you see this ghost?"

"Last week. Tuesday and Thursday. Around midnight."

"Why were you up at midnight?"

"I was answering the call of nature."

"Where did you see the ghost?"

She motioned behind and beyond him with her eyes, over toward the island. She paused for effect, then pointed to a small clearing, surrounded by red and white mangroves. Her eyes got even bigger, and she spoke in a low, conspiratorial tone. "I was returning to bed when I heard a noise outside. Out of the corner of my eye, I saw a flickering light, so I went to investigate. When I looked out, I saw a ghostly figure on the island -- a creature with a dark veil over its face. It was digging a hole, or a grave, and it kept wiping its eyes as if it were crying. I watched for a while, maybe two or three minutes, and then I turned on a lamp. The light must have spooked it, because when I got back to the window, it was gone."

Gold had risen from his chair and paced briefly around the room, throwing himself back into a reading chair by the back door and looking across the table at his mother. He looked at her as if she were a simple child. "I don't think you can spook a ghost."

"Excuse me?"

"Technically speaking, they're already spooked."

"You're making jokes?"

"Just an observation."

She gazed at him with a slack expression. "Nobody likes a smart aleck."

"Was this creature male or female?"

"Male."

"Tell me about your second encounter."

"Same as the first, only longer. I watched for a full ten minutes before I..." Her words trailed off, and an uncomfortable silence ensued. Finally, she said, "Before I fell asleep."

Gold nodded, as if he understood. "When did you wake up?"

"I'm not sure. Somewhere between three and three-thirty in the morning. In any case, the creature was long gone."

"So you ran out and bought a pair of binoculars."

"The very next day."

"Have you seen it again?"

"No, but that doesn't mean that it won't be back." She rose and started pacing. "The island is haunted. There's no question about that."

"Haunted?"

"By the ghost of a famous mobster!" She pulled a newspaper article out of a drawer and passed it across to him. The article was from the *Sun Sentinel*, a local paper published in Broward County.

Most of it dealt with the recreational opportunities on Deerfield Island. The park, operated by the state of Florida, offered a marina, nature trails, and primitive campsites.

Gold read a couple of paragraphs, then looked at her questioningly. "Would you like to go camping?"

She sighed heavily, closing her eyes on the exhale. When she opened them, she took another weary breath. "The locals don't refer to the place as Deerfield Island. Around here, they use the original name." Her smile was flat and tight. "Capone Island."

CHAPTER SEVEN

What am I getting into here? Gold thought as he sipped his morning coffee. Last night, as a favor to his mother, he'd spent three hours by the window, watching and waiting for someone -- or something -- to appear on Deerfield Island. Three hours of sheer boredom. Three hours of lost sleep. Naturally he'd seen neither hide nor hair of a ghost, or anything else that might be deemed suspicious. Nothing. Nada. Zip. Truth was, he hadn't expected to see anything, least of all an apparition with a shovel.

Sometimes, Gold realized, you just had to play along. You didn't necessarily need to believe a story. You just had to listen and keep an open mind.

Who knows, maybe there was a logical explanation.

Maybe. Maybe not. Time would tell.

Lost in his own thoughts, Gold didn't notice that his mother was standing in the doorway, waiting for him to acknowledge her presence. Finally, she cleared her throat and said, "Good morning."

Gold smiled wearily. "Morning, mother."

"You're up early."

"Busy day."

Harriet poured herself a cup of coffee and joined him at the table. She took a sip, then raised her brows in a politely quizzical expression. In a low, anticipatory voice, she said, "How did it go?"

"How did what go?"

"Last night. Did you see anything?"

"Nope."

"Nothing?"

"I'm afraid not."

"That's too bad."

Gold found himself oddly touched by her tone. "You sound disappointed. Or should I say dispirited?"

"Again with the jokes?"

"Never let a day go by."

There was a short silence, Harriet drumming on the table with her fingers. Finally she said, "How long did you watch?"

"Three hours."

"That's all? Just three hours?"

"What did you expect?"

"I would have stayed up longer."

"You fell asleep after ten minutes."

"Don't start."

Gold finished his coffee, set the mug carefully down on the mat, smiled, and said, "You'll be happy to know that I finish what I start, so even though I have my doubts, I'm going to look into this matter. Hopefully Plan B will put your mind at ease."

"Plan B?"

He threw a quick glance toward Deerfield Island. "I'm gonna visit the scene of the crime."

"By yourself?"

"Would you like to come with me?"

"Certainly not."

"I didn't think so. What time does the park open?"

"I have no idea."

"Do you know how to get there?"

"Not exactly."

"I need exactly. I'll ask for directions when I call."

Harriet shook her head, and Gold braced himself for a lecture. Instead she said, "Be careful. I don't want to lose a son."

Gold almost smiled. "I knew I was your favorite."

The park didn't open until 10:00 a.m., and since it was only a two-mile walk, Gold decided to hoof it. The exercise would do him good, and he would also have a chance to think. The route was circuitous, starting on Alexander Palm Road, then heading south on US-1, east at Hillsboro Boulevard, and left onto Riverview Road. Walking at a leisurely pace, it took him less than forty-five minutes to reach his destination, and he arrived in time to catch the first boat shuttle of the day. The shuttle was free, but it operated on a first-come, first-served basis. Fortunately there were only a handful of visitors waiting to board.

A deckhand gave Gold a brochure and asked him to review the "Customer Code of Conduct." The rules and regulations were clearly spelled out, and among the activities that were prohibited were entering or remaining in the park after hours, defacing, destroying, or altering park property or grounds, and destroying or mutilating any park landscape, plants, or soil.

These were serious violations, so if Harriet Gold was right, somebody was taking a big risk.

Who and why were the $64,000 questions.

Gold found a shady spot on the shuttle and read the rest of the brochure, intrigued by the history of Deerfield Island Park, a.k.a. Capone Island. The fifty-plus acres that made up the island were once part of a peninsula bordered by the Spanish River to the east and the Hillsboro River to the southwest. The peninsula didn't become an island until 1961, when the Royal Palm Canal was dredged in order to connect the Intracoastal Waterway and the Hillsboro Canal.

The link to Al Capone dated back to June of 1930, when Vincent C. Giblin, the gangster's attorney, announced that he was looking to purchase property in Palm Beach County. Giblin was described as a "colorful character" whose roots stretched back to Mobile, Alabama. Both of his parents had died before he was fourteen, but even though he was left an orphan, he managed to finish high school and then enroll and graduate from Notre Dame's law school -- without attending a single undergraduate class.

After moving to Florida, Giblin practiced law for the next nine years in Escambia, Duval, and Broward counties. He moved to Miami in 1929, and shortly thereafter he was engaged by Capone. The Chicago mobster hired Giblin to fight against those who wanted to prevent him from acquiring property, and the list included the governor, the citizens of South Florida, and every law enforcement agency in the state.

When the press and the police continued to hound Miami's most famous persona non grata, he decided to move north, hoping to find a remote location to set up shop. A fifty-acre tract a half-mile from the closest road -- and inaccessible by car -- seemed ideal.

According to the brochure, the tract was purchased on June 7, 1930, and a few weeks later, it was reported that Capone intended to build a $250,000 mansion on the property. Another $125,000 would be spent on a large swimming pool.

Needless to say, the plan provoked a storm of outrage, and nobody was more angry than Clarence Geist, the owner of the Boca Raton Hotel and the gent who owned half the town's properties. Geist and some of his rich friends (Henry Flagler and Addison Mizner) were prepared to fight Capone in court, but they never got the chance. In October of 1931, a criminal court sentenced Capone to ten years in federal prison for income tax evasion.

Unpaid taxes began to accumulate on the property, and in 1934, the land was purchased by the Florida Inland Navigational District at a tax foreclosure sale. They, in turn, conveyed the property to the state, and the rest, as the brochure stated, was history.

Gold was so absorbed in his reading that at first he didn't notice that his fellow passengers were getting antsy. A small, balding man with thick, black spectacles slid into a chair across from him, wiping a stream of sweat from his face. "Hell of a way to run a railroad," he muttered.

Suddenly a white BMW convertible pulled into the parking lot, and a young man wearing a park ranger uniform and a wide-brimmed hat got out, checking his appearance in the side view mirror. Gold studied him for a moment. He was in his early thirties with blonde hair pulled back into a ponytail that hung over the back of his collar. Gold guessed he liked the outdoors. His skin had an even tan, and he didn't seem to be the least bit bothered by the heat. He jogged toward the boat, and after jumping onboard, he apologized for being late.

It was only a five-minute ride from the marina to the island, but during that time, Gold struck up a conversation with the park ranger, curious about his background. The young man was happy to discuss his education and experience, and as he spoke, Gold began to wonder if they'd met before. Where and when escaped him, but he was certain that their paths had crossed.

So much for never forgetting a face, Gold thought.

They were just about to disembark when the ranger, whose name was Skip Taylor, mentioned that he'd recently been transferred from a northern post. When Gold asked about that, Taylor explained that he'd spent the last two years in Virginia, working as a Civil War tour guide. When he mentioned the town of Chancellorsville, Gold suddenly remembered where and when they had met.

One year earlier, Gold had gone to Chancellorsville to view the grave of Thomas "Stonewall" Jackson, or more precisely, to view the grave where the general's *arm* was buried. Taylor was the one who had conducted the tour and answered Irene Kaminski's question about the gravesite. During the tour, Gold had learned that Confederate pickets had accidentally shot Jackson at the Battle of Chancellorsville. If Gold remembered right, the incident had occurred in total darkness as the general and his staff were returning to camp. Under a moonless sky, they were mistaken for Union cavalry by a squad of soldiers from North Carolina. Shots rang out, and despite frantic shouts from Jackson's staff, a second volley was fired. The general, on horseback, was hit by three bullets –– two in the left arm and one in the right hand.

Due to the severity of his injuries –– and a delay in receiving medical attention –– Jackson's left arm had to be amputated.

Most severed limbs were discarded, but Taylor told the group that Jackson was something of a legend, so his arm was accorded a military burial.

Gold had no way of knowing it at the time, but the tour would drag him into the dark and dangerous world of brazen grave robbers. While investigating a claim, he would also become entangled with a scheming Southern belle and a psychopath who specialized in the murder of Thoroughbred horses.

Just a typical day at the office, he said to himself.

Taylor was still slim and handsome, but his hairline had begun to recede, accentuated by the way he combed back his hair. He'd had some dental work, too, and when he smiled, he displayed a mouthful of porcelain veneers.

Gold removed his sunglasses and grinned at him. "I think we've met before."

The statement, put so matter-of-factly, startled Taylor into silence. He shifted in his seat and did not say anything for a while. Then in a slightly strangled voice he said, "You think so?"

"I never forget a face. Well, almost never. I had a little trouble remembering where we met."

"Where was that?"

"Virginia. About a year ago. I was taking a tour of Chancellorsville. You were my guide."

The muscles around Taylor's mouth twitched an imitation of a smile. "You've got a good memory."

"Yeah, but like everything else, it's starting to fade. What brought you down to Florida?"

"The weather," Taylor said, standing and wiping away a drip of sweat that had coursed down the side of his face from his hatband. "Best in the nation. Two hundred and forty-nine annual days of sunshine. How can you beat that?"

"You could move to Las Vegas."

"Don't bet on it."

Gold's gaze swept the area. "The island looks deserted."

"It better be. We don't open until ten o'clock." He paused, acutely aware of how intently Gold was watching him. "First visit?"

"Yep."

Taylor thought for a while, squinting. "I'd be happy to give you a tour. Are you up for a hike?"

"Any ghosts on the tour?"

"The only things you have to worry about are mosquitoes, snakes, and alligators."

"Sounds like fun."

Taylor secured the boat to the pier, chuckling to himself as he helped the passengers disembark. One by one they took off in different directions, maps in hand, anxious to cover as much ground as possible before it got too hot. After a quick call to the manager's residence, Taylor explained that there were two trails on the island. The Mangrove was the longest trail, and it led to a 1600 foot boardwalk that was used to observe wildlife. The Coquina Trail made a circular tour of the eastern half of the island, with a lookout over the Intracoastal Waterway. Gold chose The Mangrove, hoping to find the spot where his mother had seen a ghostly apparition.

While Taylor rambled on about the flora and fauna, Gold made some mental notes: distances from the pier, locations of things, obstacles, and possible places to hide. He had no intention of coming back after dark, with or without a guide, but anything was possible. *Never say never*, he told himself.

When they reached the boardwalk, Taylor pulled a pair of binoculars out of his knapsack and surveyed the water in front of them. He was hoping to spot a tarpon rolling on the surface, but all he saw were some snook. He grinned mischievously, then said, "I'd love to catch a tarpon, but we're not allowed to fish."

Gold frowned slightly and looked around, struck by the beauty of the place. "No fishing on the island?"

"No fishing, no firearms, no camping, no drinking, no drugs, no pets." He paused for effect, then added, "No exceptions."

"You folks run a tight ship."

"That we do."

"Ever get bored out here?"

"Once in a while, but it still beats sitting in an office."

"How's the pay?"

Taylor told him that the pay was lousy, averaging around $30,000 per year, or roughly $12.50 per hour -- less than the minimum wage at McDonald's. Of course, some rangers made more than others, and those that made the most had college degrees. Advancement came quicker for the students who had majored in park administration, natural resource management, or wildlife science.

Certain skills were also of value, and the more a ranger mastered, the more he or she earned. By and large, the Division of Parks and Recreation sought applicants who could handle carpentry, electrical, and mechanical repairs. In addition, they preferred employees who enjoyed public speaking and knew how to work with computers and make software presentations.

The downside, in addition to the low pay, was that rangers also had to have "shift flexibility." Regardless of their rank, they had to be willing to work on weekends and holidays, and often at night.

The nighttime requirement intrigued Gold and raised a few questions about Taylor's schedule. He wondered if the ranger had been on the island at night during the past week, and if so, had he heard or seen any suspicious activity. He started to ask about that, but was interrupted by a call from the ranger residence. From what he was able to gather, one of his fellow passengers had injured himself, and Taylor had been summoned to provide first aid.

Taylor let his irritation show. He looked at Gold, then at his cell phone, shaking his head. "Injured tourist," he muttered. "Fell off a log. There's one in every crowd. Never fails." He heaved a great sigh. "I've got to go, but you're welcome to finish the tour on your own. You can't get lost. Just stay on the trail and follow it back to the pier."

"What if I see a ghost?"

"If I were you, I'd leave him be."

CHAPTER EIGHT

Leaving was exactly what Gold had in mind, especially when the mosquitoes began to attack, some of them big enough to have their own landing strips. Walking quickly helped, but without bug spray or protective clothing, it was a lost cause. Every time Gold veered off the trail looking for a freshly dug hole, a swarm of insects engulfed him, making life miserable. The heat was also miserable, and with the sun directly overhead, there was almost no shade.

Goddammit, Gold thought. The trail seemed to go on forever, with no end in sight. Truth was, he'd only walked about two hundred yards, but with the bugs and the heat, every step seemed like a mile. Finally, he reached the northern tip of the island, the area where his mother had seen someone digging. Gingerly he walked through the underbrush until he came to the shoreline. Shielding his eyes from the glare, he looked across the Royal Palm Waterway and saw his mother's house directly in front of him.

Turning, he noticed a mound of dirt, a mound that resembled a freshly dug grave, but without any marker or headstone. He peeled off his sunglasses and studied the size and shape of the mound, and as he did, an uneasy feeling crept over him. He'd seen this type of rise before -- up close and personal in Mississippi -- and he knew it was an alligator den. He could have -- perhaps should have -- gone back to the trail, but he'd come too far to turn around now. He decided to tiptoe around the den, hoping not to disturb its inhabitants. Foolish mistake. The moment he stepped forward, he heard a hissing sound followed by a telltale "head slap" on the water -- signs that he was getting too close to the den. When he glanced backward, he saw a large alligator partially submerged in the water.

One look was enough to convince Gold that it was time to get out of Dodge, and that's precisely what he did. There was no time to choose an escape route, so he just ran forward, weaving his way through the thick underbrush. He was close to the trail when he lost his footing and stumbled, headfirst, into a tree. For an instant, he saw stars spinning around his head, and then he collapsed and passed out.

Five minutes later, he regained consciousness, of a sort. He opened his eyes, unsure of where he was or what had happened to him. He thought he might be dreaming, but he was unsure of that, too. When he touched his forehead, he felt a knot, and then he remembered falling -- and that goddamn tree. How long had be been unconscious? No matter, he was still alive. He tried to breathe but could take only short, shallow breaths.

And then he remembered the alligator.

A great sense of impending doom spread over him, but fear is often a great motivator, and in this case, it enabled Gold to stand up and walk back to the trail. The morning light had darkened to a somber gray by the time he reached the pier, and off in the distance, a summer squall was making its way toward land. Suddenly showing his fatigue, Gold brought his hand up to his head and rubbed his eyes before pressing his fingers to his temple. Regaining his composure, he straightened up, then grinned to make himself look amicable.

Scowling, Taylor sat back against the boat rail and crossed his arms. "Enjoy your hike?"

Gold sat down wearily without looking at him. "Wonderful way to start the day."

"What happened to your head?"

"I ran into a tree limb."

"Need an ice pack?"

"No, it only hurts when I laugh."

"I'm glad you find it amusing."

"I've got a strange sense of humor."

"You didn't wander off the trail, did you?"

"Don't be silly."

"A lot of folks do."

"Not me."

Taylor showed his teeth in what was definitely not a friendly smile. "Did you read about our buried treasure?" He didn't wait for an answer. "Some folks think that Al Capone stashed some of his loot out here. Illegal proceeds from his Chicago operation. Somewhere between three and five million dollars. I'd sure like to get my hands on that kind of money." He smiled again, a cautious effort that did not quite extend to his eyes. "Of course, I'd rather find the strong box and those magical keys."

Gold tried to stifle a yawn. "What are you talking about?"

Taylor let him dangle a moment longer, and then he told him that before Capone went to prison in 1932, he had stashed almost $100 million dollars under assumed names in safety deposit boxes in banks in the United States and in Cuba. The keys to each box were tagged and the name used on the accounts written on the tags. According to legend, all of the keys were placed in a strong box and buried.

Buried somewhere on Capone's property.

Either on Palm Island in Miami, or on Capone Island.

After Capone was released from prison in 1939, he returned to South Florida to find the strong box, but supposedly, he couldn't remember where he'd buried it. He continued searching for several years, but the box was never found.

"A lot of folks have tried to find those keys," Taylor said. "I can't blame them for trying, but if you dig out here, you're asking for trouble. Especially this time of year."

"Why now?" Gold asked.

"May and June are the months that alligators mate, and during that time, the males become very aggressive."

"You don't say."

Taylor was having trouble keeping a straight face. "By the way, the Florida state record for a male gator is 14 feet, 3½ inches in length. If I remember right, that bad boy weighed about 1,000 pounds. A monster that size could swallow a man in one gulp."

Gold muttered something under his breath, then said, "What time does the boat leave?"

Taylor glanced at his watch without really looking at the time. "Anxious to get back?"

"I could use a drink."

"If I were you, I'd make it a frozen margarita." He tapped his forehead with his index finger. "You could use some ice."

"I could use some tequila, too."

"Well, at least you didn't break anything."

"The day ain't over yet."

Slipping on his shades, Taylor said, "Look on the bright side. You got a free souvenir."

"Lucky me."

"Actually, you did have some luck. If you hadn't been able to walk, you might have become an entree selection."

For a moment Gold didn't respond. *He can't be serious*, he thought, but his gaze was absolutely steady. "You mean figuratively, of course."

"No," Taylor said. "Literally."

"There's a pleasant thought."

"Look, I'm not trying to ruin your day, but running into a gator is no laughing matter. Alligators are most active when temperatures are between eighty-two and ninety-two degrees Fahrenheit. Right now it's eighty-eight. You're right in the sweet spot. Need I say more?"

Gold digested this information. Then he took a deep breath and looked directly at Taylor. "You sure know how to cheer a guy up."

"Just doing my job. Educating the public."

"I suppose so."

Taylor stood, stretched. "Well, time to shove off."

"Thanks for the tour –– and the lecture."

"I hope you'll come back."

"You never know. I just might."

After returning home, Gold took a quick shower and grabbed a beer out of the refrigerator. He went out on the pool deck, found a lounge chair, and closed his eyes. He thought about putting on some music, maybe a little Elvis to cheer himself up, but he decided a nap would be even better. His mind momentarily shifted to Capone Island and the way Taylor had tried to put the fear of God into him. What the hell was that all about? Educating the public or dissuading treasure hunters? Maybe both?

Harriet Gold returned from her weekly Mah Jongg game about an hour later, and when she saw the bruise on her son's head she gasped, and the blood drained from her face. "Oh my God," she said. "What happened to your head?"

"Don't worry, it's just a scratch."

Harriet's face sort of expanded, her eyebrows launching up while her jaw dropped. "*Excuse* me? A scratch? You're kidding, right? That's more than a scratch. That's a welt. A wound. A contusion. Maybe a concussion."

"Slow down, Mom. I'm almost on my death bed."

"You're making jokes?"

"I don't know whether to laugh or cry."

She stared at him, unsure of what to do next. "I should get some ice."

"I had a cold beer."

"You don't need alcohol."

"I didn't drink it, I held it against my head."

She cleared her throat and did her motherly best not to look worried. "How did this happen?"

"Believe it or not, I ran into a tree."

"Why were you running?"

"My boat was leaving. I knew you'd be upset if I didn't come back." He smiled at her. "Was I right?"

She pulled over a chair and faced him, her expression one of disbelief. "Tell me the truth. Does this have anything to do with that ghost?"

"There is no ghost. What you saw was some knucklehead digging for treasure. Al Capone supposedly buried some loot on the island, and folks have been trying to find it for years."

"I know what I saw."

Gold sighed, rubbed his tired eyes with his knuckles, and said, "You told me that a flickering light caught your eye. Treasure hunters use lanterns. Lanterns flicker. When you looked closer, you saw a figure with a dark veil. The veil was probably a mosquito net. The island is crawling with insects. The creature, as you referred to it, was digging a hole, not a grave. You can't find buried treasure without some digging. Shall I go on?"

"Why was that... that thing wiping away tears?"

"Those were not tears. That was sweat."

"Why dig at night?"

"Because it's against the law to dig on a nature preserve."

Harriet looked away a while, examined her fingernails, and finally directed her gaze back to her son. "You've got an answer for everything."

"Almost everything. I still don't understand why people risk their lives on such nonsense. I guess Barnum was right. There's a sucker born every minute."

"Speaking of suckers..." She rummaged through her purse, trying to find something, but came up empty-handed. "Where did I put that damn thing?"

"What are you looking for?"

"A business card. I've been approached by a realtor. A nice young man from Fort Lauderdale. He thinks he can get top dollar for my house."

Gold gave her a small, disbelieving frown. "Are you thinking of selling?"

"No, but there's no harm in testing the market."

"Your house is thirty years old. I doubt you'd get top dollar."

"I said the same thing, but the realtor told me that he has contacts in Cuba. Some rich clients that are anxious to invest in South Florida. According to him, money is no object."

"Sounds good," Gold said. "Too good to be true."

"Well, as your father used to say, it never hurts to listen." She finally found the card and gave it to him. "Why don't you give him a call? Tell him who you are, and ask if you can stop by his office. You'll be in Fort Lauderdale for your interview. Maybe you can kill two birds with one stone."

Gold slumped back in his chair, suddenly looking dazed and confused. "It's not possible," he murmured. "It can't be." He sat still for a moment, composing himself and staring at the card. "What the hell is going on here?" He let out a burst of fake-sounding laughter and clapped his hands together. "Ricardo Paz? Sun Coast Realty?"

"Something wrong?"

"Very wrong."

"You look like you've just seen a ghost."

"Maybe I have." With some difficulty, Gold got up from the lounge chair and walked toward the door. "I'll see you later."

CHAPTER NINE

There were no hard and fast rules about how to deal with a sleazy insured, but resorting to violence was definitely frowned upon. Too bad, Gold thought, because it would be nice to slap Ricardo Paz around for annoying his mother. It would also be nice to slap him around for filing a frivolous claim, but in both cases, Gold would be breaking the law –– and risking his license. There was no sense overreacting until he eliminated the possibility of a coincidence. But what were the chances?

The traffic was heavy on Interstate 95 headed south, Broward County saying goodbye to its last snow birds and the tired day workers that had knocked off early. Gold kept the windows closed and the air-conditioning on and played a CD of elevator music he'd found in the glovebox. The traffic was less dense on Commercial Boulevard, the Fort Lauderdale exit that led to the beach.

Sun Coast Realty was located on Tradewinds Avenue, in the heart of Lauderdale-By-The-Sea, a pricey town straddling the Intracoastal Waterway. Gold was initially concerned when he found the front door ajar, but when he peeked inside, everything seemed to be in order.

Almost everything.

The lights were on, but nobody was home.

Not a soul in sight.

Gold knocked on the door, then stepped inside, wondering why nobody was around at four o'clock in the afternoon. Inside, the place smelled musty. Maybe that was the reason the door was cracked open. There was a reception desk in the middle of the room, and behind it three more desks, side by side in a row. Each desk was covered with real estate brochures, contracts, and flyers. Further back, a door with the company name led to a private office. A sign on the door instructed employees to knock before entering. Gold was about to knock when the door swung open and a pretty brunette, slightly disheveled and wearing too much makeup, walked out. When she saw Gold, she stopped dead in her tracks, failing to conceal her surprise and displeasure.

"Oh my God," she said. "You almost gave me a heart attack."

"Sorry about that. I knocked two times."

Her gaze swept the room. "How did you get in here?"

"Through the front door. I believe that's the customary fashion."

"Jesus Christ, I told that *idiota* to lock the door."

"By *idiota* you mean Ricardo Paz?"

She brushed back her hair, squared her shoulders, and said, "How can I help you, sir?"

"I'd like to speak to the boss."

"Do you have an appointment?"

"Nope."

"Mr. Paz is very busy today."

"All tied up, huh?"

"I'm afraid so."

"Must be a hot market."

She ignored the gibe and sat down, crossing her legs and letting her skirt slip back liberally on her bare thighs as she sat farther back in the chair. "Would you like to leave your name and number?"

"I was hoping you could... squeeze me in."

She put her hands behind her head, a coy little gesture that made her all the more enticing. "Don't get your hopes up."

Gold brushed off the put-down and studied the voluptuous thirty-something woman with her snug-fitting blouse, short skirt, and platform shoes. He guessed she was of Cuban descent, since she spoke with a slight accent and the name plate on her desk read: "Morella Perez." He cracked a small smile, then said, "Forgive my boldness, but you missed a button."

"Excuse me?"

"On your blouse."

She looked somewhere between perplexed and amused. "Thanks for pointing that out."

"Any time."

Blushing, she buttoned her blouse, then picked up a pencil and began to twirl it between her fingers like a baton. It was meant to convey boredom. A signal that she was tired of the clever repartee. "Why don't you leave your card, and I'll have Mr. Paz call you when he's free. How does that sound?"

"Not too good. You see, I'm only in town for a short time."

"Maybe I can be of service. Are you buying or selling?"

"Neither. I'm investigating."

"Investigating?" She looked at him warily. "You don't look like a cop to me."

"Is that a compliment or an insult?"

"Neither. Just an observation."

"Well, you happen to be right. I'm not a cop. I work for the Anchor Insurance Company." He gave her a card. "Mr. Paz filed a claim, and if he wants to get paid, he'll have to talk to me. I suggest that you tell him I'm here."

She hesitated, but only for a moment. Just long enough to convey her displeasure. After tossing his card to the side, she picked up the handset of her phone and punched a couple of numbers on the dial pad. "Ricardo, *tienes un visitante.* Adam Gold. *Compañía de Seguros Anchor. Vestirse y venir aquí. Con rapider. Sí, rápidamente.*"

After she hung up, Gold said, "I'm glad you told him to put his pants on."

Glaring at him, she said, "You speak Spanish?"

"*Solo un poco.* Just enough to stay out of trouble."

"I've got a feeling trouble is your middle name."

"I don't have a middle name."

"Nobody's perfect."

"Amen, sister."

Perez leaned back and tapped her perfectly white teeth with a pencil eraser, then said, "Would you like something to drink? Some coffee or a bottle of water?"

Gold shook his head and reached for the picture frame on her desk. It contained a photograph of a teenage girl playing volleyball. The girl was wearing a St. Brendan High School uniform, and she bore a stark resemblance to Morella Perez. "Your daughter?"

She took the picture frame back. "That's right."

"Beautiful girl."

"She takes after her mother."

Gold smiled. "What's her name?"

"Benita."

"Blessed."

"Muy bien."

"I've got two daughters. They both played volleyball. One was a wing spiker and the other a middle blocker."

"Benita is a setter. All County two years in a row."

"You must be very proud of her."

"She's my pride and joy."

"Is there a Mr. Perez?"

"Why do you care?"

"Just curious."

She straightened herself in the chair. "I don't discuss my personal life with strangers."

"What about your public life?"

"What do you want to know?"

"How long have you been working here?"

"I got my real estate license two months ago."

"Do you like your job?"

"It beats waiting tables."

"You used to be a waitress?"

"What's wrong with that?"

"Nothing. In fact, I'm very impressed. You've come a long way. You should be proud of yourself."

She smiled demurely. "How long have you been an investigator?"

"Longer than I care to remember."

"You like your job?"

"Most of the time. I handle some interesting claims, and the pay's pretty good. I also meet a lot of interesting people. Some good, some bad, all memorable."

She batted her eyes at him. "What will you remember about me?"

Gold thought for a moment, then said, "Your cheerful disposition." He braced himself. "What will you remember about me?"

"Besides your wit?"

"In addition to that."

She beckoned him closer, then whispered, "Not a thing."

Touché, Gold thought. Her reply had been bitchy, but he had it coming after commenting on her disposition. Miss Morella Perez had obviously graduated from the school of hard knocks, and she wasn't going to take any crap from a stranger. Switching gears, Gold inquired about the local real estate market, but even there he had a hidden agenda. "How's the market in Palm Beach County?"

"Depends on the area. Some communities are hot, some are not. You know the old saying: location, location, location."

"What about Boca Raton?"

"Boca's on fire."

"I beg your pardon?"

"Sizzling hot."

Gold was genuinely surprised. "Even with all those high-priced mansions?"

"Don't be fooled by what you hear. Boca's much more affordable than you think." She turned on her computer and brought up a page of demographics. Surprisingly, the median sales price in Boca Raton was slightly over $300,000. "That's roughly $183 per square foot. Not bad for South Florida."

Gold shook his head. "How do you like that. I was under the impression that the place was unaffordable."

"Well, to be perfectly honest, the prices do fluctuate. If you want to live near the water, you'll have to pay a lot more. Some of the numbers can be astronomical."

"I think I passed one of those places on the way down here. A lovely community on the left side of US-1."

"Do you remember the name?"

"I think it was called Royal Palm Yacht and Country Club."

"Near the Boca Raton Hotel?"

"Just south of it."

"Yeah, I know the place. Real hoitsy-toitsy."

Gold smiled. "Haven't heard that word in a while."

"They get big numbers up there."

"How much do the homes go for?"

"I'm not sure. We don't handle the room to roam palaces."

"Say what?"

"The Gold Coast crowd. We stick with the little people. Less commission, but fewer headaches, too." She turned off the computer and waited for him to say something, but Gold remained silent. "If you're dying to see the place, I could recommend an agent."

Gold smiled ruefully. "No thanks. I've already got one in mind."

CHAPTER TEN

When Paz made his grand entrance, Perez handled the introductions, and she seemed relieved when she was asked to hold down the fort while the two men talked in the private office. Paz, on the other hand, was anything but relieved. He had not been expecting Gold, or anyone else from the Anchor Insurance Company, and he was not prepared to be questioned by a claims investigator. Of course, that was precisely why Gold had not bothered to call and set up an appointment.

Paz looked Gold up and down a long moment, as if sizing him up, and said, "You caught me at a bad time. I've got my hands full today."

Rather than make a crack about Perez, Gold said, "All work and no play makes Jack a dull boy."

Paz frowned at this statement. "I don't have time to play games." He gave a fake yawn and said in a clearly uninterested tone, "What can I do for you, Mr. Gold?"

Gold kept his expression polite and as casual as possible. "You recently filed a claim with my company, and I've been asked to conduct a preliminary investigation. I'd like to ask you a few questions about the loss."

Paz resented being quizzed but had better reasons for answering than staying silent. Twenty thousand reasons. He glanced at his watch, then said, "What would you like to know?"

Gold put his duffle bag on the desk, opened it, and took out the portable lie detector. He made a show of assembling the device and plugging in the wires. When he was done, he pulled out a notebook and a pen, arranged them next to the lie detector, and paused, acutely aware of how intently Paz was watching him. "Sorry about the delay." He smiled to be polite. "Do you have any objection to taking a lie detector test?"

"You want me to take a *what?*" Paz asked, staring at him, astounded.

"It's standard procedure. No big deal."

"You gotta be kidding."

"It's not mandatory. If you feel uncomfortable, we can just have a friendly chat."

Paz nervously adjusted his tie and considered his options. He didn't believe that "friendly chat" crap for a second. He fixed Gold with a wary look, then said, "I don't understand why you're here. I bought a policy, I had a loss, and now you clowns owe me some money. Simple as that."

Gold laughed, but there was no levity in it. "I'm afraid it's not that simple. The loss report was a little vague about the cause of the fire. I may have misread the report, but I think it stated that you smoked the cigars."

Paz sat with his arms crossed over his chest, his eyes focused somewhere a foot or two above Gold's head. From time to time he'd draw a breath, but nothing so deep as a sigh. There was resignation in his voice, but also a hint of arrogance. He nodded as if to say "you're damn right." A moment later, he gave Gold a weak facsimile of a smile. "Yeah, I smoked them, and I enjoyed every puff. They were Cohiba cigars from Cuba. I grew up down there, so I know how good they are."

"Yeah, but quality doesn't come cheap."

"They're worth every penny."

"I'll have to take your word for that. Eight hundred bucks is above my pay grade."

"Mine too. The cigars were a gift."

"Generous gift."

"From the owner of our firm."

"Generous owner."

Paz's dark eyes showed no amusement as he smiled. "I'm sorry about the claim, but shit happens. You know what I mean?"

Gold showed no reaction, not the faintest hint of emotion, but inside his head, the wheels were turning quickly. He had just stumbled upon a way to deny Paz's claim. God, he loved those eureka moments. He formulated his next sentence carefully. "You know what I was wondering? Is there a correct way of smoking a great cigar?"

Paz gave him a blank stare for a long moment and then said, "What do you mean?"

"Do you have to follow a certain procedure?"

"No, but I do. I treat a great cigar like a beautiful woman." A small grin formed on his lips. "I hold her gently and run my fingers across her body. Then I inhale her fragrance and study her form. When I'm ready, I set her on fire and enjoy her taste."

Gold acted like that was the most clever thing he'd ever heard and shook his head in admiration. "Do you use a match or a lighter?"

"I prefer a match, but it makes no difference. A flame is a flame."

Still smiling, Gold said, "Do you go through all that trouble every time you smoke a cigar?"

"Only with a Cohiba. They deserve special treatment."

Gold sighed and rubbed the bridge of his nose. "Well, I'm glad you enjoyed them, but I'm afraid we'll have to deny your claim."

Paz watched him closely, wariness gathering inside him. What the hell was this about? "You're denying my claim? On what grounds?"

"You just confessed to a crime."

"What the hell are you talking about?"

"You caused the fire that destroyed the cigars."

"Huh?"

"You lit the match."

"So?"

"We call that arson, and in the state of Florida, that's a felony crime."

"Arson?"

"Second-degree. Punishable by up to fifteen years in prison and a fine of up to ten thousand dollars."

The blood seemed to drain from Paz's face. *"Fifteen years? Ten thousand dollars?"*

Gold scratched his face, thinking. "Unless they add insurance fraud. Then you're looking at twenty years."

Paz exhaled heavily and seemed to slump in on himself. The cocky facade disintegrated. He rubbed his face in a weary gesture. "I don't believe this shit."

Gold began to pack his duffle bag, pretending to be distracted. "You know what sucks? After you serve your time, you'll probably be deported. Those INS folks are heartless bastards. If I know them, you'll be on the first boat to Cuba. No citizenship, no career, no nothing. All your dreams, up in smoke." A smirk thinned his lips. "No pun intended."

"Maybe I should call a lawyer."

"Or a travel agent."

Paz glared at him. "You think this is funny?"

"Frankly, my dear, I don't give a damn."

Paz sat in silence for a moment. He felt emotionally drained. Part of him wanted to run home and lie down. But he was too proud. Who was this *gringo* to threaten him with prison? Suddenly furious, his self-control deserted him and he lunged across the desk toward Gold. He did not move fast enough. Gold blocked his lunge and hammered a fist into Paz's right kidney, doubling him over and dropping him to the floor. Paz got up slowly and swung at him but caught nothing but air as Gold stepped back from the punch and braced himself for another swing. Paz swung with his other arm and missed again, but this time Gold landed a hard right to the jaw. Paz stumbled backward, tripped over his own feet, and fell to the floor.

Gold stood over him, shaking his head. "Arson, insurance fraud, assault and battery. Jesus, you're a one-man crime wave."

Paz spat the blood from his mouth, looked directly into Gold's eyes, and said, "Fuck you, *gringo*."

Gold wagged a finger at him. "Uh-uh-uh, let's not be vulgar. I was just about to offer you a deal. How would you like a Get-Out-of-Jail-Free Card?"

Paz crawled back to his chair, wondering what that meant. Having grown up in Cuba, he didn't understand the reference to the game of *Monopoly*. "I don't understand what you mean."

"I'm going to make you an offer you can't refuse -- unless you're a moron. If you withdraw your claim I'll forget about the arson and fraud charges, and we can both live happily ever after. What do you say, *amigo?*"

Paz studied him with suspicion. "For real?"

"I kid you not."

"Why are you being so nice?"

"Didn't your *madre* ever tell you not to look a gift horse in the mouth?"

"No comprendo."

"Don't push your luck, pal."

Paz said nothing but was staring daggers at Gold now. "Maybe you don't have such a strong case, huh? Maybe you're trying to push me around. I think this arson thing is bullshit."

"You don't say."

"I just did."

"Turn your computer on, *amigo.*"

"Why?"

"I want you to look up the definition of arson."

Paz was more than happy to oblige, but when he looked up the word on Google, he turned white. He tried to swallow, but his throat was too dry. All he could manage was a whispered curse word. *"Hijo de puta."*

A slow, knowing grin spread over Gold's face. He recited the definition without looking at the screen. "The willful and malicious burning or charring of property... including setting fire to one's property with fraudulent intent -- such as to collect insurance money."

Paz stared at him for a long moment. "I don't know what to say."

Gold continued, an edge to his voice. "You criminal masterminds never cease to amaze me. Did you really think we were going to fork over twenty grand?"

Paz was frowning thoughtfully. "I never wanted to file a claim. My employer talked me into it."

"Your employer's a schmuck."

"Whatever you want me to sign, I'll sign. Just give me the waiver, and then get out."

"Not so fast," Gold said. "We still have some unfinished business." He rummaged through his pocket and found the business card that Paz had given his mother. "What's this all about?"

Paz's confusion was evident as he looked from his card to Gold. "How did you get my business card?"

"My mother gave it to me."

"Your mother?"

"Harriet Gold. She lives in Boca Raton. In the Royal Palm Yacht & Country Club."

Paz was already shaking his head. "I don't do business up there."

"Too hoitsy-toitsy?"

"Huh?"

"Never mind." Gold paused for a moment, looked down at his hands and spoke quietly. "How do you explain the card?"

"Beats me. Maybe my employer gave it to her. He handles the Gold Coast crowd."

"Maybe you should ask your employer to give me a call."

"If you insist."

"I do."

"No hay problema."

"Unless he forgets to call. If that happens, you've got a big problem. If that happens, the deal's off and you start packing for Railford. Understood?"

"No need to get nasty. I'll have him call you as soon as he gets back."

"Back from where?"

"He's out of town."

"Where'd he go?"

"I'm not sure."

"You're not sure?"

"Am I my boss's keeper?"

Gold looked highly skeptical. "You guys run a tight ship. One hand doesn't know what the other is doing."

Paz sighed. "I think he went to Naples."

"I hope you don't mean Naples, Italy."

"West Coast. He should be back in a day or two."

Gold looked at him gravely. "I sure hope so."

CHAPTER ELEVEN

Gold drove back to Boca Raton on US-1, which was less congested than I-95 but actually more dangerous. In fact, the Florida section of the highway was the least safe in the nation, with 1,079 fatal crashes in the last ten years. Tailgating at high speed was a problem throughout the state, but on this section, in Broward County, tailgating usually involved a slow-driving senior citizen.

Gold was doing the speed limit, and then some, yet a black Suburban had been on his tail from the moment he'd left Sun Coast Realty. At first he thought Paz had forgotten to tell him something, but the vehicle following him two car lengths back, was definitely some sort of official government vehicle. The license plate was blue and white, and there was a department emblem on the lower left corner. When Gold slowed down and the Suburban drew closer, he saw that the emblem was from the Department of Homeland Security.

Hoping to avoid a scene, he drove past the entrance to his mother's community and continued north on US-1. When he reached Taverna Kyma, a popular Greek restaurant, he pulled into the back parking lot and waited for his new friends to arrive. Five minutes later, with no sign of the Suburban, he decided to take advantage of the restaurant's generous happy hour –– two-for-one drinks at the bar.

The bartender, a pretty young woman from Argentina, took his order and placed a menu in front of him. By the time she returned with a chilled martini, there was a lady sitting beside Gold. Smiling sweetly, she reached for Gold's glass and held it up to the light. "Let me guess," she said calmly. "Bombay Sapphire Gin. Ice and olives on the side." She winked at him. "Did I get it right?"

Gold turned all the way around and looked at her, and when she removed her sunglasses, his mouth fell open. He could scarcely believe his eyes. "Holy sh—." He pulled his chair closer and lowered his voice. *"Sally?"*

She smiled affectionately. "We meet again."

Sally Ridge, a long-lost friend, was the last person on earth Gold expected to see at Taverna Kyma. Five years earlier, he'd saved her life while working on a claim in Tupelo, Mississippi. Back then, she was Lieutenant Ridge, a detective in the Felony Crime Division of the Tupelo Police Department. Two years later, their paths crossed in Texas, where they were both investigating crimes linked to a sadistic cult leader.

The Texas adventure had ended rather abruptly –– and awkwardly –– and Gold never knew what happened to her.

She never called.

She never wrote.

She simply vanished.

And now she was here, sitting beside him, as if the past had been a dream.

They sat for a moment in completely awkward silence. Well, it was completely awkward for Gold. Ridge seemed fine with it. But he didn't like the silence. It made him feel as if he might blurt out something inappropriate. Which is exactly what happened. "Jesus Christ," he finally said. "I thought you were dead."

Ridge shrugged weakly, then ordered a gin and tonic. "The rumors of my demise were greatly exaggerated."

He stared at her for a long minute, then gave her a hug. "You look great."

"You look like you've just seen a ghost."

"A ghost? Don't mention that word to me."

"Huh?"

"Never mind. Long story. How the hell are you, Sally?"

"Doing well."

"I heard you jumped out of a plane and vanished. Somewhere over the Davis Mountains."

"Actually, it was over the Van Horn Mountains."

"Everyone assumed the worse."

"Wishful thinking." She reached over and patted his hand. "Except on your part. The rest of those folks were glad to get rid of me. I guess I pissed them off."

"Well, you did fly off with their prisoner."

"So I did."

"Without a warrant, I might add."

"This is true."

"I think they were very embarrassed."

"I think you're right."

"Well, you know what they say. All's well that ends well."

Ridge reached for her drink and pushed the ice around in her glass with her index finger. Sitting back now, an ankle on its opposite knee, she let the silence hang for a few seconds. "It didn't end well for Eric Krugman. The son of a bitch ran into some bad luck. When the plane stalled, I was forced to bail out. As fate would have it, there was only one parachute, and it was strapped on my back. The child molester went down with the ship." She sighed theatrically. "Such is life."

Gold was frowning, shaking his head from side to side. "Karma's a bitch."

They clinked glasses.

She leaned closer, then said, "It was a long way down, but I landed on my feet, so to speak. I was picked up by the Border Patrol and escorted to El Paso. From there, I made my way back to Tupelo and laid low for a while. Before long, the feds came knocking, but instead of questioning me, they offered me a job. Seems they were looking for a Native American tracker, and I fit the bill. Choctaw. Female. Law enforcement background. The whole nine yards."

Even while he was listening to the interesting news, Gold found himself watching her with fascination, concentrating his attention first on her dark eyes, which seemed to sparkle with energy, then on her expressive mouth, then on the way the light fell on her long brown hair. He didn't want to interrupt her, but he was famished. He said, "Why don't we order some food?"

"Sounds good to me."

He showed her the menu. "What would you like?"

"I don't know. What do you think?"

"We could start with tzatziki and spanakopita, and then order moussaka and souvlaki. How does that sound?"

"It's Greek to me. Go for it."

Gold broke into a grin. "I'll order for us." The bartender materialized and took the order without writing anything down. Bartenders with good memories were another sign of a well-run establishment, he told himself. When they were alone, he said, "How long have you been with DHS?"

She dabbed her mouth with a napkin. "How did you know..."

"The emblem on your plate."

"Of course. When did you spot us?"

"When I turned onto Commercial Boulevard. How long have you been following me?"

"Since you left Capone Island." She had been about to take a swallow of her drink but she paused, the glass a few inches from her mouth. "I've been with DHS for five years. Would you like to know how you got on my radar?"

"First things first. I interrupted your recruitment story. Finish what you were saying."

Ridge propped her elbows on the bar and steepled her fingers. She told him that she'd been recruited by ICE –– Immigration and Customs Enforcement –– to serve in the Shadow Wolves, a tracking unit composed of Native Americans, based on the Tohono O'odham Indian Reservation in southern Arizona. The name of the tribe meant "Desert People," and its members were highly proficient trackers, a skill passed down from generation to generation.

The name "Shadow Wolves" referred to the way the unit hunted, which was like a wolf pack. When a wolf –– or tracker –– located its prey, the rest of the pack joined the hunt. In this case, the prey consisted of smugglers operating in arduous desert and rugged mountain terrain.

She went on to say that the job required a special skill set –– the ability to master a technique called "cutting for sign." In essence, "cutting" meant searching for and analyzing "sign," physical evidence that included footprints, tire tracks, items snagged on branches, bent or broken twigs, and fibers of clothing left on the ground.

The fifteen-member unit, the Department of Homeland Security's only Native American tracking unit, was responsible for patrolling almost three million acres of land.

"We're the best in the business," she said proudly. "The drug smugglers hate us. So do the scum that engage in human trafficking. I don't mean to brag, but we've taught our ancient tracking skills to customs officials and border guards in Kazakhstan, Uzbekistan, Latvia, Lithuania, and Estonia."

Gold stayed silent for a full minute, then said, "How come I didn't get a postcard?"

"I was working undercover. Incommunicado with the outside world."

"For five years?"

"Most of that time."

Gold wasn't buying, but he didn't push it. "You haven't aged a day."

"You need glasses."

"I'm serious. You're as pretty as ever."

"You need binoculars."

"Don't mention that word either."

She leaned over and kissed him tenderly on the cheek. "Are we having a bad day?"

"Two bad days."

"How can I help?"

"Two-for-one drinks should do the trick."

"Are you down here on business or pleasure?"

"Mostly business."

"Working on a claim?"

"A real doozy."

"Tell me about it."

"Excuse me?"

"I'd like to hear about the claim."

"Really?"

"If you're involved, it's got to be interesting."

Gold hesitated, reluctant by habit to disclose information about his work. He knew that Ridge could be trusted, but it just felt odd to discuss the details of an ongoing investigation. Of course, she had just confided in him, so it wouldn't be fair to hold back. *Screw protocol,* he thought. *If you can't trust a DHS agent, who can you trust?* He leaned closer and spoke in a whisper, telling her everything, leaving nothing out. When he finished talking, she threw her head back and laughed out loud. "What's so funny?"

"I can't believe he smoked the cigars. What a clown."

"Takes all kinds."

"Your response was priceless. How did you think of the arson angle?"

"I don't know, it just hit me like a bolt from the blue."

"Divine intervention."

"I don't know about that, but the result was divine. Paz signed a waiver and withdrew his claim. What more could I ask for?"

"Well, this calls for a celebration."

"We are celebrating."

"Next round's on me."

"Trying to get me drunk?"

"It crossed my mind."

Gold summoned up what he hoped would pass for a friendly smile. "You still owe me an explanation."

"I beg your pardon?"

"Why have you been following me?"

Ridge took in a breath and let it out slowly. This was going to be the hard part. She'd never been much of a sharer, not when it came to a particular case. Her job was finding and arresting the bad guys, not holding hands and singing *Kumbaya*. She said what needed to be said and then captured or killed the people who needed to be captured or killed. Simple as that. However, in this situation, she'd reached a dead end. She had hit the proverbial brick wall. Her expression transformed into something between a frown and a smile. "I need your help, Mr. Gold."

"You need *my* help? Well, that's a switch. How can I be of service?"

"You'd better order another martini."

CHAPTER TWELVE

The bar was getting crowded, so Ridge and Gold moved outside and found a secluded spot on the patio. Between bites, she asked him if he was familiar with the term "Whirling Dervish" as it applied to law enforcement. When he shook his head, she explained that DHS used the term to describe someone who was involved in numerous criminal activities. At the present time, she was after one of their most notorious "Dervishes," a man who was involved in drug smuggling, human trafficking, and child pornography.

Gold shook his head. "Sounds like a bad dude."

"The worst of the worst."

"What does this have to do with me?"

"More than you might think."

"I don't follow."

"The man I'm after is the owner of Sun Coast Realty. The creep that gave Paz the cigars." She paused for a moment as if to make certain he was following her explanation, then she continued. "His name is Nicholas Russo. Ring a bell?"

Gold was quiet, thinking. "I used to work with a guy named Joey Russo. In fact, he was the reason I came to Tupelo. He was working on a claim, but he died suddenly. I took over. Any relation to your boy?"

"Joey Russo was Nick's uncle."

"Uncle?"

"Yep."

"Son of a bitch."

"My sentiments exactly."

Gold felt goosebumps run down his arms. He seemed worried, and with good reason. Joey's brother –– and Nick's father –– was a Jersey mobster named Sal Russo. Five years ago, the don, who thought of himself as a Don Juan, assaulted the wrong woman and ended up on the wrong end of a gun. The woman who shot and killed him was Annette Russo, Joey's widow. In an act of compassion –– some might say foolishness –– Gold helped her stay out of jail by concocting a story about rape.

Gold swore again and then heaved a resigned sigh. "I always wondered what happened to Sal's son."

"Now you know. He's been keeping up with the family tradition."

"Like father, like son."

"The apple doesn't fall far from the tree."

"Especially a rotten apple."

Ridge managed a brief smile. "I didn't know that you were involved in this mess until I saw you on Capone Island. We've had the place under surveillance for several weeks, hoping that Russo might show his face."

Gold frowned darkly. "Why would he go out there?"

"To look for the treasure."

"Capone's treasure?"

"An informer told us that Russo is a true believer. I wouldn't be surprised if he heard the story on his father's knee. In any case, he's planning to use the money to finance his criminal activities."

"Never underestimate the stupidity of the criminal mind."

"Amazes me, too."

"How does Nicky plan to get around the park rangers?"

"He doesn't have to get around them."

"Why not?"

"He owns them. Skip and his buddies are on Russo's payroll."

"Skip Taylor?"

Her expression grew sober. "I call him Skip Town. The poor boy never stays in one place too long. He makes ends meet by selling stolen artifacts. Russo pays him and his pals to look the other way when they go on digs."

Gold forced himself to laugh, but it wasn't easy. "Are you sure you've got the right guy?"

"I'm positive."

"He seemed like a nice young man to me."

She leaned across the table and placed her mouth right next to his ear, then whispered, "Situational awareness."

"What about it?"

"Not your strong suit."

"What's that supposed to mean?"

"Didn't you wonder why a park ranger was driving around in a new BMW? Those babies cost a bundle."

"Ever hear of a lease?"

"I don't think he leased those dental caps, and he's got a mouthful."

"Yeah, I noticed."

"For future reference, a Beemer convertible is around fifty grand, and those caps are no bargain either. They cost about a thousand bucks apiece."

"I get the point."

Ridge was smiling as she spoke. "By the way, Skippy is also a homeowner."

"Where does he live?"

"In a swanky neighborhood in Delray Beach. A place called Addison Reserve."

"I know it well."

"You do?"

"My brother lives there."

"How do you like that."

"I don't like it. Not one bit. I can't believe that punk kid bought a home in Addison."

"He used a local realtor. Would you like to guess who that might be?"

"Sun Coast Realty?"

"Give that man a cigar! Oops, make that a Kewpie doll. I forgot about the claim."

"No problem. I got the waiver. That's all that counts."

"Your boss will be very happy."

"My boss will be thrilled."

She ordered her second drink, then said, "You never told me why you went to Capone Island."

"You never asked."

"I'm asking now."

So he told her. Starting with the ghost, and then the binoculars, and then his visit to the island. He even told her about his accident, how he ran into a tree and knocked himself out. He expected her to laugh or make a snide remark, but she resisted the temptation. He was grateful for that. Out of the corner of his eye, he noticed a change in her expression. It was small and subtle. But he was certain it was there –– an expression of sympathy. He managed a weak smile in return. "Here's the weird part. I met Skip Taylor a year ago, during a trip to Virginia. He was working for the Park Service in Chancellorsville. He gave my boss and me a tour of the battlefield, and showed us some interesting graves."

"Small world."

"I never took him for a thief."

"Looks can be deceiving. Would you like to see his file?"

"He's got his own file?"

"He's no Al Capone, but he's heading in that direction." She reached into her bag and pulled out a two-page dossier. "Read it and weep."

Taylor's file contained a number of disturbing revelations, but the most revolting part was his obsession with child pornography. As Ridge explained, Taylor was a sick low life who was hoping to become a player in Florida's booming porn industry. Nationwide, Americans spent $14 billion a year on various forms of smut, and of that amount, $3 billion was spent on child pornography. She went on to tell him that 55 percent of the images of children were produced in the United States, and at the present time, there were over 600,000 porno traders in the country.

State and federal laws prohibited the production, distribution, importation, reception, and possession of any image of child pornography, and in most cases, it was a felony offense to violate the law.

"By the way," she added, "each violation is punishable by a long prison sentence and a hefty fine."

"I would hope so," Gold said. He wondered how the industry continued to flourish. "Don't the feds go after the major dealers?"

"Sometimes."

"Sometimes?"

"Less than 1 percent of the dealers are investigated or pursued."

"Why so many?" Gold asked sarcastically.

"Not a priority."

"Children are not a priority?"

"Not when we have to deal with terrorism. Those ISIS bastards suck up most of the funds and much of our manpower. The porn merchants know the score and act with near impunity."

"Wonderful."

"If you ask me, it sucks." She closed her eyes for a minute. Told herself to calm down. *Breathe through the mouth. Deep, steady breaths.* "Every now and then we catch a break. Last year, the FBI arrested and prosecuted the creep who ran the world's largest child pornography website. The site had 150,000 users around the world. The son of a bitch got a thirty-year prison sentence."

"I hope he gets a cellmate named Bubba."

"Well, it doesn't matter. He won't last long. The prison population frowns upon child molesters and pornographers."

"Honor among thieves?"

"More or less."

"Nice to know they have some standards."

"Incidentally, that creep I mentioned was a resident of the Sunshine State."

"Whereabouts?"

"Naples."

"Small world."

"How so?"

"Paz told me that Russo went to Naples. He's supposed to be back in a couple of days."

Ridge gave a cheerless grin. "A lot could happen in forty-eight hours."

Gold wiped a napkin across his mouth and then said, "We could drive over to Naples. Take a look around. Or we could start in Miami."

"Miami?"

"Annette Russo lives in Miami. Somewhere out west. We could stop by her house and have a chat. Maybe she could point us in the right direction."

Ridge pulled her chair closer and lowered her voice. "Who's Annette Russo?"

"Nick Russo's aunt."

"Aunt?"

"She was married to my colleague, Joey Russo. After Joey died, she sold her house in Bensonhurst -- Brooklyn -- and retired down here. She's a stand-up gal, if you know what I mean."

"Mama mia, this case is getting more interesting by the minute. You think she'd be willing to help us?"

"Yeah, I think so. She owes me a favor. A big favor."

"I'm listening."

Gold shook his head. "You don't want to know."

"Sure I do."

"Why are you so nosy?"

"I sense a tale of intrigue and romance."

"Intrigue, maybe. Romance, no. Joey was a friend of mine, and I don't fool around with my friends' wives."

"Well, you must have done something lovely, but I won't pry." She drew a deep breath, then exhaled noisily. They had played this game before, and Ridge was sure the rules weren't going to change now. He wasn't going to tell her anything, so there was no point in pressing him, even if she pretended to be hurt. She stayed silent, and more than a minute passed. Finally, she said, "All right, Sir Lancelot, let's start in Miami. Give me your address. I'll pick you up tomorrow morning. Ten o'clock sharp."

"Tomorrow morning? I thought you were anxious to get started."

"I have to be in Tallahassee at nine o'clock tonight. Urgent meeting with the top brass."

Gold glanced at his watch. "You'll never make it in four hours."

"Don't worry, I'll make it."

"They've got speed limits in this state."

"I'm not driving. I'm flying."

Gold looked at her with a quizzical expression in his eyes. *"Flying?"*

"I still have my pilot's license." She popped an olive into her mouth and chewed thoughtfully. "After we speak to your girlfriend, we can fly over to Naples together. How does that sound?"

"Not very good." Gold looked incredulous and exasperated at the same time. "The last time we flew together you ran out of gas."

"Yes, I remember. Faulty gauge." Her smile became a little brittle. "Fortunately, I've got a new plane. Well, actually it's a vintage aircraft, but it's in very good condition. Have you ever flown in a Dust Cropper?"

Gold smiled but felt a sick feeling in his stomach. "Where the hell is that martini?"

CHAPTER THIRTEEN

Naples, Florida, the jewel of the west coast, was quite different from its Italian namesake. Unlike *Napoli,* it was one of the wealthiest cities in the world, with the highest per capita income and the second highest proportion of millionaires per capita in the United States. The city had long been a haven for the rich and famous, and with its year-round tropical savanna climate and its eighty or so championship golf courses, it was an ideal place to play or work.

Nick Russo had done both in Naples, and now he was on his way back to Miami, anxious to take care of some unfinished business with his aunt. Driving at night across Alligator Alley had become a risky proposition, requiring a driver's full attention. A recent hurricane had caused some road damage, but the bigger hazard, the one that sent a chill down the spine, was the prospect of running over an enormous snake.

To be more precise, an enormous Burmese python.

The car-length reptiles were all over Florida's wetlands, slithering into Everglades Park in record numbers and causing great concern among residents and visitors alike.

Russo hated snakes, even the harmless ones, which were few and far between in this part of the world. Earlier in the day, he'd read a bone-chilling article in the *Naples Daily News*, describing how the python had become the state's most vexing invasive species. The situation had deteriorated to the point where the Florida Wildlife Commission was sponsoring a "Python Pickup Program." Anyone who caught or killed a snake and provided proof of the snake's location through GPS was eligible to win a prize.

Roadkill excluded.

Live pythons were preferred, and they were to be double bagged and placed into a secure container marked "dangerous reptiles."

To Russo, they were a bunch of suckers. All they got for their trouble was a lousy T-shirt. If a hunter won the monthly prize drawing, he also received a thirty-two-ounce stainless steel coffee mug with the Python Pickup Program logo on it.

Big friggin' deal, Russo thought.

A stupid mug.

All that proved to him was that his old man was right: there was a sucker born every minute. Two per minute in the Sunshine State.

Nicholas Francesco Russo was born in New Jersey, and he was nobody's fool. The way that he conducted his business proved that he was a cut above the average wise guy. When the porn market became saturated with Russian dealers, he branched out, focusing on the lucrative fields of drug smuggling and human trafficking. The feds called him a "double dealer," an entrepreneur who combined the two crimes, using abducted girls to unwittingly transport drugs.

Unfortunately for law enforcement, business was good. Very good. Americans seemed to have an insatiable appetite for anything that was illegal or immoral, regardless of the cost. Nowadays, drugs provided the greatest income, with Floridians spending the most on marijuana, opioids, and cocaine. Russo preferred to push opioids, but he wasn't content to distribute Vicodin and OxyContin, or the more potent opioids, Fentanyl and Carfentanil. Those drugs were popular, but the hard-core addicts wanted something stronger, a substance that could deliver more bang for the buck.

A substance called "gray death."

Almost overnight, Russo became the largest purveyor of the deadly drug, which was a mixture of several synthetic opioids. In its most potent form, gray death combined Fentanyl, which was designed to treat severe chronic pain, Carfentanil, which was used to tranquilize large animals like elephants, and a dose of heroin, cocaine, or crystal meth.

Every now and then, there would be a rash of overdoses, and the DEA would temporarily disrupt the marketplace. On those occasions, Russo would simply switch gears and concentrate on human trafficking, another lucrative endeavor. Like child pornography and drug smuggling, there were state and federal laws against human trafficking. Most of these laws defined the crime as soliciting, recruiting, harboring, transporting, or otherwise obtaining another person to exploit him or her for labor, domestic servitude, or sexual exploitation.

The penalties for breaking the law were severe, but as always, Russo just didn't give a shit. He was going to become a *grosso colpo* –– big shot –– by hook or by crook. Only then would he be able to say that he'd fulfilled his father's expectations and restored the family name.

A life of crime had made Russo rich, but he was still grieving about his old man. Still bitter about the way he was killed. One way or the other, he had to make things right, and in his sick mind, that meant tying up a couple of loose ends.

Loose ends named Annette Russo and Adam Gold.

By the time Russo reached his aunt's house, it was ten o'clock, and most of the homes on her street were dark. He pulled into the driveway and parked beside a screened-in porch, leaving his lights on for a full minute before turning off the engine. The side door was unlocked, so he let himself in and knocked on the back door.

When Annette Russo looked through the peephole, she felt a knot in her stomach, but she forced herself to open the door. Her lips moved slowly, as if finding each word was a major struggle. "Nicky, what are you doing here?"

Russo, sensing her uneasiness, took a tiny step back. "I meant to call, but my cell phone died."

She eyed him warily, wondering what he was up to. The sneaky bastard was always up to something. What could it be this time? She glanced at her watch, then said, "Kind of late for a visit."

"I just came from Naples. I thought you might like some pastries." He gave her a small, white box. "I got Biscotti, Sfogliatella, and Zeppole. They were all out of Cannolis." He gave her a reassuring smile. "I know you miss the old neighborhood, so I brought a box of Bensonhurst."

Annette's lips were tightly compressed, and for a moment she resisted answering. Then she relented. "How thoughtful."

"Hey, we're family, and families have to stick together."

She gave a noncommittal shrug. "Thank you. They won't go to waste."

Russo took the comment in stride, his smile never wavering. He detested his aunt, but he had to admit that she was still a handsome woman. Tall, voluptuous, attractive but with a hard edge and a clenched jaw telegraphing *don't mess with me*. He ran a hand over his mouth, wiping away the sweat that was glistening over his lip. "I sure could use a cup of coffee before I get back on the road."

"I was just about to turn in."

"Turn into what? A pumpkin?" He leaned closer, as if someone might be listening. "Come on, Annette, it's only ten o'clock. One cup and I'll be on my way. What do you say?"

She looked uncomfortable. The skin around her eyes creased, and she looked at him and then outside, at the vast, dark Everglades. She wished she could run into the swamp and hide from him, but that was a silly idea. Hell, she wouldn't last five minutes out there. She held his gaze for a minute, then motioned him toward the kitchen. "One cup," she said firmly, "and then I'm off to bed."

Russo breathed a sigh of relief, then stepped inside. "You always were my favorite aunt."

She was tempted to call him a liar, but instead of insulting him, she told him that he had a strange way of showing his affection. She reminded him that he hadn't shown his face for over a year. "To tell you the truth, I was about to write you off."

"I've been working like a dog."

"You must be doing well. Fancy suit. Rolex watch. Alligator shoes. Who says crime doesn't pay?"

Russo's hands clenched and unclenched at his sides. A shadow slid across his face. He chuckled a little under his breath, then said, "You don't approve of my work?"

"What do you think?"

"I think you're entitled to your opinion."

"I'm glad you feel that way."

"I also think that opinions are like armpits. Everybody's got a couple, and they usually stink."

She held his gaze, trying to show him that she would not be intimidated -- trying to *feel* that she wasn't -- but she saw something in his eyes that frightened her. She took a deep breath, obviously trying to remain civil. "You and I have been down this road before, and we both know it's a dead end. Why don't we change the subject?"

"What would you like to talk about?"

"Anything but business."

"How about *famiglia?*"

"Family?"

"Yeah, we could talk about my father. How does that sound?"

"Did you come here to upset me?"

"No, I came to make things right."

A small tremor passed through her body. She blinked and let a long, slow breath out through her nose. "What's your problem, Nicky?"

"I've got a lot of problems, Annette. First and foremost, I need to figure out what to do about you and that fucking Jew. You see, I know damn well that you and Adam Gold concocted that rape story. My father was a lot of things, but not a rapist. I think you got lonely and scared after Uncle Joey died. Maybe you thought my father was the next best thing, so you came onto him but then changed your mind. Am I getting warm?"

"No, you sick bastard, you're getting out!" Her face turned red with anger. "Get out of my house, or I swear to God, I'll call the police!"

"Calm down, sweetheart."

"You heard me, Nicky!"

Russo stood still for a long moment, his feet planted to the floor. "Jesus, you never change. You're always calling the cops on someone."

"I mean it, Nicky. I want you to leave, and I don't ever want to see you again."

"Whoa, is that any way to talk to your favorite nephew?"

"*My favorite nephew?* You make me sick. You've been a bum since the day you were born. Why do you think you were sent to reform school? Because you were special? You stabbed a teacher in the eye with a pencil! The judge gave your parents a choice: reform school or prison. You could have made something of yourself later on, but you chose to follow in your father's footsteps." Suddenly she laughed. It was a bitter sound. "You want to make things right? You'd better start with your mother. Why do you think she killed herself?"

Russo grabbed her arm with a surprisingly strong grip. "Shut up, bitch!"

She pulled her arm free and glared at him. "No, big shot, you need to hear the truth. Your mother knew that you were a violent hoodlum, and it broke her heart. She was ashamed that you were her son. After you went to prison, she began to drink, and eventually she drank herself to death." She set her mouth and drew a determined breath. "You drove that poor woman to an early grave."

"Goddammit!" Russo yelled out loud. "I told you to shut up!"

"The truth hurts, doesn't it?"

"Spare me the sob story. My mother was a lush most of her life. She didn't drink because of me; she drank because she loved booze."

"Jesus, you don't have the brains you were born with."

"I'm smart enough to plan the perfect crime." He pulled out a .45 Colt Automatic and pointed it in her direction. "Need I remind you that payback's a bitch?"

She gave him a long, hard look. "Are you out of your mind?"

"Nah, I've finally come to my senses."

She stood still for a moment, breathing hard, fighting down panic. Part of her wanted to scream, but she didn't. Instead, she steadied herself against a counter, trying to remain calm. Her palms grew sweaty and her mouth dry. "You'll never get away with this, Nicky."

Russo made a dismissive gesture with his hand. "Do you know that 30 percent of all homicides remain unsolved? No shit, 30 percent." He cocked the hammer and took aim at her chest. "Those are pretty good odds."

Annette's eyes went wide with panic. She put her hands out in front of her. "Oh my God, don't. No, please."

For the briefest moment there was no response. Then, almost as if he had shifted into some other gear, Russo's eyes sharpened, his shoulders came back, and he stood erect. He shook his head and chuckled, the fat jiggling under his arms and his chin. "God, he said softly, "I was hoping you'd beg." He gave her his most arrogant smile, then pulled the trigger.

CHAPTER FOURTEEN

Gold hadn't slept very much at all. Every time he had started to fall asleep, he had jerked himself awake, wondering if someone was digging on Capone Island. He ran to the window at least three times, but he never saw a damn thing. When morning came, he showered, shaved, and wiped the vapor from the mirror. It was as though the mist that hung over the island had crept into his room. Taunting him. Reminding him that catching a ghost is no easy task.

Sally Ridge arrived early, and by the time Gold made his grand entrance, she was on her second cup of coffee. Harriet Gold was sitting beside her, reminiscing about her life in New York while munching on a buttered bagel. The ladies barely acknowledged Gold, even when he poured himself coffee and sat down at the kitchen table.

Gold actually found that amusing. "Good morning, ladies. I hope I'm not interrupting your stroll down memory lane."

Between bites, Harriet said, "I didn't know that Sally's an American Indian. Did you know that?"

"I knew there was something different about her, but I couldn't put my finger on it."

"She's a full-blooded Choctaw."

"You don't say."

Ridge winked at him. "Now you know why I have high cheekbones."

"You'd be cheeky with or without the bones."

"Don't be fresh," Harriet said. "She's also a federal agent."

"So I've heard."

"She works for the IRS."

"DHS," Gold said. "The Department of Homeland Security." He glanced at Ridge. "What did you do, tell her your life story?"

"Only the good parts," Ridge replied. "I didn't mention Mississippi or Texas, or how you keep showing up like a bad penny."

"I'm the bad penny?" He sipped his coffee and then had a sudden thought. "You're the one who got shot in the leg and jumped out of an airplane."

Like an embarrassed child, Ridge mumbled. "Nobody's perfect."

"You can say that again."

"Yeah, well, you were there on both occasions. Coincidence? I think not."

"Wait a minute. Are you blaming me?"

Harriet held up a hand, silencing them. "All right, children, let's not argue. Who wants breakfast? I've got fresh bagels, vegetable cream cheese, and lox."

"I'll pass," Gold said, smiling at Ridge. "I don't like to argue on a full stomach."

"Neither do I," Ridge said. Her face took on almost a pained expression. "I'm not a breakfast eater, but it was sweet of you to offer."

Characteristically, Harriet wasn't deterred. "Don't you kids know that breakfast is the most important meal of the day?"

"Not for me," Gold said. "I'm a lunch person."

"I prefer dinner," Ridge said.

Harriet's patience was clearly starting to wane. In a last-ditch effort, she tried to make them feel guilty. "Maybe you two don't know it, but people are starving in Bangladesh."

Gold sputtered with laughter. "Have you ever been to Bangladesh?"

"No, but I watch CNN."

"CNN stands for "Clearly Not News." For your information, the country of Bangladesh is loaded with telephone operators, and most of them make a pretty good living."

She looked at him with a stricken expression. "My son, the know-it-all. Very well, suit yourself. You'll be sorry you didn't eat something."

"News flash, Mom. They have restaurants in Miami."

"Don't be fresh," Ridge said. "She's only trying to help."

Harriet frowned. "You're going to Miami?"

Gold nodded. "I'll be back this afternoon."

Harriet glanced at Ridge, who was doing an admirable job of concealing her amusement over what had just transpired, then gazed outside. She lapsed into a brooding silence, but it didn't last long. "What's in Miami?"

"Annette Russo."

"Joey's wife?"

"Joey's widow."

"Why do you want to see her?"

"She's an old friend. I'd like to see how she's doing." He saw a momentary flash of what he knew was disappointment on her face. "We won't be long. We'll take you to lunch when we get back. Ridge is buying."

Ridge smiled. "I'd be happy to take your mother to lunch, and if you behave yourself, you can join us."

Harriet leaned back in her chair, thinking. "What about that other business?"

Gold frowned. "What other business?"

"Capone Island. The ghost."

Gold stared down at his hands, which he had placed in his lap. His legs were stretched out in front of the chair. He took a deep breath, but before he could say anything, Ridge cut in. "Your mother told me about the ghost, and I've been giving it some thought as we've been talking. Would you folks like to hear my theory?"

Looking relieved, Gold said, "By all means."

Ridge stood up, coffee cup in hand, and walked over to the back door. Pointing to Capone Island, she said, "I know all about that place. In fact, that's part of the reason I came to Florida. DHS is concerned about homegrown terrorists, so we've decided to erect motion detectors around the island. You know what they say, an ounce of prevention is worth a pound of cure." She returned to the table and sat beside Harriet, placing an arm around her shoulder. "Our installers work at night –– for security reasons –– so you probably spotted one of our crews. Your vigilance is greatly appreciated."

Harriet beamed. "See something, say something."

"Precisely."

"I'm glad I spoke up."

"You're a model citizen."

Harriet looked at her son. "Did you hear that, Mr. Know-It-All? I'm a model citizen."

Gold smiled. "You're one of a kind, that's for sure."

Harriet dismissed the levity with a wave of her hand. "I don't understand why you won't eat something. Your father always ate a full breakfast."

"I'm not hungry."

"What does hunger have to do with eating?"

"I think there's a connection."

"You'll be sorry."

Gold shot a bewildered look at Ridge, then said, "Think of it this way, mother. If people are starving in Bangladesh, and I eat a big breakfast, there'll be a lot less food. Do you really want that on your conscience?"

She gave him one of her patented scowls. "I've got some ironing to do." She pushed her chair away from the table and stood. "Drive carefully. I'll see you kids later."

Gold blew his mother a kiss as she walked out of the kitchen, and after she was gone, he spread a road map across the table.

"Annette Russo lives way out west, close to the Everglades. The fastest route would be the Florida Turnpike south to Tamiami Trail."

Ridge glanced at the map, then said, "Sounds good to me. Do you think we should give her a call to let her know we're coming?"

"Nah, let's surprise her."

"You sure about that?"

"Who doesn't like surprises?"

"I don't."

"Since when?"

"Since I put on a badge." She stood up to put her coffee cup in the sink and remained standing, her back to him. "Knowledge is power, and it's the small details that often count the most. You'd be wise to remember that."

"Are you trying to tell me something?"

"I was wondering why you didn't mention Morella Perez. A woman like her is hard to forget."

Gold looked down at his coffee, lifted the cup and took a sip, then put it down carefully. "She's just a realtor."

"A realtor who works for Nick Russo."

"So?"

"So that's an important detail. What do you know about her?"

"Not very much. She's a single mom. One child. A teenage daughter. The kid's name is Benita. She goes to St. Brendan High School in Miami." He let out a bored sigh and then said, "Perez has a few rough edges, but she's a hard-working woman trying to make ends meet. She used to be a waitress but recently obtained a real estate license. I don't know anything about her personal life, but I do know that she's involved with Ricardo Paz."

"Involved?"

"Office romance."

"How do you know that?"

Gold hesitated, but only for a moment. "I, uh, interrupted the afterglow."

"The afterglow?"

"They forgot to lock the front door."

"Jesus, you're something else. No wonder you didn't mention her."

"They should've locked the door."

"Do you know where Perez is from?"

"I think she's from Cuba, but I'm not sure. She might be from Puerto Rico."

Ridge turned around, eyes lit up, although she tried to keep any sign of enthusiasm out of her face. "Two Cubans in the same office. What do you make of that?"

"Nothing."

"I beg your pardon?"

"There are plenty of Cuban-Americans in South Florida."

"Yes, I know. About 800,000 or so."

"You've done some homework."

"Yeah, I have, and I'm concerned about your new friend."

"Why's that?"

"Her background is troubling."

"Her background? How do you know about..."

Ridge raised her hand, cutting him off mid-sentence. "She's been on our radar for several months. As a matter of fact, she's the reason I was summoned to Tallahassee. For your information, Perez was born in Matanzas, Cuba. Ever hear of the place?"

"Nope."

"Matanzas is about sixty miles east of Havana, on the north shore of the island. The city is called "the City of Bridges," because there are seventeen bridges that cross the three rivers that traverse the province. One of those bridges leads to a facility called Camp Matanzas, just outside of the capital. The camp is run by the *Dirección de Intelligencia* -- the DI -- a group that collects foreign intelligence. Your friend is a graduate of their training program, which has produced some very bad actors, including a scumbag named Ilyich Ramirez Sanchez -- better known as Carlos the Jackal."

"Son of a bitch," Gold whispered under his breath. "Perez is a spy?"

"Why do you find that so hard to believe?"

"She didn't strike me as the cloak and dagger type."

"Looks can be deceiving."

"Tell me about it."

"After she left Cuba, she moved to Moscow and lived in a *Khruschyovka* near Lubyanka Square. Have you ever been to Russia?"

"No, I haven't."

"A *Khruschyovka* is a three-to-five-story apartment building. Most of them were built in the 1960s, during the time of Nikita

Krushchev, hence the name. Perez lived in a building that was popular with former KGB agents. We think she might have been recruited by the Federal Security Service, which replaced the KGB. We don't know if she's still active or who she's really working for, but her connection to Russo is troubling. Very troubling."

Gold fell silent for a moment, his lips pressed tightly together. He felt as if he had been kicked in the stomach. He saw this was going to be more difficult than he had imagined. A lot more difficult. He twisted his neck from side to side, then said, "Well, this is another fine mess you've gotten us into."

She cleared her throat loudly, startling him. "You don't have to tag along if you don't want to."

Gold put his hand on Ridge's shoulder and looked her in the eye. "One request. No airplanes."

She gave him a sunny smile. "Don't forget the map."

CHAPTER FIFTEEN

There was nothing particularly funny about the old KGB, but that didn't stop Ridge from repeating the only joke she'd heard about its brutal tactics. "Did you know that the KGB owned the tallest building in Lubyanka Square? You could see Siberia from its basement."

Gold managed a half-smile. "Gulag humor?"

"Similar to gallows humor."

"Just as funny."

Ridge nodded pensively. "Why the long face?"

"I'm a little confused. Who the hell does Perez work for, the Cubans or the Russians?"

"Probably both."

"Both?"

Ridge explained that the DI had a close relationship with the KGB, which sought to use the Cuban government as a proxy agent around the world. Shortly after the Cuban Missle Crisis in 1962, Moscow began to train a large number of DI agents, and those agents were involved in many covert operations. Leftist movements were aided successfully in Chile, Grenada, Nicaragua, Puerto Rico, and Venezuela. She was tempted to ramble on, but out of the corner of her eye she noticed that Gold was rubbing his forehead. "Too much information?"

"A lot to process. I feel like I'm heading down the rabbit hole."

"If I were you, I'd keep my eyes on the prize."

"What prize?"

"Nick Russo."

"Oh, the booby prize."

"The CIA will deal with Perez. We need to find Russo."

"Then what?"

"Then we arrest him, try him, put him in jail, and throw away the key."

"Sounds like you've got an airtight case."

"We do, but I'm not at liberty to discuss it."

"I understand."

"I don't." She gave him a weary smile. "I don't understand anything about these people. How they're raised. How they become monsters. How they can live with themselves." Her voice was soft, passionless, but Gold could feel the pent-up emotion in it. "None of it makes any sense to me."

On impulse Gold stroked her hair, fondly, almost absently, as one would a child's. "Aren't road trips fun?"

"I'll let you know in a few minutes."

Annette Russo's house was twelve miles west of Florida's Turnpike, perched on the edge of the Everglades National Park, a 1.5 million-acre wetlands preserve made up of coastal mangroves, sawgrass marshes, and pine-covered forest. The homes on her block were modest but well maintained. No lawns or shrubs gone to seed. No cars or trucks parked on the grass. No broken down boats in the driveway. Nothing out of the ordinary -- except for one small detail.

Yellow crime-scene tape had been stretched across the driveway and stapled to pieces of hammer-driven lath.

For a moment Gold stared, unbelieving, trying to absorb the scene. His stomach lurched, a reaction he tried to hide as he began to deal with the situation.

Ridge sighed, and her voice grew suddenly somber. "What do we have here?"

Gold swore under his breath and then said very slowly, "Nothing good."

A uniformed officer scrutinized them for a moment and then shuffled over, irritated by their staring. "Move along, folks. Nothing to see here."

Ridge stepped out of the car and flashed her badge at the officer. "What's going on?"

"Homicide investigation," the officer replied. "One victim. Female Caucasian. Shot once in the chest."

Gold's face was expressionless, but inside the sinking feeling had taken the bottom out of his stomach. *Damn,* he thought. *Damn! Damn! Damn!*

Ridge breathed deeply. She needed to stay calm, and more importantly, she needed Gold to remain calm. She forced her game face back into place, then said, "Who's in charge?"

"Sergeant Grimes. He's inside, talking to the medical examiner."

Ridge and Gold walked toward the house, each lost in thought. They were stopped at the back door, which was standard procedure since no one was supposed to enter or leave without authorization from the crime scene investigator. Inside, the M.E. was examining the chest wound and making notes about livor mortis and rigor mortis. Nearby, a police photographer was snapping away, taking photographs of the crime scene from all angles.

Detective Grimes was sitting at the kitchen table, ignoring the chaos that surrounded him. When Ridge knocked on the door, he glanced up from the copy of the *Miami Herald* he was reading. His face showed nothing. It rarely did. He was a slender man with ebony skin and eyes darker than his hair. In keeping with his stoic demeanor, his look was neither friendly nor hostile. Mostly it was solemn, and a .40 caliber semiautomatic prominently displayed in his hip holster, added its own note of seriousness.

Two hours earlier, Grimes had gone through his checklist, noting the seemingly mundane details of the crime scene. These were the details that were often overlooked by rookie detectives. He made note of the light switches -- which ones were on and which were off -- the thermostat setting, the locked and unlocked windows and doors, and the beverages and food on the counter and table. He also eyeballed the victim's mail, her cell phone, her computer, and her answering machine.

Finally, he took the time to look for the things that should have been there but weren't. These items included jewelry, keys, purses, and pocketbooks.

Oddly enough, the killer had only taken one thing.

Annette Russo's life.

Grimes stood up, put his hands on the small of his back, and twisted his torso. He glared at the intruders standing in the doorway. Coming closer, he said, "What are you two selling?"

Ridge displayed her badge again. "Special Agent Ridge. Homeland Security. My colleague, Adam Gold." There was a dead silence. Unperturbed, Ridge continued. "We picked up a 187 on the radio."

"Nice to know your equipment's working."

"Sorry to barge in like this, but we're working on a case."

"What can I do for you, special agent Ridge?"

Ridge rubbed her long, thin fingers together, drew a deep breath and said, "What happened here?"

"What happened here? A woman got shot in the chest. One bullet. Straight through the heart. That's what happened." He put his face in front of hers, and said in a slow, distinct tone, "Did you drop by to lend us a hand?"

Ridge thought of several sarcastic replies, any one of which would send him off the deep end. She said, "My colleague knew the victim."

Grimes looked at Gold. "How well?"

Gold looked at him, irritated –– he didn't like the sergeant's tone –– and then let it go. The man was just doing his job. "Well enough," he answered. "I can make a positive identification."

Grimes stepped aside. "Be my guest."

Gold made a vague gesture with his hands to suggest that the medical examiner turn the victim's head. He rubbed his temples slowly, staring at the lifeless body of Annette Russo. Then he turned around and looked outside, at nothing. "Annette Russo."

"You sure?"

Gold slumped in despair. "Yeah, that's her."

Grimes let out a rough laugh. "What's left of her. The killer shot her with a .45 Colt. The bullet passed through her body and made a mess of her internal organs."

Gold got a little better control of his emotions and said, "How do you know it was a Colt?"

"We found the murder weapon."

Gold looked incredulous. *"You found the weapon?"*

"The perp dropped the gun as he was making his getaway. We found the weapon outside, near the driveway."

A wide-eyed Gold looked at Ridge. "How's that for luck?"

With raised eyebrows and a stern expression, she reminded Gold that she was not a big believer in luck or coincidence. "May I see the weapon, sergeant?"

"We sent it to the crime lab to be checked for prints. They're also checking the serial numbers. Who knows, maybe we'll catch a break and find the owner."

Ridge rubbed her chin thoughtfully. "Did you find any prints in the house?"

"Nope. No fingerprints or footprints."

"That's odd. Any sign of a struggle?"

"Nope, and no sign of forced entry."

"Which indicates that she knew her killer."

"Maybe, maybe not."

"Anything taken?"

"As far as we can tell, not a damn thing. No jewelry. No money. No credit cards. No nothing."

"Well, I guess we can rule out robbery."

Grimes rubbed a kink out of his neck, picked up a container of coffee and took a gulp. "The killer wasn't a pro, if that's what you're thinking. Not only did he drop his weapon, but he also left tire tracks on the driveway. Looks like he drove through a puddle just before he got here. Careless mistake. We took some photos and sent them to the FBI. The feds are also checking the plates."

Gold brightened. "You got a plate number?"

"A partial number. The last three digits."

"How'd you get those?" Ridge asked.

"A nosy neighbor spotted the car. When the killer pulled into the driveway, he left his lights and radio on for a few minutes. I guess he was having second thoughts. In any case, the neighbor got a look at the vehicle and the plates."

Gold almost smiled. "What type of vehicle?"

"Black Mercedes. Late-model sedan."

"Thank God for nosy neighbors."

"We got lucky."

Ridge stared at a large blood stain on the floor, motionless, off in another world. "More luck," she mumbled. "You guys should buy some lotto tickets."

Bristling, Grimes said, "It's not polite to stare."

"Excuse me?"

"You're staring at the murder victim."

"Actually, I was looking at the blood stain. The spatter indicates that the blood fell from a distance of at least seventy-two inches."

"You don't say."

She looked at the medical examiner. "Would you concur?"

The M.E. nodded, but said nothing.

Grimes took another gulp of coffee, smacked his lips, and said, "You feds don't miss a trick." He gave the M.E. a sideways look that she couldn't read. "Hold that thought, Agent Ridge. I'm getting a text message from headquarters."

When Grimes stepped outside, Ridge turned to Gold and said, "The distance the blood drops fell suggests that the shooter was about six feet tall, since the bullet went straight through the heart." She went on to say that Grimes knew his stuff but had made one serious blunder. A blunder that could hinder the investigation. "He keeps opening and closing the back door."

Gold leant closer, as if someone might be listening. "So?"

"They're letting in flies."

"Flies?"

"The insects feed on the blood of the dead, and they can easily contaminate a crime scene." Pensive, frowning, she scanned the room, then settled back on the late Annette Russo. "I don't know if they've done a Luminol test, but if they have, they're going to find minute specks of blood all around the kitchen."

Gold digested her words for a minute, then shook his head. "Jesus, maybe we should say something."

"Maybe, maybe not."

"Does that happen a lot?"

"More often than you might think." She told him that after flies consume blood they usually move to a warm area to regurgitate their meals as part of the digestive process. The most common areas were lamps, ceiling lights, and windows. During this process, tiny blood specks from the flies' feet were left around the room, and the more flies, the more blood specks. "The blood specks resemble a high-velocity blood spatter, and they can easily confuse an investigator."

Gold drew in a tiny breath, giving himself a moment to think. "Grimes doesn't seem like a novice to me."

"No, this is not his first rodeo."

"I guess we shouldn't interfere."

"Probably not."

When Grimes returned, he was in a much better mood and almost pleasant. His emotionless expression didn't waiver, but Ridge and Gold detected just the slightest excitement in his voice. "Well, we're off to the races. The lab found some prints on the gun slide. A pretty clear set of prints."

"Only on the slide?" Ridge asked. "Not the trigger?"

"They didn't mention the trigger."

Ridge gave Gold a look that told him she was puzzled. She just said, "Huh."

Grimes wiped his mouth with the back of a bony hand and said, "The prints belong to a licensed gun owner, and the serial numbers match the application form. A black and white has been dispatched, and the suspect should be downtown by the time I get back. I don't know what you're up to, but you're welcome to join the party."

Ridge gritted her teeth. "We wouldn't miss it for the world."

CHAPTER SIXTEEN

Sergeant Grimes didn't know the name of the suspect who was being picked up in Miami, but Gold was sure of the killer's identity. He told Ridge he'd bet the farm that Nick Russo had pulled the trigger. Ridge was not as certain, her doubt based upon past experience and a habit of not rushing to judgement. There were a number of things that didn't make much sense to her, and when pressed to explain, she began with the murder weapon.

"We don't know the identity of the gunman," Ridge said. "It might not be Russo."

"Trust me. He's our boy."

"Most likely, but Russo's a career criminal. He wouldn't drop a gun unless he wanted the police to find it. That's the part that troubles me."

A worried frown flickered across Gold's face. "Why would he want the gun to be found?"

"I'm not sure. Maybe he's trying to frame somebody."

"Somebody like who?"

"I don't know, maybe a competitor."

"I don't buy it."

"I'm just trying to think outside the box. The crime lab found prints on the gun slide, but not the trigger. That's unusual. It suggests that the owner of the gun might not be the shooter. The serial numbers will tell us more, but I've got a hunch that Russo planted the weapon."

"I'm not big on hunches."

"Yeah, I remember, but what about situational awareness?"

Gold rolled his eyes. "Here we go again."

"Do you think a guy like Russo, a career criminal, is going to pull into a driveway and leave the lights and radio on by accident? Before he whacks someone? No way, Jose. He was trying to draw attention to the vehicle, and just for good measure, he made sure to leave some tire tracks." She scratched at the corner of her mouth, a smile playing around the lips. "Don't be surprised if the gun owner and the vehicle owner are the same person, and that person isn't Nick Russo."

Gold stared at her in amused disbelief. "You're stretching, Sally. The frame job doesn't make sense. If Russo wanted to get rid of a competitor, he'd whack the guy himself."

"You never know with these wiseguys. They enjoy playing games. Outwitting the cops. I never met a hoodlum who didn't think he was a criminal mastermind."

Gold stuck to his guns, but didn't push it. "Well, we'll know for sure when we get downtown."

"Until then, we should use our time wisely."

"What do you mean?"

Ridge allowed herself a thin smile, but it faded quickly. "I think you know more than you're saying. Why don't you tell me why Annette Russo was killed? I'd like to know the real reason."

Gold chewed pensively on his lip. Her request seemed reasonable, especially under the circumstances. Besides, if he couldn't trust Sally Ridge, who could he trust? He took a beat deciding where to begin, then told her everything, starting with the incident that got the ball rolling. "Nick's father, Sal Russo, was the head of a New Jersey crime family. The old man was old school, caught up in family honor and all that other wiseguy bullshit. Annette was married to Joey Russo, who happened to be a colleague of mine at the Anchor Insurance Company. After Joey died, Sal decided to become Annette's guardian angel, but he turned out to be a jealous devil. If somebody tried to get close to Annette, he'd intervene using intimidation or threats. One day he crossed the line and seriously injured one of her friends. Somebody very close to her. They had words, and before you could say *arrivederci*, Sal got shot in the chest."

Ridge shook her head. "Just like Annette."

"Similar."

"Where do you come in?"

"I arrived on the scene after the fact -- but before the police got there." He slumped, sitting back, and let his head lean against the headrest. "I didn't want Annette or her friend to suffer because of Sal. I knew they'd be dragged into a lengthy court case if she was arrested, so I concocted a story about rape. I was hoping the cops wouldn't look a gift horse in the mouth, and as it turned out, I was right. As far as the authorities were concerned, it was goodbye and good riddance. They were happy to be rid of Russo."

"You're crazier than I thought." There was grudging admiration in her voice. "Much crazier."

"I know the wheels are turning. Are you searching for the right cliche?"

"I was going to go with, 'Oh! What a tangled web we weave when first we practice to deceive'."

"I'm glad you restrained yourself."

"Seriously, though, have you given any thought to what comes next?"

"What do you mean?"

"You're next on the hit parade. If Russo's our killer, you need to be extra careful. In his sick mind, it's one down, one to go."

"Now there's a pleasant thought."

"I'll give you another one. If my hunch is right, and Russo sticks to his modus operandi, he'll do the killing, but somebody else will take the fall."

"Any idea who that might be?"

"Your guess would be as bad as mine."

A faintly amused smile flitted across Gold's face. "Are you trying to cheer me up?"

"Just keeping it real." She glanced at his face for a moment with a keen, assessing look. "By the way, I'm sorry about Annette Russo. I know she was your friend."

"Yeah, Annette was a good egg. I liked her a lot. She was a proud Italian. Catholic to the core. Wednesday night Bingo, fish on Friday, Sunday mass." There was a pause. The silence stretched out. Eventually he turned to her with a smile on his face. "Her lasagna was legendary. The best in Bensonhurst."

"Whatever happened to her friend? The one that was seriously injured?"

"His name is Lou Feretti. Oddly enough, he became a priest."

"Why is that odd?"

"Because before he became a man of the cloth, Feretti was an NYPD detective. He gave up his badge and gun late in his career, which is not an everyday occurrence -- especially in the City that Never Sleeps."

"Interesting."

"I met Feretti shortly before I met you. Back then he was a homicide detective, and a damn good one. He led the investigation into Joey Russo's death, which is how he met Annette. They spent a lot of time together, but their relationship was strictly platonic. Anyway, after he recovered from the bombing..."

"Hold on one second," Ridge said, getting her mind around the situation. "He was injured by a bomb?"

"A car bomb. Curtesy of Sal Russo. The son of a bitch used more napalm than explosives, otherwise Feretti would have been a dead man." He noticed the serious look on Ridge's face and said, "I guess you're familiar with those devices."

"I've had some training. Sounds like Russo used a basic device, something wired to the car's ignition system. Those type of bombs have become passe. Nowadays the bad guys prefer to use bombs that are magnetically fixed to the underside of the car, placed underneath the driver's seat, detonated by the opening of the door or by pressure applied to the brakes or accelerator." Her expression darkened, and she said, "Was Feretti hurt badly?"

"He sustained second-degree burns, but he made a full recovery with minimal scarring."

"Lucky guy."

"Russo wasn't as lucky. After he sent Feretti a message, Annette sent one of her own. Actually, she sent two messages at point blank range, and they both hit home. I had the pleasure of watching Russo take his last breath."

For a long moment Ridge said nothing, and it was clear she was turning everything over in her mind; finally she glanced at him and said, "Too bad it didn't end there. We still have to deal with the prodigal son."

"You mean the problematic son."

"No good deed goes unpunished."

"Apparently not."

"So what became of Feretti?"

"Last I heard he was teaching at St. Edward's University, a Catholic school in Austin, Texas."

"You still keep in touch?"

"We exchange holiday cards, but that's about it."

"You gonna tell him about Annette Russo?"

"I hate to be the bearer of bad news, but he deserves to be told."

"Absolutely."

Gold sighed. "Would you like to make the call?"

"Me? I don't even know the guy."

"Well, that's true, but he once did you a big favor."

"How do you figure?"

"Remember our Texas adventure?"

"Only too well."

"Feretti played an important role in our investigation."

"How so?"

Gold had to tread lightly since their investigation had dealt with the murder of Ridge's niece, a teenage runaway. He reminded her that they had hit a brick wall during their investigation and did not have enough evidence to make an arrest. Feretti had been involved from the outset, not as a former detective or priest, but as a college professor who'd taught Ridge's niece. He was the one who had suggested that there might be an audio recording of the autopsy performed on the niece. It was during the autopsy that the medical examiner had been killed, so if a tape existed, it could become the proverbial smoking gun.

"Which it did," Gold said. "There was an overhead mic, and the killer was caught on tape."

"Feretti's a smart cookie."

"You can say that again."

"How'd he get so smart?"

"Twenty-five years on the force. Most of it spent in the homicide division. In my humble opinion, he was one of the best detectives in the N.Y.P.D."

"One thing's for sure. He knew the importance of small details."

"Yeah, he was a sharp guy."

"Well, when you call him, send my regards, My sympathy, too."

Gold smiled grimly. "If I know Feretti, he won't be looking for sympathy, or in this case, even justice. The only thing on his mind will be revenge."

"You think so?"

"Once a cop, always a cop."

"Tell me about it."

CHAPTER SEVENTEEN

The Miami Police were headquartered in a modern facility on NW 2nd Avenue, in an area known as the Central District, halfway between Little Haiti and Little Havana. Murder suspects were usually interrogated by the Criminal Investigations Division, but in Annette Russo's case, the interrogation was handled by Detective Sergeant Grimes, who was assigned to the Special Investigations Section. Special Investigations dealt with a broad range of criminal cases, but they primarily focused on crimes that involved money laundering, high level narcotics trafficking, weapons violations, and terrorism related activities.

Ridge and Gold were surprised by the added attention, but they knew that there had to be a reason -- a good reason -- for the Special Investigation Section to be involved in a homicide case. They were even more surprised to learn who was being interrogated. Sitting in front of them, on the other side of a two-way mirror, was Ricardo Paz. The poor guy was pale as a ghost, shaking like a leaf. Grimes was sitting across from him, slouched in his chair, reading a dossier.

"How do you like that," Ridge said. "I'm right again."

Gold stared at Paz for several moments, then looked at Ridge, who purposefully avoided looking back. He mumbled unintelligibly, then said, "You're starting to get on my nerves."

“Because I’m always right?”

“That’s one of the reasons.”

“Do I detect a note of envy?”

“All right, Sherlock, you were right, and I was wrong. Make yourself comfortable. The show’s about to begin.”

The “show,” as they both knew, was an intricate game of cat and mouse, designed to produce a criminal confession. In most cases, the psychological manipulation began before the actual interrogation, starting with the placement of the light switches and thermostat, which were out of the suspect’s reach or control. The physical layout of the room was purposefully designed to maximize a suspect’s discomfort and produce a sense of powerlessness. The room was small and drab, furnished with a metal desk and three uncomfortable chairs. The walls were gunmetal grey and unadorned, creating a sense of exposure, unfamiliarity, and isolation.

All in all, the last place on earth that Paz wanted to be.

Gold wondered which interrogation technique Grimes intended to employ. The Reid Technique was the most common, but the wily detective might have another trick up his sleeve. Either way, Paz was in for a rude awakening, about to be turned every which way but loose.

In the United States, 80 percent of suspects waive their rights to silence and counsel, a common mistake that allows the police to question a suspect at length. When Paz waived his rights, Grimes stopped reading the dossier and tossed the folder on the chair beside him. In hopes of developing a rapport, he adopted a folksy tone and initiated a casual conversation about baseball. For the next five minutes, he rambled on about the Miami Marlins, speculating about their chances of winning a Pennant or the World Series. The ploy was part of the Reid Technique, and it gave Grimes an opportunity to observe the suspect's posture and eye movement.

Grimes made a mental note of the way Paz reacted, then said, "Do you like baseball, Mr. Paz?"

"Sure, it's our national pastime."

"Are you referring to America or Cuba?"

"Both."

Grimes rubbed his chin. "I thought playing dominoes was the national pastime of Cuba."

"Maybe I should have said national sport."

"You a Marlin fan?"

"No, I like the Yankees."

"*The Yankees?* There's a surprise. I thought Cubans shouted 'Yanqui Go Home?'"

"In the old days. Not now."

"Live and learn," Grimes said. He showed Paz most of his teeth in a broad smile. "Were you read your Miranda Rights?"

"Yeah, but I don't know why."

"Well, that's why I'm here. To explain the situation. To ask a few questions. To help you come to terms with the truth."

"I don't know what you're talking about."

"I think you do."

"No, I don't."

"Let's not get off to a bad start. Would you like something to drink? Some water or coffee?"

"No thanks."

"I'd offer you a soda, but the vending machine is broken."

Paz raised his hands to his forehead and massaged it, pressing his fingertips hard against his scalp. "What the hell is going on? Why am I here?"

"You're being held in police custody."

"Why?"

"You have no idea?"

"Is this about parking tickets?"

Grimes managed to keep his anger in check, but barely. "Listen up, *amigo*. If you play ball with me, you might avoid the death penalty. The choice is yours." He leaned forward, resting his elbows on the table. *"Entiendes lo que quiero decir?"*

"No, I don't understand. What do you mean, play ball? What do you think I've done?"

"What I think doesn't matter. What I know is a different story, and what I know is that you murdered Mrs. Russo."

Paz paused, stared into near space for a moment before focusing on Grimes again and saying, "Who?"

"Annette Russo. The nice lady in West Miami."

"Never heard of her."

"Maybe you didn't have a chance to ask her name."

Paz fired back. "Maybe I don't know what the fuck you're talking about."

"Wise up, pal. Florida's a death penalty state. Either you cooperate or we put a needle in your arm."

"Are you out of your mind?"

Grimes sat back, watching for the telltale signs of guilt: fidgeting, licking of lips, nervous grooming. Each was indicative of deception, and together they could tell him if he was on the right track. "Did you ever hear that confession is good for the soul?" He let this register a moment before asking the next question. "Why don't you tell me what happened?"

Paz would have burst out laughing if the situation hadn't been so serious. "I have nothing to confess. I don't know the woman you mentioned, and I didn't kill anyone. You've got the wrong man."

Grimes folded his arms across his chest and spoke quietly. "If you're the wrong man, why did we find your gun at the crime scene?"

"You found *my* gun?"

"I'm afraid so."

"I don't believe that."

"I kid you not."

"There must be some mistake."

"*Au contraire*. I believe you own a Colt .45 1911 pistol?"

"Me and three million other people."

Grimes gestured toward the two-way mirror, and a uniformed officer came into the room and placed a Colt .45 on the table. After the officer left, Grimes picked up the pistol and read off the serial numbers. "Sound familiar?"

"I didn't memorize the numbers."

"No, but you did fill out a gun permit application, and the weapon you registered is the weapon we found at the crime scene –– and the weapon that killed Annette Russo. How do you think that will look to a jury?"

Paz was thinking as fast as he could, trying to figure out how his gun had ended up at a crime scene. He was sure he'd locked it in his desk drawer at work. He tried to recall the last time he saw the gun, but nothing was coming to him. "There must be some mistake," he said at last. "I keep the gun under lock and key."

"Your prints were found on the weapon."

"You sure they're mine?"

"A perfect match."

"By the way, would you like to see the ballistics report? I'd be happy to show it to you." He continued to look steadily at Paz. "Guns and bullets leave a lot of damning evidence. Bullet casings, bullet holes, spatter patterns, and in your case, even a dropped weapon. Maybe you don't know it, but every gun barrel is rifled at the factory. Rotating grooves allow the bullet to spin, which improves accuracy. Unfortunately for you, those grooves also leave markings on the bullet. The striations can identify a type and model of firearm, and that evidence is admissible in court. Have you heard of hidden fingerprints? We found those, too. You see, when a person loads bullets into a cylinder or magazine, they leave tiny quantities of salty sweat on the casing. When a bullet is fired, heat vaporizes the moisture and the salts become molten. The chemical reaction etches the shooter's fingerprints into the casing, and voila, you've got a conviction. Fascinating stuff, don't you think?"

Sweating, breathing hard, Paz stared at him for the longest moment, then lowered his head in dispair. It took him a while to find his voice, but he finally said, "Somebody must have stolen my gun."

Grimes rolled his eyes at Paz as if to say, "What kind of dumbass do you think I am?" A short silence ensued. In a more strident voice, he said, "Please don't insult my intelligence. I hate when perps do that."

Paz held his temper but not without clenching his teeth. He could feel the heat in his chest radiating up to his neck. "I'm telling you the truth. I keep my gun locked in a drawer, and I'm the only one with a key."

"Well, there you go."

"Somebody must have made a key."

"One of your coworkers?"

"I don't know."

"Maybe the cleaning lady?"

Paz wanted to say, *Get the hell off my back, you son of a bitch.* Instead he shook his head and said, "I just don't know."

Grimes exhaled sharply and gave Paz a look that said he was running out of patience. "What kind of car do you drive?"

"Mercedes-Benz."

"Which model?"

"CLS."

"What color?"

"Black."

"Nice wheels."

"It's a company car. Part of a fleet."

"Do you remember your license plate number?"

Paz thought for a moment, but he could only remember the last four digits. The last three were the most important, and for Grimes, they were music to his ears. "You don't have a very good memory."

"I'm under a lot of stress. Besides, I also drive an SUV."

"Why do you drive two vehicles?"

"Sometimes I have to chauffeur a family."

"Which one are you driving today?"

"The SUV."

"Where's the Mercedes?"

"Back at the office."

"I'm afraid not."

"Excuse me?"

"We checked. The vehicle is gone."

"Somebody might have borrowed the car."

"Without your knowledge?"

"Like I said before, it's a company car. Part of a fleet. Duplicate keys are kept in the office."

"My goodness, you've got an answer for everything. Well, almost everything. Maybe you could explain why a black Mercedes was spotted at the crime scene. The killer was not very bright. He parked in the victim's driveway, and a nosy neighbor got a look at the license plate. The last three digits match the ones on your car."

Shifting nervously, Paz said, "What does that prove?"

Grimes gave a sad little laugh. "It proves that you're not very bright." His eyes now bored in on Paz. "By the way, the FBI found your Mercedes. One hour ago. The vehicle was parked in a handicapped spot at Town Center in Boca Raton. Another dumb move. The feds were able to match the tires with the tire marks found in Mrs. Russo's driveway. And that's not all. The radio was set on a Cuban music station. What kind of music do you listen to?"

"Depends on my mood."

Grimes leaned across the table and bent close to Paz's ear and his breath went inside it with his words. "I don't know about you, but I'm in a bad mood. A very bad mood. No more games, slick. You either tell me what happened or you can tell it to the judge. Makes no difference to me."

"There's nothing to tell. I swear to God, I didn't kill that woman."

Grimes laughed a nasty patronizing laugh, and he realized that it was time to develop a "theme," which was step two of the Reid Technique. He now had to get inside the suspect's head and figure out why he became a murderer. How did Paz excuse or justify his actions? Did he blame the victim for some real or imaginary slight? A clever interrogator would offer several themes, hoping that the suspect would latch on to one and spill his guts. The hard part, especially for Grimes, would be lowering the heat and speaking in a soft, soothing voice in order to appear nonthreatening and lull Paz into a false sense of security.

Gold didn't think Grimes was up to the task.

Ridge knew different, and as usual, time would prove her right.

CHAPTER EIGHTEEN

Grimes was right 99 percent of the time when it came to judging other people. It was one of the things that made him so good at his job, but Paz was difficult to figure out. He seemed so sincere, even though he was lying through his teeth. *A tough nut to crack*, Grimes thought. He took a moment to figure out a diplomatic way to put it, then said, "You can talk in a minute, but right now I need you to listen. I'm tired of all your denials. We've got a murder weapon that belongs to you and bullets with your fingerprints on them. We've also got the getaway vehicle, a plate match, tire marks, and a radio station that plays Cuban music. Around here that's called a slam dunk." He let Paz chew on that a moment, then said, "If you don't confess, you're the one who's gonna get slammed and dunked. You catch my drift?"

Paz didn't respond at first, but then his words came out with a tone of urgency. "Jesus Christ, you're asking me to confess to a crime I didn't commit."

Grimes raised his hand in the air, demanding silence. He reached for the Colt .45, pulled back the slide, and examined the empty chamber. Then he began to fiddle with the safety, as if he'd never seen one before. With surprising calmness, he said, "These

Colts are very well made. Easy to operate. Sometimes too easy. This one has a trigger pull weight of four pounds. Do you know what that means?"

"Of course."

"Explain it to me."

"It takes four pounds of pressure to pull the trigger."

"Exactly."

Not having a clue where Grimes was going with this, Paz gave him a half smile and said, "What's your point?"

"You don't know?"

"Explain it to me."

"A child could pull a four-pound trigger. In fact, they do it all the time. Did you know that guns kill 1,300 children each year?"

"No, I didn't."

"Well, it's true. If you ask me, the triggers are too sensitive, especially on some of the automatics. If they increased the trigger pull weight, there wouldn't be as many accidental shootings. You see where I'm going with this?"

"No, as a matter of fact, I don't."

Grimes shook his head pityingly. "I don't think you meant to shoot Mrs. Russo. I think you were robbing the house when she stumbled into the kitchen and caught you by surprise. You probably panicked and pulled out your gun, intending to keep her at bay. Unfortunately, your finger touched the trigger and the gun discharged. The next thing you know, she's lying dead on the floor."

Gold glanced over at Ridge, then said, "Damn, this guy's good."

"Never doubt me," Ridge said. "Do you know what he's doing?"

"Yeah, he's leading Paz down the garden path."

"Straight to the death house."

Paz sat mopping his face, afraid to say anything. The silence stretched out. Eventually he gathered his thoughts, then said, "I don't know what you're trying to pull, but that's not the way it happened. I didn't shoot that woman. I'm no murderer."

Grimes gave his head a small, decisive shake. No. He wasn't falling for that. He knew that Paz was good for the murder. Stopping denials and overcoming objections were steps three and four of the Reid Technique, and after Grimes gave them a shot, he turned to step five, getting the suspect's undivided attention. In order to accomplish this, he stood up and walked behind Paz, touching him on the shoulder and patting his back. "I know this looks bad, but deep down, I still think we've got an accidental shooting. Maybe I'm being naive, but you seem to be a decent guy. I think that you were in the wrong place at the wrong time, and you panicked. And let's face it, you're no firearms expert."

"American guns are new to me."

"I understand. To be perfectly honest, some of our weapons are poorly designed, and others are poorly made." There was a beat before Grimes cleared his throat and said, "Have you ever heard of products liability?"

"Yeah, but I'm not sure what it means."

Swearing to himself, and by now a little worried, Gold said, “Here comes the lifeline.”

“More like an anchor,” Ridge said. “Paz won’t know what hit him.”

“All part of the game.”

Ridge glanced at him, squirming with uneasiness. “Only this is not a game.”

A seasoned interrogator like Grimes knew when to employ the next step, which was designed to break down the suspect’s resolve and lead him to a confession. He could tell just by looking at Paz that he was starting to weaken, his body language indicating that he was almost ready to surrender. Or so Grimes thought. If he could get Paz to admit that he fired the gun –– supposedly by accident –– the true account would surely follow. Offering a socially acceptable alternative went hand in hand with the previous step, and in this case, the culprit was the weapon itself.

Grimes returned to his seat and did a little drumroll on the table. “Product liability refers to a manufacturer being held liable for producing a defective product. For instance, a pistol that has a defective trigger. A trigger that is too sensitive and discharges on its own, causing severe injury or death. Hell, you can’t blame a gun owner for that sort of thing.”

Paz nodded in agreement. “No, that wouldn’t be the owner’s fault.”

“Of course not,” Grimes said. “That wouldn’t be fair.”

“Not fair at all.”

“Let me tell you something. Just between us girls, there are plenty of accidental shootings in this country. Almost fifteen thousand last year. I'm not saying that all of the guns were defective, but let's face it, a large number were. Who knows how many bad triggers are out there? My brother-in-law is an insurance broker, and he handles plenty of product liability cases. According to him –– my brother-in-law –– a firearm can be defective in three ways: if it's marketed with inadequate instructions or warnings, if it's produced with a manufacturing defect, and if it's defective in its design. Do you see where I'm going with this? Maybe one or more of those things apply to your situation."

Ridge sat back and looked at Gold. For almost a minute, she didn't speak. Her mind was filtering through all of the trickery she'd just heard, none of which she particularly liked. In her view, Grimes was awfully close to entrapment, but as Gold pointed out, the detective was telling the truth.

"Grimes is right on the money," Gold said. "If a firearm is defective in the way that it's marketed, manufactured, or designed, and someone is injured as a result of that defect, then the manufacturer will be held liable. I've handled a number of those claims. I know what I'm talking about."

"All well and good," Ridge said. "But that's beside the point. Grimes is using insurance mumbo jumbo to trick Paz. He wants Paz to think that he won't be held responsible for shooting Annette Russo, and you and I know that's bullshit."

"Maybe so, but all is fair in love and war."

"You don't really believe that."

"I believe half of it –– the latter half."

Several moments passed, and then another uniformed officer came into the room and handed Grimes a note. He read it slowly, then turned his cold stare on Paz. "Tell me about Annette Russo. Why did you pick her house?"

"I told you before, I've never heard of the woman."

"Never try to crap a crapper."

"I'm telling you the truth."

There was a dead silence. Grimes looked at him, blank-faced. "You need to stop this nonsense. You're making a fool of yourself." He waved the note in front of Paz, regarding him with contempt. "Your vehicle, the black Mercedes, is registered to a man named Nicholas Russo. Same last name as our murder victim. I assume that's your boss?"

"That's right."

"The owner of Sun Coast Realty?"

"Yeah."

"How long have you worked for Mr. Russo?"

"About six months."

"You like him?"

"Of course."

"Most employees hate the boss."

"Not me."

"You're an enigma."

"What's that?"

"A person that is difficult to understand. What do you like about Mr. Russo?"

"He takes good care of me."

"Is that why you took care of him?"

"Huh?"

"Did you kill Mr. Russo?"

"No, of course not. Are you crazy? I wouldn't harm a hair on his head." The sick feeling in Paz's stomach intensified. "Is he really dead?"

"You tell me."

"How would I know?"

"I think you know more than you're saying, but to answer your question, we don't know if your boss is dead or alive. We only know that he's missing."

Paz frowned, evidently baffled by this new revelation. "Jesus Christ," he whispered. "I don't believe this shit."

Grimes took a deep breath and plowed forward. "Workplace violence is very common. Sometimes understandable. Employees are often overworked and underpaid. You know the drill. Lift that bale, tote that barge. Too much stress. Hell, I might snap, too."

Paz hesitated, unwilling to rise to the bait. "What are you getting at?"

"I'd like to know why you killed your employer's aunt."

"Aunt?"

"Let me guess. You didn't know that Annette and Nicholas were related. Is that what you're saying?"

"Good lord," Paz whispered in a feeble, failing voice. "I had no idea. Oh my God, that's terrible. Just terrible."

Now Grimes paused for a moment, wondering if he was missing something, if there was something else going on. He finally decided that Paz was just a good actor. Losing patience, he jumped to the final step of the interrogation, pushing for a confession that could be used in court. "Listen to me, Paz. Sooner or later you'll have to face the truth. I've got all the time in the world, but why not make it easier on yourself? Man up, *amigo*. It's the right thing to do."

Paz glared at him. "You're wasting your time. I have nothing to confess."

Grimes barked a quick, short burst of laughter. "You're as pure as the driven snow."

"I didn't say that."

"You're getting on my nerves, Paz."

"Believe me, I know the feeling."

"What time did you get home from work last night?"

"The usual time."

"When would that be?"

"Seven o'clock."

"Did you eat dinner at home?"

"Yeah."

"When did you leave the house?"

"Who said I left?"

"You didn't run out for a pack of cigarettes?"

"I don't smoke."

"Did you leave your house for any other reason?"

"Nope."

Was it Grimes's imagination, or was Paz enjoying this battle of wits? In the past, Grimes had always held the upper hand, always set the pace and tone, often through intimidation. Paz was playing by his own rules, stubbornly maintaining his innocence and showing no sign of surrender.

Very annoying, to say the least.

The rules of engagement allowed Grimes to lie during the interrogation, but there were limits to his deception. For instance, he could tell Paz that his fingerprints had been found in the victim's house or claim that they had found incriminating DNA evidence when they had none, but he couldn't bend the rules about a defendant's legal rights. Specifically, he couldn't tell Paz that his incriminating statements would not be used to charge him with a crime.

Physical force was also out of the question.

If Grimes wanted to obtain a legal confession, he would have to go about it the old-fashioned way, which meant that it was time to get back to the basics.

CHAPTER NINETEEN

After two hours of jousting, Grimes was ready to pull his hair out, but he was too stubborn to call it quits. There was simply no way that he was going to let some smartass Cuban get the best of him. No way in hell. Rather than give up, he decided to try a different tactic -- something that had worked in the past. He brought in a colleague and tried the good cop/bad cop routine. For the next half hour, the new guy bombarded Paz with questions and accusations, and Grimes defended him at every turn. It was entertaining to watch, but it did not produce the intended result.

There was no admission of wrongdoing.

No confession.

At this point, Ridge had heard enough, and she suggested that they adjourn to the nearest watering hole and console themselves with some adult beverages. She didn't have to ask twice, but Gold advised her that they should head back to Boca Raton lest they get stuck in rush hour traffic. Ridge agreed, so they drove back to Taverna Kyma, hoping to partake in another happy hour.

On the way north, Gold asked about the interrogation. He was curious about the procedure. "How long can they question him?"

"Twenty-four hours. After that, they'll be on thin ice, legally speaking."

"How long before they have to file charges?"

"Well, that depends on the venue –– where a person gets arrested. The laws vary from state to state, but as a rule, prosecutors have up to seventy-two hours to bring charges."

Gold sat brooding for a half minute and finally said, "A lot could happen in three days."

"You worried about Paz?"

"Yeah, a little. I'd hate to see him take the rap for something he didn't do."

"You should worry about yourself."

He digested that for a moment and then said, "Are you trying to tell me something?"

"I've already told you, but it bears repeating. You've moved up in the world. You're now at the top of Russo's hit list, and you can't let your guard down."

"I don't intend to."

"Russo's a sneaky son of a bitch. He could come at you from any direction. Even a direction that seems safe."

"What do you mean?"

"You should tell your mother to remain vigilant. Make sure her doors and windows are locked. Tell her not to admit any strangers."

Gold exhaled and clasped his hands behind his head. "I'm afraid that ship has sailed."

"What?"

"I think that Russo already got a lay of the land."

Ridge glanced at him, then did a double take. "What are you talking about?"

Gold told her about the business card his mother had showed him -- the one from Sun Coast Realty. "I asked Paz about the card, and he claimed he never gave it to her. I believe him. He doesn't handle Royal Palm properties."

"So you think Russo gave her the card?"

"Who else could it be?"

"Did you get a description?"

"I forgot to ask. I was in a rush."

"Tsk tsk."

"I had a lot on my mind."

"You need to follow-up on that."

"As soon as I get home."

There was a short silence between them, and then Ridge said, "I forgot something, too. I meant to tell you this earlier, but I got distracted by the interrogation. I think that Russo is on to us, or at least to me. DHS has been plagued by leaks, and nobody in Washington knows how to keep a secret any longer. I have reason to believe that Russo was tipped off, and that's why he's gone underground. I could be wrong, but I think he's gone dark and plans to ride out the storm."

Gold didn't like the thought of that, and he say so. "Damn, that's not good. He's the kind of rat that could find a lot of holes."

"We'll have to flush him out. We have no other choice."

"How do you propose we do that?"

"Do you know anything about rats? Real rats?"

"Not my field of expertise."

"Nor mine, but I do know a few things about their behavior. For instance, I know that rats act aggressively when threatened. Sometimes they get too aggressive, and that's when they get caught. If we keep the pressure on our rat, he might get careless and fall into our trap."

"From your mouth to God's ears."

"I also know that rats are known to travel great distances and are wary of unknown objects in their path."

"Meaning?"

"Russo could be anywhere in the state, hiding where he knows the terrain and feels safe. We shouldn't limit our search to Miami-Dade, Broward, and Palm Beach Counties."

"Well, we have to begin somewhere, so what do you suggest?"

"I suggest we pull out all the stops. Shut down his operation. Cut off the money supply. Make life miserable for his family, friends, and business associates. Sooner or later, somebody will turn on him."

"Sounds like a lot of work."

"Piece of cake for DHS. We've already cancelled his passport and put him on the no-fly list."

"Good move."

"Tomorrow we freeze his bank accounts."

"Jesus, you're like a dog on a bone."

"For good reason. I've been down this road before. I've dealt with drug dealers, gun smugglers, and human traffickers. I know how they operate. How much pain they cause. I've felt that pain myself."

Gold fell silent for a moment, then said, "Are you referring to your niece?"

Ridge sighed heavily. She started to answer, and then stopped, and then started again when she realized that Gold was staring at her. She was clearly distraught, but she was determined to explain her feelings. Even so, she had trouble finding the right words.

Gold had never met her niece, whose name was Jenny Ikaho, but he knew that her life had been short and sad, the stuff that nightmares are made of. After a traumatic childhood, she left the Pearl River Reservation in Neshoba County, Mississippi, and fell into the clutches of a psychotic cult leader. A short-lived affair led to more abuse, and when she tried to leave, she was brutally murdered.

In many ways, Jenny Ikaho was a product of her environment — an environment that had shrunk from six billion acres to only fifty-two million acres thanks to the questionable management of the Bureau of Indian Affairs. Jenny was born and raised in Pearl River, the largest of eight Choctaw Indian communities in the state. Like the other communities, Pearl River had numerous infrastructure problems, including antiquated electric, telephone, and sewage connections. The poverty rate was roughly 39 percent, and unemployment fluctuated between 25 and 50 percent.

Sadly, these were not the only social challenges.

Year after year, the reservation had high rates of school dropout, child mortality, suicide, and teenage pregnancy.

Both of Jenny's parents had been casino workers, which meant that they were absentee parents. Her mother dealt Blackjack, and her father worked the Roulette wheel. Between shifts they gambled with their freedom, selling drugs to tourists. When they got busted, Jenny was more or less on her own, and easy pickins for the cold-blooded killer who recruited her.

When they got to the restaurant, they sat outside, and as soon as they had their drinks, Ridge dropped the other shoe. "I volunteered for this assignment. I had to call in some chits to get the job."

"Jesus, you're a glutton for punishment."

"Maybe, but this is something I have to do."

"Why?"

"My niece was a victim of human trafficking. That's how she got involved with the cult. In my view, there's a special place in hell for those bastards, and I mean to send down as many as I can."

"I can't say that I blame you."

Ridge glanced around, lowered her voice a notch. "You might think I'm overreacting, but the numbers speak for themselves. Last year, DHS received over two thousand reports of human trafficking. That happens to be a 54 percent increase from the previous year." She sat back, kneading her fists into her thighs. "I don't know about you, but that makes me sick to my stomach."

"Well, that explains why you're willing to use me as bait."

"Come again?"

Gold's expression grew sober. "If Russo wants to get to me, he'll have to crawl out of his hole. Isn't that why you want me to tag along?"

"You don't mince words, do you?"

"No, but let's get something straight. I have no intention of becoming mincemeat, so don't ask me to stick my neck out. We're a team. We work together. You watch my back, and I'll watch yours. Agreed?"

"I wouldn't have it any other way."

"I've heard that before."

Ridge smiled sweetly. "Have I ever put you in harm's way?"

There was no hint of levity in Gold's voice when he leaned over and said, "Did you forget about our flight to West Texas? If I recall, we ran out of gas at three thousand feet."

"I think it was two thousand feet."

"Whatever."

"Altitude matters."

"So does attitude, and in my view, it's preferable to land with the engine running."

"You're so picky."

Gold gave her a blank stare. "How many planes have you crashed?"

"Just one."

"How did you manage to keep your license?"

"I guess you've never handled aviation claims."

"Nope."

"Well, for your information, there are thousands of general aviation accidents each year."

"How comforting."

"Mostly due to pilot error. According to the NTSB, loss of control is the major cause of crashes."

"I would think so. Where do faulty gauges rank?"

"Equipment failures are rare. The bigger problem is switching from VHR into IMC. That's aviation lingo, meaning Visual Flight Rules into Instrumental Meteorological Conditions."

"Run that by me in English."

"A situation where an unqualified pilot is forced to fly by instruments in bad weather or low visibility."

"A la JFK, Jr."

"Precisely."

"Do you have an instrument rating?"

"I certainly do."

"That's good to know."

Ridge's voice cut into his thoughts, as she reminded him that thirty thousand people died in traffic accidents each year, compared to the four hundred or so who perished in general aviation accidents. "I'd take a plane over a car any day of the week."

"Not me."

"You only live once."

"I hope you'll keep that in mind. Are you hungry?"

"Yes, but I've got to run. I've got another meeting in Tallahassee." She finished her drink, then stood. "You were supposed to take your mother to lunch. If I were you, I'd buy her a nice dinner."

"I was hoping you could join us."

"I'll have to take a rain check."

"I understand."

"By the way, don't forget to call Father Flanagan."

"Who?"

"Your detective friend. The one who became a priest."

"I think you mean Father Feretti."

"You need to call him."

Gold flinched reflexively, forcing a smile. "I intend to." He was surprised by her concern. He studied her for a moment and registered her look as completely sincere. "Don't be surprised if he shows up in Florida."

"We need all the help we can get."

"Be careful what you wish for."

CHAPTER TWENTY

There were plenty of good restaurants in Palm Beach County, but when her son was in town, Harriet Gold insisted that they dine at the Boca Raton Resort and Club. She enjoyed the atmosphere and food, but more importantly, strolling through the grand lobby gave her a chance to show off her son and brag about his handsome salary. *De rigueur* among the moneyed set.

The "Pink Hotel" was Boca's most famous landmark, and by coincidence, it opened in 1926, the year that Al Capone made his first visit to South Florida. The hotel was designed by Addison Mizner and built during the Florida land boom of the 1920s. The original hundred-room hotel was the most expensive hotel ever built at the time, and among its first guests were the ranking hierarchy of Wall Street, Hollywood, and the international social set. The register included people named du Pont, Vanderbilt, Whitney, Jolson, and Ziegfeld.

During World War II, the hotel was commandeered by the government and transformed into "the most elegant barracks in history" for a few hundred Army Air Corps officers. After the war, the hotel was purchased and renovated by Arthur Vining Davis, one of the founders of Alcoa.

Due to its location in the heart of Florida's Gold Coast, the hotel had become the perfect spot to see and be seen, which was why Gold disliked the place. When they finally sat down in the main lounge, Harriet ordered some sort of tropical concoction, and Gold asked for a Bombay Sapphire martini –– ice and olives on the side.

When the waiter was out of earshot, Gold said, "I thought you drank champagne."

"You only live once."

Gold smiled. "You sound like Sally Ridge."

"Too bad she couldn't join us."

"She had to fly to Tallahassee."

"What's in Tallahassee?"

"The State Capitol."

"Tell me something I don't know."

"Such as?"

Harriet sat back, leveled her gaze at him. She put her hand over his, squeezed it gently, and spoke in her sweetest tone. "How does a nice Jewish boy become friends with a Choctaw Indian woman?"

"First of all, I'm not as nice as you might think. Second, Sally is not a full-blooded Choctaw. If I remember right, her father's Cajun."

"What does that have to do with the price of tea in China?"

After some deliberation, he attempted to explain the Quantum Blood Laws that governed who became a member of the Choctaw tribe. He told her that a seventeen-member Tribal Council had decided that a person must have a 50 percent quantum degree of

Choctaw blood in order to be a member in good standing. He could see that his mother was slightly confused, but he went on to say that the blood laws were originally enacted by European Americans in order to define and regulate who would be classified as Native American and thus eligible to receive federal benefits.

At the present time, each tribe established its own criteria for membership, and with the growth of casino revenues and other economic development, many tribes had become quite restrictive, including the Choctaws.

Gold pretty much knew the answer to his question but decided to ask anyway. "Am I going too fast?"

Harriet was looking at him with a frown. "No, I understand. Our tribe has something similar. To be a Jew, one must be either the child of a Jewish mother or a convert to Judaism." She smiled sheepishly. "The quantum thing is a little confusing, but rules are rules."

Without exactly knowing why, Gold decided to elaborate. "As I said, each tribe has its own rules. For instance, the Cheyenne and Arapaho require one-fourth degree blood quantum. The Apache and Comanche require one-eighth degree. The Caddo nation will accept a one-sixteenth degree. Some tribes have no minimum." He flushed slightly and said, "Too much information?"

"Way too much."

The waiter returned with their drinks, and after he left, Gold made a toast. *"L'chaim,"* he said. "Always a pleasure to be with my beautiful mother."

"Flattery will get you everywhere."

"I'm only after a lobster dinner."

"Well, you came to the right place."

"The bartender makes a good martini."

Harriet's eyes lit up, although she tried to keep any sign of enthusiasm out of her face. "So tell me, what's the deal with you and Sally?"

"What do you mean?"

"Are you just friends?"

"Just friends."

"Huh."

"Did you forget that I'm married?"

"You're still a man."

"The last time I checked."

"She seems very fond of you."

"For good reason. I once saved her life."

"You saved her life?"

Gold made a vague gesture with his hands to suggest that it was no big deal. "She fell into a fish tank, so I jumped in and pulled her out."

"A fish tank?"

"A commercial tank. We were at a hatchery."

"Doing what?"

"Long story."

"You mean a likely story."

"Don't be silly."

"Did you give her mouth to mouth resucitation?"

"Yeah, but no tongue."

"Very funny."

Gold studied her carefully over the rim of his glass, amazed that she was still worried about him, still concerned that he might fall into the clutches of some Jezebel. After all these years he was still her little boy. Eventually he said, "You don't have to worry, Mom. Sally's in love with her work, and she doesn't have time to play around."

"Where does she live?"

"Wherever the job takes her. We met a few years ago, in Tupelo, Mississippi. Back then she was a homicide detective. A damn good one. We worked on a case together, and then I left. I didn't see her for a couple of years until I went to Texas to handle another claim. Sally was looking for her niece, who had joined a religious cult."

"A religious cult?"

"Another long story."

"No wonder you drink so much."

"What are you talking about? This is my first drink of the day."

"The day ain't over yet."

"Don't remind me."

"Sally's a lovely woman. She should find herself a husband and settle down. Raise a family. Home is where the heart is, or where it should be."

Gold couldn't help but smile as he listened to his mother play the role of matchmaker. "Speaking of homes, when did you meet that guy from Sun Coast Realty?"

"The real estate agent?"

"Uh-huh."

She sipped her drink, thinking. "Two or three weeks ago."

"Did he make an appointment?"

"No, he said he was driving around the neighborhood, looking for houses that might be for sale."

"What did he look like?"

"I don't remember."

"You don't remember?"

"We only spoke for a couple of minutes."

"You must remember something about him. Was he tall? Short? Heavy-set? Thin?"

"I don't recall."

Gold laughed. It was a dry, hacking cackle, the best he was capable of, but he choked it out nonetheless. "All right. Let me guess. You forgot to put your glasses on."

Harriet bristled, her back straightening. "Nobody's perfect." She let out a sigh. "Are we through playing Twenty Questions?"

"Yeah, but I want you to do me a favor. Stop opening your door to strangers. You're a senior citizen living alone in a mansion, and that makes you an easy target."

"For your information, I live in a gated community, and we have our own police force."

"Yeah, I've seen the boys in blue. Keystone Cops on golf carts."

Harriet's eyebrows furrowed in puzzlement. "Why are you so concerned about my safety?"

"I'm your son. I'm supposed to be concerned."

"You worry too much."

"I'd worry a lot less if you promised to keep your door locked."

"Fine. I'll use the intercom."

"Thank you."

She raised her eyes to meet Gold's with that intelligent, clear-eyed, piercing gaze that went right through him. "Is there something you're not telling me?"

Out of the corner of his eye, Gold saw the maitre d' signal him. "Just one thing," he said. He walked behind her and pulled out her chair. "Our table is ready."

Harriet had fallen asleep soon after they got home. One moment she was on the couch reading a magazine, and the next she was out like a light. Gold covered her with a blanket and propped a pillow under her head. He found it odd to be looking after his mother the way he would take care of a child. It made him feel old.

By the same token, it was nice to be needed.

Gold's phone didn't often ring in the early hours of the morning. Anyone who knew him well knew that he was not an early riser. So when the phone rang, he had a pretty good idea who it was going to be –– someone who didn't give a hoot about his sleeping habits. "Hello, Irene," he yawned.

"Did I wake you?"

He was silent for a moment, considering the possibilities. But he was too sleepy for wit. "Yes, but I'll recover."

"Sorry," Kaminski said. "I was worried. I haven't heard from you in a couple of days."

"I've been busy."

"Apparently so."

"What time is it?"

"Seven o'clock."

"I hope you're not calling from work."

"No, I'm home." She was quiet for a moment, probably considering where to begin. "Are you all right?"

"Yeah, I'm fine."

"How's your mother?"

"She's fine too."

"How's the weather?"

Gold seemed a bit miffed. "Fine and dandy."

"Have you spoken with Paz?"

"Yeah, we had a nice, long chat. He's an interesting character, but not the brightest bulb in the pack."

"He's smart enough to cause us trouble."

Gold assumed that she was referring to the claim, so he tried to reassure her that everything was under control. "You don't have to worry about Paz. We, er, settled out of court."

Kaminski was enraged. "You did *what?*"

"You don't sound pleased."

There was a moment of silence. Then she said, "I hope you're joking. I didn't approve any payment."

"There was no payment."

"I don't understand. You must have offered something."

"Only his freedom."

"What are you talking about?"

"I pulled a rabbit out of the hat. I made the claim disappear."

Kaminski cleared her throat. "Look, I know it's early, but you need to get your brain in gear. Stop babbling about rabbits and tell me what happened."

"We're home free. Paz signed a waiver." With some difficulty, Gold crawled out of bed and dragged himself over to a chair. He was thinking as fast as he could, wondering how much he should tell her. Knowing Kaminski, he figured she'd want to know everything. So he told her -- all about his visit to Capone Island, about his meeting with Paz, about Annette Russo's murder, and about Sally Ridge. It took a while, but he managed to cover all the bases. When he finished talking, he braced himself for the verbal barrage that was sure to follow.

But she didn't say anything.

Not a single word.

Gold stared at the receiver of the phone as if hypnotized. Neither one of them said anything for thirty seconds, then Gold put the phone back to his ear and said, "Are you still there, Irene?"

"Yes, I'm here."

"I thought we got disconnected."

"No, I heard every word."

"So, what do you think?"

There was another short pause. "I think I should keep my thoughts to myself. Our phones might be tapped."

"Tapped?"

"Your friends might be listening."

"My friends?"

"DHS."

Gold was about to laugh, but changed his mind. "Why would the feds tap our phones?"

"Maybe you should ask Sally Ridge that question. She's the one who obtained a court order requiring our company to produce all of the records, documents, and materials related to the Paz claim." She laughed, but it was not a pleasant sound. "And while you're at it, ask her what happened to our underwriter. Bill Burke has also disappeared."

CHAPTER TWENTY-ONE

Every once in a while, Gold wished he could stay in bed, pull the covers over his head, and sleep until noon. Today was one of those days. Irene's call had been a rude awakening, both figuratively and literally, and now he had to worry about Sally Ridge. Why had she obtained a court order? Why had she gone behind his back? Where the hell was Bill Burke?

Later, after showering and dressing, Gold went downstairs in search of breakfast. The kitchen was empty, but somebody, presumably his mother, had made coffee, cut up fruit, and set out English muffins. A light rain was falling on the back yard, the pool, and the tropical plants surrounding the patio.

Gold sipped at his coffee, mesmerized by the glistening surface of the Intracoastal Waterway and the gently swaying palms on Capone Island. *I should be sleeping,* he told himself. *Enjoying the calm before the storm.* But he was too keyed up to sleep. There were chores to be done, loose ends that required his undivided attention.

The most difficult chore, the one he dreaded the most, was calling Lou Feretti and telling him about the murder of Annette Russo. As expected, Feretti listened carefully, asked a bunch of questions, and then flew through the five stages of grief while they were still on the phone. One by one, he hit each stage, expressing denial, anger, bargaining, depression, and finally acceptance.

Of course, as Feretti hinted, acceptance and forgiveness were two different things.

Two very different things.

The second chore of the day took more effort. Gold felt guilty that Paz was being held for a crime he didn't commit, so he drove down to Miami, hoping to convince Sergeant Grimes that he was barking up the wrong tree. The sergeant was not in his office, but Gold obtained permission to visit Paz, who was cooling his heels in a holding cell.

A hard-looking man was standing beside a wall phone, his arms crossed, impatience etched on his face. He had a hatchet nose and a scar on his right cheek. "Mr. Gold?" he said brusquely, straightening up and holding out a badge. "I'm Lieutenant Robb, homicide. You've got ten minutes, so knock yourself out."

Gold and Paz locked eyes in some kind of shared understanding across the small space between them. Not for long, though. When the lieutenant walked away, Paz shook his head, spoke with a weary tone. "I don't believe this shit. They think I murdered some broad. It's making me crazy."

Gold, reading his mind, said, "You're a lot of things, but not a murderer."

"What are you doing here?"

"Just stopped by to say hello."

"How did you know I was here?"

"A little bird told me."

"A little bird named Morella?"

"I'd rather not say."

Paz rose and started pacing. "I should call a lawyer."

"Before you do that, you might want to pull your head out of your ass."

"What?"

"Stop playing the fool. You were framed, and you know it. You also know who's pulling the strings. Don't you, Ricardo?"

"I don't know what you're talking about."

"Really? I find that hard to believe."

"I don't care what you believe."

"You'd better start caring –– or start preparing your will. Time is of the essence."

Paz could feel a slight shaking in his hands and knew it wasn't just anger. It was fear. He felt his heart thumping, the blood darkening his face. He clenched his teeth to stop himself saying something rash. "I'm behind bars. What do you expect me to do?"

"Face facts."

"No comprendo."

"Fact number one: Russo gave you the gun that was used to kill his aunt. Fact number two: The gun was locked in your desk drawer at work, so Russo had plenty of time to make a key and steal it. Fact number three: Russo borrowed *your* vehicle, and then he left the radio on a Cuban music station. Fact number four: You help me find him, or it's *hasta la vista, baby.*" Gold was a little startled by the force of his response. Paz let out a lengthy string of expletives in Spanish, then slammed his fist into the wall.

"Hallelujah," Gold said. "You've finally seen the light."

Paz kept cursing. "The son of a bitch set me up!"

"I don't know about you, but I hate fair-weather friends."

"How could he do this to me? He was my sponsor. My mentor. My *amigo*. I don't understand."

Gold took a deep breath, knowing what he had to say was going to be hard to swallow -- and painful. "Russo was never your friend. He has no friends. You were recruited to be his stooge. Nothing more, nothing less." He did not avert his gaze. "How did you two meet?"

Paz stared at him for a long moment, then crumpled onto the bed, defeated. "I met Russo in Miami, shortly after I left Cuba. He pulled some strings and got me released from ICE. The next thing I know, I've got a Green Card. After that he offered me a job, and I became an American citizen. He was very good to me. He gave me a car, taught me real estate, and paid me well. He even introduced me to my girlfriend."

"Russo introduced you to Morella Perez?"

"Yes."

"And then he hired her?"

"That's right."

"Convenient."

"What does that mean?"

"Never mind. Let's get back to your predicament. You need to tell me everything you know about Russo. I also need a list of his real estate holdings. He could be hiding in one of his own properties."

Paz glared at him. "First things first. You need to get me out of here."

"No can do."

"Bullshit. You must have some connections. How did you get in here?"

"I know Sergeant Grimes. I mentioned his name, and they gave me ten minutes."

"So mention somebody else's name and get me out of here."

"We're wasting valuable time."

There was a long silence, and when it ended, Gold was completely unprepared for Paz's fury. "Listen to me, *amigo*. I'm going to kill that *bastardo*. I don't care if it's the last thing I do. I swear to God, that *hijo de puta* is a dead man!"

Gold stared at him and spoke slowly. "Start talking, Paz."

"Vete al infierno!" Paz said loudly. "I have nothing to say to you. I want to call my lawyer."

"You don't need a lawyer," said Lieutenant Robb. "You're free to go."

Gold turned around to find the lieutenant studying him with utter contempt, his arms folded across his massive chest. He glanced at Paz, then shook his head in disbelief. "You're letting Paz walk?"

Robb shrugged indifferently, a smirk spreading across his lips. "We've been asked to release him."

"You gotta be kidding me."

"I'm afraid not."

"Who made that request?"

"Your buddies at DHS." He unlocked the cell and waved Paz out. "I hope you people know what you're doing."

"They're not my people."

"Yeah, right."

"I happen to be an insurance investigator."

"Save your breath, hotshot. I saw you and your partner in the observation room. I was the bad cop yesterday."

"I thought you looked familiar."

"You two better leave before Grimes gets back. He's gonna hit the roof when he hears that we released a cold-blooded killer."

Paz stepped between them, trying not to let what he was thinking and feeling show in his face. "Where do I pick up my personal belongings?"

"Upstairs," Robb said. "Turn in your voucher, and you'll get your property."

"I hope it's all there."

"Start walking."

"You'll be hearing from my lawyer."

Robb gave him a cunning smile. "You might be hearing from us, too. Payback's a bitch, *amigo*."

Gold followed Paz upstairs, and when they got outside, he offered him a ride home. The offer was quickly rejected. Paz closed his eyes, trying to mentally regroup. How did he get himself into these situations? What the hell just happened? He took out his cell phone, hoping to make a call, but the battery was dead. "Son of a bitch."

Gold smiled faintly. "Trying to reach your lawyer?"

"No, *estúpido*, my girlfriend. Morella has no idea where I've been."

"If I were you, I'd keep my distance from her."

Paz stepped closer, eyes bulging a little more as his face drew taught. "What's your problem, Gold? You got the hots for my girl?"

"All I got from Morella was a cold shoulder."

"That's all you deserve."

"You deserve better."

"What?"

"I might be wrong, but I think you're being played."

"What the hell does that mean?"

"Did it ever occur to you that Morella and Russo might be a team? Think about it, Paz. She's Cuban, too. Her contacts in Havana may have told her that you were on your way to America. Right after you get here, you get picked up by ICE, and then, miraculously, you get released and offered a job." Paz started to move away, but Gold grabbed his wrist. "Didn't you tell me that Russo introduced you to Morella? Didn't he hire her to be your secretary?"

"Back off, *pendejo!*"

"She's probably the one who stole your gun."

Paz glared at him and literally spat out the words, "Fuck you, Gold. I told you before, I don't care what you think."

Gold shook his head gravely. "Love is blind."

Paz stayed quiet for a moment, then said, "When I get through with Russo, I'm gonna look you up and kick your ass!"

"We've been down that road before."

"Round two will be different."

"I can hardly wait."

Paz started to walk away, then stopped dead in his tracks and said, "Why did they release me?"

"I don't know."

"You have no idea?"

"Nothing I can prove."

"I don't get it. First they accuse me of murder, then they let me go. Something's not right."

"You can say that again."

"Who the hell is DHS?"

"Department of Homeland Security."

Paz's voice had a frustrated quality to it. Gold was smiling. "Why the fuck do they care about me?"

"If I had to guess, you're their bait."

"Bait for what?"

"They're hoping that Russo hears about your release and then makes the mistake of contacting you. That's when they pounce."

"Why are they after him?"

"He's been a very bad boy."

"What's he done?"

"Besides killing his aunt and then framing you? Well, let's see. He's been engaged in the distribution of illegal drugs, gun smuggling, and human trafficking."

"Jesus Christ."

"He's also been involved with enemies of the state."

"Who?"

"The folks who engage in espionage."

"Foreign spies?"

"*Cuban* spies." Gold watched Paz's eyes grow large and fearful as he processed what was said. There was now a growing look of terror in them. "Are you starting to connect the dots?"

Paz gave him a withering look. He felt something roiling in his stomach, and he realized that there was a hell of a lot he wasn't being told. Crossly, he said, "I'll see you later."

Gold faced him squarely. "I'll be around."

CHAPTER TWENTY-TWO

After dealing with Paz, Gold needed some downtime, so he spent a quiet evening with his mother, unaware that his early morning phone call to Lou Feretti had lit a fuse. While Gold relaxed in Florida, an American Airlines flight from Austin, Texas, made its final approach to New York's JFK Airport. Twenty minutes later, an excited throng of passengers made their way to the baggage claim area, but Lou Feretti, wearing a dark suit and fedora, walked by the luggage carousel and stood outside. He hadn't been standing there five minutes when a car, a black Cadillac, pulled to the curb and the electric window glided down.

The driver wore dark sunglasses and a baggy Hawaiian shirt, concealing a weapon. He studied Feretti for a moment, then gestured him forward. "Are you Feretti?"

"Yeah."

"Any luggage?"

"No."

"Hop in."

Feretti sat in the back, moving toward the middle so he could see the driver's face in the rearview mirror. The driver seemed happy about that, too. Neither man spoke, but in order to ease the tension, the driver inserted a Frank Sinatra CD and cranked up the volume. As daylight faded into evening, they drove west on the Belt Parkway, crossing the Manhattan Bridge and turning right onto Mulberry Street.

The driver parked in front of Angelo's, a popular restaurant in the heart of Little Italy. Directly across the street was the Caltanissetta Social Club, a private club reputed to be a mob hangout. The driver escorted Feretti across the street and opened the door for him. In the back of the club, Joe DeCarlo, the underboss of the Genovese crime family, sat on a wobbly chair, facing the entrance. There was a small table in front of him and one empty chair to his right.

Feretti was somewhat amused by the decor. The walls on both sides of the room were painted in broad, vertical stripes of green, white, and red. The stripes were meant to represent the flag of Italy, but they gave the place a carnival atmosphere.

All in all, the setting was not very intimidating, but that was okay because DeCarlo didn't want visitors to be so afraid they couldn't think straight.

Though he needed them to be a *little* afraid.

Suddenly a muzzle of a gun appeared against Feretti's left cheek. "Don't move," was the whisper. The gun now pressed against his back. "I need to pat you down."

Feretti sighed. "I'm unarmed."

A harsh whisper: "Just keep still."

After frisking Feretti, the voice told him to walk over to the table and sit down. Feretti did as he was told, lowering himself into the chair while contemplating the wisdom of stepping into the lion's den. DeCarlo eyed him closely for several seconds without saying anything. The tension in the room was palpable. Tired of playing games, Feretti looked straight into the mobster's eyes and said, "*Buonasera*, Giuseppe."

DeCarlo forced a smile but didn't offer his hand. "Father Luigi, so good to see you again. How are you doing?"

Feretti said he was doing fine, exchanged a few pleasantries, and then dropped a bomb on him. "You don't have to address me as Father. I'm leaving the priesthood."

"Che cosa?"

"In a matter of days."

DeCarlo slumped back in his chair, then shook his head like he couldn't believe what he was hearing. "You're leaving the church?"

"No, the priesthood. There's a difference."

"Why are you leaving?"

"I'm not cut out to be a priest."

"Says who? You've been a choir boy your whole life."

"Not hardly."

DeCarlo fumbled in his pocket, fishing out a cigarette pack and a lighter. He pulled a cigarette from the pack, then glowered at the ubiquitous No Smoking sign near the entrance and let the unlit cigarette dangle from his lip. "I know it's none of my business, but the suspense is killing me. Which vow is giving you *agita*? Chastity? Obedience? Poverty?" With a grim laugh, he added, "I'd have trouble with all of them."

Feretti restrained an urge to make a smart comeback. "I'm leaving for personal reasons that have nothing to do with my vows."

DeCarlo shook his head again. "I think you're making a big mistake. I'm very involved in my parish, and I know what's going on in the Catholic Church. There's a shortage of priests, and it's only getting worse each year. Did you know that there is only one priest for every two thousand Catholics?"

"Yes, I'm aware of that."

"You should keep that in mind."

"My mind is made up."

DeCarlo lit the cigarette and took several deep drags, which in a strange way seemed to settle his breathing. After exhaling a big cloud of smoke, he said, "You can't quit because you're having a bad day. You'll have to go through a long process."

The process was known as laicization, which meant that a priest was dismissed from the clerical state and could no longer perform liturgical or catechetical roles on behalf of the church. When the request was voluntary, as in Feretti's case, it was referred to in Latin as *pro gratia*, but the priest still lost rights to such things as clerical garb and titles.

Feretti took a few moments to explain the process, but the irony of the situation was not lost on him. He found it a little odd to be discussing church doctrine with a notorious mobster.

And the word "notorious" fit him to a tee.

Joe DeCarlo was the son of Vincent DeCarlo, the former *Capo di tutti capi* -- boss of the bosses -- of New York's Five Families.

During his reign, he was known as "Vinnie Caps" because of his pearly whites. According to mafia lore, he'd made his bones early in life, and until his recent death, he was the only living boss who had actually been present during the most famous mob bust in US history –– the Apalachin Meeting in upstate New York.

Back in 1957, roughly one hundred Mafiosi held a meeting at the home of Joseph "Joe the Barber" Barbara in Apalachin. Barbara, himself a boss, owned a fifty-three-acre estate in the small town, which was located about two hundred miles northwest of New York City. The agenda was designed to resolve some ongoing disputes related to mob business –– disputes that could escalate into a mob war.

The Genovese family was concerned about their lucrative operations in the east, which included gambling, loansharking, and narcotics. They were also hoping to make further inroads into the garment industry, which meant access to trucking and labor unions and the large sums of money they controlled.

Back then, DeCarlo was a bodyguard/chauffeur assigned to be a lookout during the meeting. He'd been one of the first to spot state troopers jotting down license plate numbers. When the police moved in, he tried to protect his boss, but Vito Genovese and fifty-eight others were apprehended.

DeCarlo was also arrested, but he claimed to be delivering fish and was questioned, then released. From there it was onward and upward, becoming a made man in his twenties and then being promoted to caporegime, underboss, and finally boss.

Joe DeCarlo was following in his father's footsteps, and like his old man, he saw himself as a pillar of the community. He listened to Feretti's explanation and did not interrupt him, but he was clearly unhappy about his decision to leave the priesthood. "You gave up a lot to become a priest."

"I thought it was my calling."

"Maybe it was. Serving is part of our heritage. Take a look at these walls. Those colors represent the Italian flag. The red stripe symbolizes sacrifice."

"Yes, I know."

DeCarlo stared at him, chewing on his pale lower lip for a moment, then finally said, "Where's your parish?"

"I don't have one. I teach at a Catholic university."

"Notre Dame?"

"St. Edward's University."

"Where's that?"

"Austin, Texas."

"You really get around."

"Well, you know how it works. You go where they send you."

"Yeah, and now you're here." He stubbed out his cigarette and promptly lit another. "So why did you want to see me? *Qual è il problema?*"

Feretti paused a moment, aware of what he was doing. He was about to ask a mafioso for permission to do something he absolutely didn't want to do. He didn't know if he was seeking justice or revenge, but at this point he didn't care. He had to make things right. He breathed lightly, getting a grip on his emotions, then said, "Five years ago, when your father was in charge, a man named Sal Russo asked for a sit-down. Russo wanted to get rid of me, but he was a Jersey wiseguy, so he needed your father's permission. Luckily for me, your father refused his request. Don DeCarlo knew that killing a cop would be bad for business, and as you know, business comes first. I don't know if you heard about the meeting, but that's the way it went down."

DeCarlo searched his memory. Then he remembered. One of Russo's soldiers, a guy named Cardone, stepped out of line and planted a bomb in Feretti's car. Vinnie Caps thought that was disrespectful, so he put out a contract on the guy. "Just for the record, we had nothing to do with that car bomb."

"I realize that."

"So why are you here?"

Feretti, a precise and deliberate man whose stoic expression and dark eyes could shield even a hint of emotion, was not only one of the best detectives the city had ever produced, he was a man of few words, who rarely smiled and who spoke in direct, unambiguous sentences. "Sal Russo is dead, but his son has become a problem. He's a made man. I need your permission to take him out."

"You want to whack Nicky Russo?"

"That's right."

DeCarlo's scowl deepened for an instant and then, suddenly, he found himself chuckling. "You gotta be kidding me."

"Do I look like I'm kidding?"

"Marone, sei pazzo!"

"No, I'm not crazy. I know exactly what I'm doing."

Feretti watched DeCarlo's face, already hard, turn to stone. The eyes narrowed, the lips went tight, the jaw muscle by his ear quivered. He tried to smile, but it came out crooked. Finally, he said, "I know that Russo's scooch, but why do you want to kill him?"

"He murdered a friend of mine. A civilian."

"He killed a civilian?"

"A woman."

DeCarlo shook his head disgustedly. "Not good."

"The woman was his aunt."

"Whoa, he killed his own aunt?"

"Shot her in the chest."

DeCarlo was incredulous. "Damn, that's fucked up."

"Big time."

"When did this happen?"

"A couple of days ago."

"I didn't see anything on the news."

"She was killed in Florida."

"How do you know Russo clipped her?"

"I heard it through the grapevine."

"From your buddies on the force?"

"I'd rather not say."

DeCarlo gave him a long and piercing look. "Why don't you let the cops do their thing?"

"The feds are handling the case."

"The feds?"

"Department of Homeland Security."

"*Non capisco.* Why are they involved?"

"They've been after Russo for a long time. I hear they're on the warpath. I guess you know what that means. Lots of hassles. Leave no stone unturned. Bad for business."

"Just what I need."

"Misery loves company."

The color had drained from DeCarlo's face. His eyes drifted to the back of the room as though he hoped to find some answer there. Staggered by the threat to his business –– and family –– he could do nothing but stare. He shifted in his chair and did not say anything for a full minute. It suddenly occurred to him that Feretti's problem had become his problem too. He rubbed his face with both hands, and his voice cracked with sudden anger. "Russo's been a thorn in my side for a long time. I never liked that *cafone*."

"There's nothing likable about him."

"What kind of animal kills his own aunt?"

"Beats me."

"I knew his old man. Sal Russo was a nasty prick, too."

"Like father, like son."

DeCarlo, smoke pouring from his nostrils, said, "Are you sure you want to pop him? Once you cross the line, there's no going back."

"I can't ask a stranger to do my dirty work."

DeCarlo nodded, as if he understood. "Let me ask you something. Are you still a priest in the eyes of the church?"

"For the time being."

"So you're able to hear confession?"

"Yes."

"In that case, whatever I told you couldn't be used against me in a court of law."

"Canon Law states that the sacremental seal is inviolable and that confessional privilege is absolute."

DeCarlo flashed a wicked smile. "So if I unburden my soul and confess my sins -- and then give you the green light on Russo -- you can't testify against me."

Feretti rolled his eyes, irritated. "Yeah, that's right."

"You sure about that?"

"Positive."

Ah, what the hell, DeCarlo thought. *Swing for the fences.* Grinning wolfishly, he leaned forward and whispered into Feretti's face, "Forgive me, Father, for I have sinned..."

CHAPTER TWENTY-THREE

Two days later, following a police autopsy, the body of Annette Russo was transferred from a Miami morgue to the Assumption Catholic Church in Lauderdale By-The-Sea. The church, founded in 1959, was located one mile north of Tradewinds Avenue, a short walk from Sun Coast Realty. The *Sun Sentinel* had published a lengthy obituary, indicating that a Funeral Mass would be held on Friday morning. Following mass, the deceased would be interred at Our Lady Queen of Heaven Cemetery.

Harriet Gold had left the newspaper on the kitchen table, assuming that her son would want to pay his respects to the wife of his former colleague. Gold arrived at the church a half hour early, which turned out to be a smart move, as the parking lot was nearly full. The lobby was also crowded, and when he walked past the holy water font, he was met by an usher and escorted to a pew. Almost every seat in the chapel was taken, which in Gold's view was a testament to the character of the deceased and the life she had led.

From his seat in the last row, Gold had a panoramic view of the chapel and the beautiful stained glass windows that surrounded the altar. They reminded him of the windows he'd seen at All Saints'

Church in England, the only church in the world to have all its twelve windows decorated by the great Russian artist Marc Chagall.

When the entrance hymn began, Gold pulled himself up straight in his seat, his attention now focused on the procession making its way down the aisle. He could not see any faces, but he saw that the procession included a priest, a deacon, and two altar servers. The priest and the deacon held Bibles, and the servers carried a cross, candles, and incense.

The group made its way to the altar, and when the priest arrived at his chair, he turned around, made the sign of the cross, and said, "In the name of the Father, and of the Son, and of the Holy Spirit."

Most of the people in the pews answered "Amen," but Gold just stood there, dumbstruck. He was not surprised by the words of the priest, but by his identity. He had no idea that Lou Feretti -- Father Lou -- would be conducting the Funeral Mass. He was both surprised and amused that his old friend, a former homicide detective, was now a man of the cloth.

The Lord works in mysterious ways, Gold thought. For the next half hour, he sat quietly, listening to the Act of Penitence, the Kyrie, and a couple of Scripture readings. Feretti hadn't changed much, but he now had crow's feet at his eyes, and his dark hair was a little thinner. What hadn't changed, from what he could tell, was the man's imposing stature. He still displayed an aura of gravitas, heightened by his clerical garb. And he conducted mass with the perfect amount of solemnity, distributing Communion and offering consecrated bread and wine.

After Communion, he took a few minutes to talk about the deceased, telling the congregants that Annette Russo was a close and trusted friend -- a woman who had led an exemplary life and was now at peace in the Kingdom of God.

What Feretti said, of course, was wishful thinking. But Gold felt the same way. If anyone deserved a place in heaven, it was Annette Russo. She was truly a good woman, and sadly, people like her were few and far between. Gold was thinking of her life back in Brooklyn when the service abruptly ended. A moment later, a choir singer, accompanied by an organist, began to sing a Vince Gill tune, *Go Rest High On That Mountain.*

The chapel emptied slowly, and most of the attendees, including Gold, joined the funeral cortege, escorted by two police cars. The procession drove west, stopping at Our Lady Queen of Heaven Cemetery, where the body of Annette Russo was laid to rest.

In accordance with Catholic tradition, the Rite of Committal was performed at the gravesite, and after the site was blessed, most of the mourners returned to their vehicles and drove away. Gold stayed behind, hoping to have a word with Father Feretti. He scarcely had time to gather his thoughts before a too-familiar voice behind him said, "You've got a lot of nerve."

Out of the corner of his eye, Gold saw Sergeant Grimes step over a rope post and head his way. He suppressed a smile that would have been inappropriate given the gravity of the occasion. "Sergeant Grimes. What a pleasant surprise."

"Speak for yourself," Grimes shot back. "What the hell are you doing here?"

"Paying my respects."

"You got a strange way of showing respect. First you release the victim's killer, and then you go to her funeral? Damn, that's cold."

"I had nothing to do with his release."

"Yeah, that's what you told Lieutenant Robb."

"It's the truth."

"Bullshit."

Gold's instincts had told him there was something fishy about releasing Paz. And he was definitely feeling guilty now, but not exactly about his release. According to his moral compass, Ridge should have consulted with Grimes before making her move. The detective had a right to know what was happening. He brooded about this for a moment. Then he said, "I'm sorry you don't believe me."

"Maybe I'm being too harsh. Maybe you're just a flunky. Is that it? Does your girlfriend call the shots?"

Gold's mouth tightened, the lips conveying mild distaste. "Agent Ridge works for the Department of Homeland Security. I work for the Anchor Insurance Company. As I told your partner, I'm just a lowly investigator."

"The hell you are."

Gold gave him a business card. "Check it out for yourself. My number's on the bottom."

"Don't insult my intelligence."

"The truth shall set you free."

Grimes tore up the card, then stepped closer and poked Gold's chest, right above his sternum. "Listen, hotshot, I don't give a rat's ass who you work for. Don't ever come to my office and pretend you're my friend. I'm choosy about the company I keep, and I wouldn't be caught dead hanging out with a Junior G-Man."

Staggered by the verbal assault, Gold could do nothing but stare at him. It angered him to be lectured like a schoolboy, even though he guessed he had it coming. He *had* been with Ridge at the crime scene, and again in the observation room during the interrogation. He suppressed a retort and walked away.

When Gold reached his car, his spirits improved. Lou Feretti was sitting in the passenger seat, removing his clerical collar. He glanced toward the window, then said, "I saw you in church. In the last pew. I'm glad you came."

Gold opened the door, extended his hand. "Annette was a wonderful woman. I'll miss her."

"So will I."

"When did you get in?"

"Last night."

"Good flight?"

"Good enough."

"How long will you be in town?"

"For as long as it takes."

Gold slowly turned his head, puzzled by that answer. "For as long as *what* takes?"

"Why don't we grab some lunch?"

"Any preferences?"

"Nope."

They decided to try the Biergarten in Boca Raton, a place with outdoor seating, known for authentic German fare and a wide assortment of beer. Loud conversation filled the main dining room. Waiters and waitresses glided back and forth between the kitchen and the tables with huge serving trays of food and beer. They sat outside, at the last table in the bar area. A lovely young lady dressed as a German beer garden girl took their order. When she left, Feretti lit a cigarette.

Gold looked at him with an expression of surprise on his face. "I didn't know you smoked."

Feretti tilted his face skyward and took in the warmth of the sun. "I just started."

"Midlife crisis?"

"Something like that."

Gold shook his head in a slow, disapproving manner. "Those things will kill you."

"We all have to go sometime."

"Why rush it?"

"Let him who is without sin cast the first stone."

"Well, that leaves me out."

They reminisced about old times for a while, but every memory led back to Annette Russo, casting a pall on the conversation. The only safe subject seemed to be the present, but even there Gold was on thin ice. After a few minutes of aimless chit chat, the waitress returned with their beers. When she walked off, Gold raised his stein and said, *"Prost!"*

"*Zum Wohl*," Feretti said. "To your health."

Gold smiled pleasantly at him. "The mass was very moving. You did a great job."

"First one?"

"No, I grew up in Valley Stream. Most of my friends were either Irish or Italian."

"Yeah, I forgot you were from Long Island."

"When I was a young lad, there were eighteen churches in Nassau County."

"You don't say."

"They were all nice, but not any nicer than the Assumption Church. Those stained glass windows were something else. They reminded me of a church I saw in England. In the town of Kent."

"All Saints' Church?"

"Yeah, that's the one. Every window was decorated by Marc Chagall. All twelve of them. Man, that was a sight to behold."

"It's on my bucket list."

"Do you actually have a bucket list?"

"I certainly do."

"Good for you."

Feretti stared at a spot in the middle of the table, not meeting Gold's eyes. Finally, he looked up. "Would you like to know the number one item on my list?"

"Sure, if you want to tell me."

"I want to help you find Nick Russo."

Gold's face betrayed his astonishment. For a long time he said nothing at all. The tense silence stretched. He was pretty sure why Feretti wanted to find Russo –– though he didn't know which hat he'd be wearing at the time –– priest or avenger? In any event, he didn't think it was a good idea. At last he said, "No offense, but you'd just be in the way."

"In your way?"

"No, not just mine. A whole bunch of people are looking for Russo. Local, state, and federal authorities. Believe me, they don't need your help."

"You're probably right, but that's not the point. Annette was a dear friend of mine. I owe her a great deal. I need to contribute something."

"Mass was something."

"Not enough." He sipped from his stein, thinking. "What if I just spoke to that kid?"

"What kid?"

"The one you mentioned on the phone. The park ranger."

A horrible thought suddenly shot into Gold's gut. In an effort to make conversation while half asleep, he'd said too much. He should have kept Capone Island to himself. Too late now. The cat was out of the bag. He sat up rigidly and let out a long, exasperated breath. "Not a good idea," he said quietly.

"Why do you say that?"

"The ranger's under surveillance. DHS is hoping that Russo will try to contact him."

"Which means they haven't questioned him."

"I don't think so."

"He might be willing to talk to me."

"Why would he tell you anything?"

"Because I'm a priest. He might be a Catholic."

"So?"

"I could listen to his confession and ask a few questions. He might reveal where Russo is hiding. I know it's a long shot, but it could pay off. What do we have to lose?"

What were the odds? Gold asked himself. In the end the answer to most investigations -- civil and criminal -- was always devastatingly simple. It was always right there, obvious. Hiding in facts, evidence, lies, and the misperceptions and missed opportunities of the investigators. He stared off at the horizon for a moment and didn't speak. Finally he smiled at Feretti tightly, in a very unhappy way. "God, I hope you know what you're doing."

"I know exactly what I'm doing."

"You seem pretty sure of yourself."

"In God we trust."

"You promise to be careful?"

"You have my word."

Gold nodded doubtfully, still trying to come to terms with the idea. "All right, we'll try it your way. The ranger's name is Skip Taylor. He lives in a place called Addison Reserve, up in Delray Beach." He wiped his mouth with the back of his hand, then looked carefully at Feretti once more. "Do me a favor. Don't get killed."

"Heaven forbid."

CHAPTER TWENTY-FOUR

Delray Beach was known as "Florida's Village by the Sea," but during hurricane season, it often became Florida's village *under* the sea. Since its inception in 1884, the coastal city had endured at least twenty-five hurricanes. Nonetheless, it was still advertised as "The Most Fun Small Town in America." Except for frequent traffic jams, there was a lot to love. On average, there were 235 sunny days per year, great beaches, and a vibrant downtown packed with shopping, dining, and entertainment venues.

But none of these things mattered to Lou Feretti.

Not one of them.

He had a mission to accomplish, and it was the only thing on his mind.

By the time he pulled into the gated community of Addison Reserve, it was dark, and most of the residents were in for the night. He was stopped at the entrance by a solemn-faced security guard who asked about the purpose of his visit –– and who he'd come to see. Feretti ignored his questions and held out his badge, the one he'd carried for twenty years in New York City. He let the guard have a long look, then asked for directions to Villa D'Este Way. The guard stared at the badge for several moments, then opened the gate and waved him through. Even in the darkness, the grounds were impressive, and the clubhouse was the epitome of South Florida grandeur.

It was nine o'clock by the time he pulled up in front of the home where Skip Taylor lived. The lights were on inside, but the garage doors were closed, and there were no vehicles in the driveway. Feretti waited for a few minutes and saw no activity behind any of the lighted windows. If Taylor was inside, he wasn't showing it.

Feretti left his car on the street and walked up the driveway, wondering if he'd made the long trip for nothing. He rang the doorbell, but nobody came. Two loud knocks did the trick, and when the door flew open, Taylor stepped out, wearing nothing but a pair of Bemuda shorts. He looked right and left and then directly at the man who was interrupting a peaceful evening at home.

"What can I do for you?" Taylor asked.

"Mr. Taylor?"

"That's right."

"Skip Taylor?"

Taylor's scowl deepened, his voice suddenly harsh. "Jesus, another Jehovah Witness."

"Not quite."

"What do you want?"

"Just a few minutes of your time."

Taylor squinted, trying to adjust his eyes from the dark hallway to the bright front porch. "Do I know you?"

"No, but we both know Nick Russo."

"So?"

"So I thought we could do some business."

Taylor watched him closely, wariness gathering inside him. What the hell was this about? "What kind of business?"

"I hear you're a film buff. So am I. Maybe you'd like to part with a few movies?"

"Try Redbox."

"They don't have what I'm looking for."

"Tough shit." He started to close the door, but Feretti put his foot in the way. "What's your problem, dude?"

"I'm glad you asked. I've got five grand that's burning a hole in my pocket."

"Five thousand dollars?"

"I believe that's the coin of the realm."

Taylor broke into a huge grin. "Damn straight."

Feretti smiled back at him. "What are we waiting for?"

"Not a damn thing. If you've got the money, I've got the slime." He opened the door and waved Feretti inside. "Follow me, dude. Keep your voice down. My girlfriend's sleeping."

"I'll be as quiet as a mouse."

Feretti followed a few feet behind, hesitating at each corner of the hallway as if he were expecting an assailant at every turn. The house was not as grandiose as he'd expected it to be. Most of the rooms were small, barely furnished, and possessed of an unsettling musty odor that suggested frequent drug use. The only other person in the house was a lanky teenage girl, sprawled across the living room couch, high as a kite. She didn't move a muscle or bat an eye when they walked passed her.

"This way," Taylor whispered as he turned left down a darkened hallway.

They walked into another dimly lit space that seemed to be the master bedroom, and once again, it was sparsely furnished and reeked of marijuana. There was a lava lamp on the floor, and a large built-in bookshelf took up an entire wall. The shelves were filled with kiddie porn -- mostly DVDs, but also magazines and photographs.

An involuntary shiver raised the hairs on Feretti's arms. He could feel his blood pressure rising, and for one fleeting moment, he was tempted to grab Taylor by the throat and choke him to death.

Taylor leaned closer and whispered that he was welcome to check out the titles. "Try not to drool on the merchandise."

The merchandise was part of an industry that produced three billion dollars in revenue per year, catering mainly to pedophiles and hebephiles. In Feretti's day, as now, two-thirds of the offenders were single, and about one-quarter had problems with drugs and alcohol. Taylor appeared to have a serious drug problem, and like the majority of offenders, he was over twenty-six years old. The odds were good that he was also a child molester.

Eighty percent of pornography traders fell into that category.

Feretti knew the numbers by heart. Prior to joining the homicide division, he'd spent several months on the vice squad. He was well aware of the dangers posed by child molesters, and the havoc they wrought on society. In New York City, less than 1 percent of molesters were convicted through traditional means -- which meant child abuse reports, arrest, and prosecution. Sadly, only 5 to 8 percent of the victims reported abuse, and only a small number of these reports led to arrest.

The reason was painfully clear: children don't make credible witnesses, as they are often too terrified to testify.

Feigning a nonchalance he didn't feel, Feretti folded his arms over his chest and said, "Quite a collection."

Taylor gave a laugh and rubbed his hands in glee. "Best in Palm Beach County."

"You'd better hope you never get busted."

"What?"

"If I remember right, a first time offender convicted of transporting child pornography faces five to twenty years in prison."

"What are you, a fucking lawyer?"

"God forbid."

Taylor just stared at him, the prison comment far beyond his tolerance level. "So what are you looking for, boys or girls?"

"Neither."

"Huh?"

"Adults interest me."

"Sorry, pal, you came to the wrong place."

"I don't think so. I think I'm right where I'm supposed to be. You see, I'm interested in one particular adult. A creep named Nick Russo."

"You must be high."

"Only on life. I need an address, Skip."

"You need to get the fuck out of my house. That's what you need to do."

Feretti held up a finger like a teacher demanding silence. "I'd like a phone number, too."

"Go fuck yourself."

"Wrong answer."

"Do I have to throw you out?"

In one smooth and swift move, Feretti pulled a Glock pistol from under his shirt and slapped Taylor in the face with the barrel. What happened next was purely reflexive. Feretti didn't even stop to think, but simply reacted. With his free hand, he grasped Taylor's wrist, twisting him around, then pushing him onto the bed. He heard Taylor yell, "Stop it! You're breaking my arm!" But Feretti was operating on automatic now, slapping handcuffs on a perp, the way he'd done a hundred times before. Only this time there was rage fueling him, making him tighten the cuffs harder than he had to, making him want to hurt this child molesting freak. Hurt him badly.

Taylor was in pain, but he was smart enough not to move. He did manage to take a deep, steadying breath. Then he said, "What the hell are you doing?"

"I need to find Russo. I think you know where to look for him."

"Even if I knew, I wouldn't tell you. The crazy bastard would kill me."

"I'd be a millionaire if I had a dime for every time I heard that line."

"It's the truth."

"Maybe so, but I still need an address."

"Are you a cop?"

"What do you think?"

"I think you broke my nose."

"What a pity."

"You also forgot to read me my rights."

"You don't have any rights. The only thing you've got is an opportunity to avoid traction."

Taylor made the mistake of laughing. "I'm shaking in my boots."

Feretti pushed Taylor's face into the mattress, cutting off his air supply. Taylor cried out in surprise, then struggled wildly, trying to get a breath. His chest heaved as he fought for air. Feretti shifted his pressure to the neck area, shutting off the blood flow to Taylor's brain, causing him to panic. He thrashed and kicked and almost fainted before the pressure stopped.

After a while, Taylor turned his head and looked toward the door. A tear trickled from the corner of his eye and slid onto the mattress. "You're a dead man," he whispered. "Do you hear me? A dead man! You have no idea who you're dealing with. Russo is going to come for you and everything you love!"

"He already has," Feretti said wearily. "Now it's my turn. You ready to talk?"

Taylor cursed out loud, then told him that Russo was a gypsy. A *paranoid* gypsy. The man owned houses in Palm Beach, Broward, and Dade counties. He never slept in the same house more than a week, and nobody ever knew where he'd show up next. The routine was tiresome but, up to now, rather effective. A moving target was hard to hit, and in Russo's line of work, only the cunning survived.

Feretti glanced at the bookshelf. "You and your partner seem to have cornered the market on kiddie porn."

"Help yourself to a free sample."

"No thanks. Not my cup of tea."

"To each their own."

Feretti snorted derisively. "Where do you make your movies?"

"We don't make them. We buy them."

"From who?"

"The Russians."

"How does that work?"

Taylor was about to answer when his girlfriend snuck into the room and pushed the business end of a Taser into Feretti's back. Two probes shot out, delivering an initial charge of 1,800 volts -- four times more voltage than a defibrillator. The shock caused an immediate and total disruption of his muscular system, and he fell forward, striking his head on the bedpost. Sleeping Beauty kept her finger on the trigger and delivered another dose of high voltage, but by then, the world was spinning out of control.

Spinning and turning dark...

CHAPTER TWENTY-FIVE

When Feretti regained consciousness, he found himself sitting on the ground, tied to a tree. He had no earthly idea where he was, but it certainly wasn't Delray Beach. He was tied to a mangrove tree, and the ground beneath him was damp. The odor of decomposing plants filled his nostrils. He guessed he was in a swamp, but it was too dark to know for sure. After a while the world began to clear again, and he was able to piece together what had happened. He'd let his guard down. He'd missed a clear and present danger, and now he was a hostage.

A goddamn hostage.

He cursed himself for being so careless.

In a swamp, the warmth of the day turns to damp coolness. The sounds of civilization are silenced behind impenetrable vegetation and strange-looking trees. Shadows fall everywhere. There are things that go bump in the night.

All in all a god-awful place to spend the night.

Especially tied to a tree.

An hour went by before Feretti heard footsteps and saw a flickering light coming toward him. He nudged himself upward, waiting for it to come into view. When it finally did, he saw that it was a kerosene lamp. He opened his mouth, about to call out, then shut it. Tight. Finally, he said, "Just my luck."

Russo locked gazes with him and, in a folksy voice, said, *"Buonasera, amico mio. Come va?"*

Feretti took a deep breath, trying to keep his cool. "I'll write you a letter."

"Not enough time. I'm on a tight schedule."

"I'm not going anywhere."

"No, you're certainly not. How do you like my office?"

"Where are we?"

"Broward County."

"This doesn't look like Broward to me."

"Welcome to Capone Island. My home away from home."

"Fits you to a tee. How did I get here?"

"You were shot with a Taser. Eighteen hundred volts. Up close and personal."

"Who do I thank?"

"Taylor's girlfriend."

"The couch zombie?"

"She was finally good for something."

"Which is more than I can say for you."

Russo let out a belly laugh. "You haven't changed a bit."

"You've gotten uglier."

"You don't look too good, yourself. By the way, try not to move. Your right leg is broken. You busted it when you fell."

"You should have seen the other guy."

"I did see the other guy. He's the one who brought you here."

"Where's wonder boy hiding?"

Russo paused and smiled slyly. "Taylor is down by the water. Lying next to his girlfriend. They're both dead."

"Dead?"

"I'm no detective, but it looks like they were killed in a shoot-out. Their bodies are riddled with bullets. Seventeen bullets, to be exact. All fired from the same gun. *Your* gun. A Glock 17."

Feretti glared at him contemptuously. "Why did you kill them?"

"I didn't kill them. You did. Your prints are on the gun, not mine. I had nothing to do with this business."

"Why did you kill them, Russo?"

"Well, if you really must know, Taylor had become a loose cannon. I warned him about the drugs, but he wouldn't listen. You know those millennials. They think they know everything. Anyway, if you can't trust a person, why keep them around?"

"Was the girl a loose cannon, too?"

"No, she was just loose. Just a dumb slut who would open her legs for anyone. She won't be missed."

"I see."

Russo's mouth turned upward briefly in a parody of a smile. "You won't be missed either."

"Don't be so sure. I've got a lot of friends."

"Yeah, you do, and I intend to kill a few of them. Adam Gold is *numero uno*, and then I'm gonna whack that Indian squaw who's been breathing down my neck."

"You always were a big talker."

"Talk is cheap. I'm a man of action."

"You've got it all figured out, eh?"

"No, not all of it. I know why you came to Florida –– to seek revenge –– but did you forget that I was a made man? You can't step out of line with a guy like me. It's against the rules. That's not the way this thing of ours works."

Now it was Feretti's turn to smile. "Jesus, I forgot how stupid you are."

"What?"

"I hate to be the bearer of bad news, but you're not as well-liked or respected as you think you are. You might be a big earner, but to the Commission you're still a *cafone*. They were more than happy to approve a hit."

"You're full of shit."

"You think so? Maybe you should ask around. Talk to one of your goombahs. You might learn something."

"You should learn to keep your mouth shut."

"As they say, the truth hurts."

Russo looked at him with contempt. "What do you know about the truth? Your whole life has been nothing but a lie. Just one big lie. You know why that *puttana* shot my father. My aunt wasn't being raped –– she was trying to protect you, her secret admirer. She was afraid you'd get hurt again, maybe killed. You knew that, but you kept your mouth shut and played along. Do you know what that makes you, Feretti? A willing accomplice. A crooked cop."

"I'm sorry you feel that way. If there was something I could say or do..."

Russo cut him off in mid-sentence. "Save your pity. I don't need it. You didn't lay a glove on me. My parents were the ones who got hurt. After my father was killed, you and the bitch destroyed his reputation. He became a rapist. My mother already had a drinking problem, but my father's death pushed her over the edge. Do you know what happened to my mother?"

Feretti took a moment, then spoke, softly. "I heard she killed herself."

Russo nodded, his face flushed with rage. "She had a nervous breakdown, and the shrink sent her to Trenton Psychiatric Hospital. One of the orderlies, a fucking moolie, raped her. After that, she drank anything she could get her hands on. Anything that contained alcohol. One day, she stole a bottle of witch hazel, and the rest, as they say, is history."

Feretti glanced at him, meeting his eyes for only a second, but that was long enough for him to understand the depth of his anger and to be frightened by it. "Why did your mother have a drinking problem?"

"How the fuck should I know?"

"Your aunt thought that you and your father were to blame."

"Who cares what that whore thought?"

"A life of crime takes a heavy toll on a family."

"Don't try to pin the rap on me. It's not gonna work."

"I'm not blaming you alone. All I'm saying is that the mansion of your soul has become a haunted place."

"There you go again. Pretending you're a priest. You need to stop lying to yourself. You're not a man of God, and you never will be."

"And you're not an innocent bystander."

Russo folded his arms across his chest and just stared at him. "You know what I think? I think you're trying to piss me off. You gotta get over this obsession for revenge. My aunt was *un traditore*, a traitor to the family. She got what she deserved. She had to answer for her sins."

"We all have to answer for our sins. Even you, Russo."

"Jesus, you don't give up. Stop pretending you're a man of the cloth. A real priest could turn the other cheek. Not you, Feretti. You believe in an eye for an eye, and that makes you a fake, a phony, and a fraud. You wouldn't know God if he walked up and handed you wings."

"I know the devil when I see him."

"I'm no devil, Feretti. I'm just a son who loved his father. A man with a long memory. A stand-up guy who knows how to make things right."

"You wouldn't recognize right if it punched you in the face."

"Watch it, Feretti, or I might punch you in the face!"

"Like I said before, you're a big talker."

Russo was about to make good on his threat when they heard the sound of sirens. All of a sudden the Intracoastal Waterway was lit up by a powerful spotlight on the shore. A moment later, two police boats sped by, heading for the dock on the island.

A short silence stretched between them. Neither moved or looked away. Eventually Feretti said, "I forgot to tell you something. Taylor's been under surveillance by the feds. They were hoping that you would contact him. I guess the party's over."

Russo smiled broadly, affording Feretti a repugnant view of uneven, gapped teeth stained by tobacco. "Ye of little faith. Didn't I just say that I was a man of action? I knew the feds were slinking around. I'm ready for the grand finale."

"Good luck with that."

"I'm a great believer in luck. The more I plan the more I have of it."

"That might be the smartest thing you ever said. As a matter of fact, that might be the *only* smart thing you've ever said."

"I've got something else to say." He reached into the bushes and pulled out a duffle bag. "So long, sucker." He tore off his clothes and tied them into a bundle. Then he opened the bag and took out a snorkel, a mask, a wetsuit, and a spear gun. He put on the wetsuit, attached the snorkel to the mask, and then tossed his clothes into the bag. "Well, it's been nice chatting with you, but it's time for me to leave." He picked up the spear gun and pointed it at Feretti's chest. "Any last words?"

Feretti dropped his eyes to the ground and sadly shook his head. "You won't find peace by killing me."

Russo let out a short, aborted chuckle. "I know, but you miss the point." He pulled the trigger and the spear flew into Feretti's chest, killing him instantly. "No pun intended."

CHAPTER TWENTY-SIX

By the end of May, most of the snowbirds had flown north, eager to escape the heat and humidity of South Florida. After the migration, life returned to normal, and it was once again possible to enjoy a leisurely breakfast at a place like the Olympia Flame Diner in Deerfield Beach. When Gold poked his head inside, he saw Sally Ridge sitting in a booth, nursing her second cup of coffee. He sat across from her, bracing himself for an update or something else -- something that would ruin his appetite.

"Sorry I'm late," Gold said. "I had to run an errand for *mi madre*."

"Everything okay?"

"Fine and dandy."

"How's Mom doing?"

Gold looked at her, his head cocked to one side. "You tell me."

"Excuse me?"

"I spotted the guards you posted. The ones that were posing as gardeners. You should have used Floridians. Your agents were too pale."

"A keen observation."

"Situational awareness."

"Touché, mon ami."

Gold winked at her. "Thanks for the extra security."

"Better safe than sorry. Do you want some breakfast?"

"Just coffee."

Ridge signaled for the waitress. "I'm sorry I missed the funeral mass. I know it was a sad day, but I'm glad you went."

"Well, Yogi Berra said it best. You should always go to other people's funerals; otherwise they won't come to yours."

She smiled faintly. "How was the turnout?"

"Full house."

"Did you see any familiar faces?"

Gold hesitated a moment, waiting for the waitress to take his order. After she left, he said, "I ran into Sergeant Grimes. He was livid about Paz. Pissed about his release."

"He'll get over it."

"What was all that about?"

She spoke as if to herself, saying, "Paz might be a con artist, but he's no killer. I couldn't leave him in jail for a crime he didn't commit. That wouldn't be right."

Gold grimaced slightly, making a face. "Are you telling me that you released him out of the goodness of your heart?"

"More or less."

"Come on, Sally, I know you too well. When it comes to doing your job, you don't have a heart."

She bit the corner of her lip, lowered her head demurely, and looked out the tops of her eyes at him -- her little girl look. Convincing, too. "Paz is a petty criminal."

"Yeah, but Russo's a different story, and I think you'd do just about anything to capture him -- and that includes sacrificing a pawn or two. Look, I'm no Boy Scout, but I'm not sure the ends justify the means."

"Why don't you let me worry about that?"

"You have enough worries."

"Yes, and Paz isn't one of them."

"Not yet. But what happens if he gets himself killed?"

"I'll cross that bridge when I come to it."

Gold felt a bitter smile tug the corners of his mouth. "Famous last words."

Ridge was frowning deeply, sitting all the way back in her seat, her hands on her lap, her legs straight out and crossed at the ankles. Hesitantly, the words started to come. "Have you forgotten who we're chasing? Russo's a monster. Let me remind you how evil that bastard can be." She leaned closer, resting her elbows on the table. Her voice dropped to a whisper. "Who else did you run into at the cemetery? One of your old buddies from New York?"

Gold stared at her, jaw dropping slightly. "How do you know about Feretti?"

"How do you think I know?"

"Another security detail?"

"Watching your every move."

"I guess I should be thankful."

Ridge nodded slowly, and then asked the million dollar question. "What was Feretti doing there?"

There was a full thirty seconds of silence –– an embarrassed silence –– as if Gold had been caught with his hand in the cookie jar. "I called Feretti a few days earlier to let him know about Annette Russo. I didn't know he was in town until I saw him at the church. As you probably know, he conducted the funeral mass and the graveside ceremony."

"Odd time for a reunion."

"I told you he was unpredictable."

"So you did."

Gold looked at her with a strange expression on his face. "What does this have to do with Russo?"

She ignored the question and asked one of her own. "Did you tell Feretti about Skip Taylor?"

"Yes, I did."

"Why?"

"Feretti wanted to help, to contribute something to our investigation. I didn't want him going after the big dog, so I threw him a bone." He sipped his coffee, studying her reaction over the rim of his cup. She didn't say a word or move a muscle, which worried him. "Do you think I made a mistake?"

"Your intentions were good, but you know what they say about the road to hell."

"Are you trying to tell me something?"

An undecipherable expression flitted across her face. She patted Gold's hand solicitously and raised an eyebrow. "Sometimes this job sucks. Sometimes you have to tell people what they don't want to hear. Sometimes you have to show them things they shouldn't have to see." She tossed a five dollar bill on the table, and then she stood. "Why don't you take that coffee to go?"

Gold instinctively looked over his shoulder in the general direction of the parking lot. Then he stared at Ridge. "Where are we going?"

"Down the road apiece."

Gold felt something twist in his abdomen. "I was afraid you'd say that."

There wasn't much traffic on South Federal Highway, so Gold had no problem keeping up with Ridge, who drove like a bat out of hell. He was more than a little puzzled by their sudden departure, but when they turned right at Hillsboro Boulevard, he knew exactly where they were going.

Capone Island.

When they pulled into the parking lot, they encountered a small army of law enforcement officers. Local, state, and federal units were on the scene, and a large tent had been erected near the pier. Ridge led the way, and as they drew closer to the tent, Gold realized that it was a makeshift morgue. Three body bags were lying on stretchers, and a group of medical examiners hovered over the corpses, engaged in a lively debate.

Gold glanced nervously toward Capone Island, which framed a portion of clear blue sky, where white sea gulls periodically swooped and capered. His shoulders slumped visibly as the world seemed to settle on him. "What's going on?" he asked.

"Triple homicide," Ridge said.

"Anybody we know?"

"Unfortunately." She led him inside the tent and then unzipped the upper portion of two of the bags. "Skip Taylor and his girlfriend. They died from gunshot wounds."

Gold, eyes narrowed to slits, nodded slowly. "Who's behind door number three?"

Ridge's tone was businesslike. "Lou Feretti."

Gold shut his eyes an instant to organize his head. "Also shot?"

"He was killed with a speargun."

Gold scowled as his brain struggled with the words. *Did she say a speargun?* For some reason, the words didn't compute for a moment. He thought he'd misheard. He didn't mean to stare, but he couldn't believe that Feretti was dead. Steeling himself, he put a hand on the stretcher and used the tail of his shirt to wipe the sweat out of his eyes. Taking a deep breath, he unzipped the top of the body bag, and his eyes widened with recognition. The color drained from his face. "This is my fault," he whispered. "I should have kept my mouth shut."

Clumsy as always in the realm of emotions, Ridge tried to comfort him. "Don't punish yourself. Feretti knew what he was doing. He understood the risk."

"I wonder if he did."

"Well, stop wondering. You'll drive yourself crazy."

"Just move on. Is that the way it works?"

"What else can you do?"

Gold pressed his fingertips hard against the sides of his forehead in an attempt to stop the throbbing in his right temple.

Another bad morning, another splitting headache. "When were they killed?"

"Late last night or early this morning."

"In the parking lot?"

"No, over there." She pointed to Capone Island. "I can show you the crime scene."

"I'd like to see it."

Ridge commandeered a police boat and asked the pilot to drop them off on the western side of the island. As they stepped out, the tall sawgrass swished around their knees, camouflaging the damp soil that sucked at their shoes. Jesus, the mosquitoes were out in full force. Not more than ten yards away was a small clearing surrounded by bald cypress trees.

Ridge told him that this was the spot where the police had found Feretti leaning against a tree. "There was a spear embedded in his chest."

Gold let out a deep sigh and let his sad eyes drop to the ground. A few feet away, flies congregated over a small pool of blood, buzzing incessantly, but they were no match for the buzzing in his mind. "What happened out here?"

"The police think it was a drug deal gone wrong. Two of the victims were drug users, and the third was an ex-cop. Of course, you and I know the truth. Russo killed all three of them." In her mind's eye, Ridge had a distinct picture of what had occurred, and she was more than happy to share it with Gold. "Taylor and his girlfriend were shot first. The color and texture of the bloodstains on their clothing indicated that they were killed several hours before Feretti. Their bodies were found near the shoreline, but they were killed where you're standing."

"How do you know that?"

"The sawgrass is bent in one direction, and there are heel marks in the mud. They were dragged toward the water, but I'm not sure why. Maybe Russo thought they'd be taken by gators." She went on to explain that *cladium jamaicense* -- sawgrass -- often formed rivers of grass and grew in dense clusters in wet sites that were low in phosphorus. The plants were typically long and narrow and, when trampled, left a visible trail. "It's not easy to fool Mother Nature."

Gold chewed a fingernail, sweat trickling down his cheek as he studied the area. There were few people in the world who knew more about killing than Ridge. A rifle shot from a thousand yards was beyond her skill, as were explosives and poisons and weapons of mass destruction. Her expertise was all about up close and personal.

The way Feretti had been killed.

"Feretti was shot at close range," Ridge said. "From above. The spear was on a downward angle, which meant that Russo was standing over him. There was no shoot-out. Feretti was tied to a tree and murdered in cold blood."

"How can you be so sure?"

She walked behind one of the trees and then signaled him to follow. "Take a look at the bark on that bald cypress. Do you see those rub marks? Those were made by a rope -- the rope that was tied around Feretti. He struggled to break free, but he never made it."

Gold's eyes darkened. "Russo will pay for this." He moved to the edge of the clearing to look across the water. "How did the bastard escape? By boat?"

Ridge took her time replying, like she was deciding whether or not to answer. "They came by boat," she said eventually. "The keys were found in Taylor's pocket. Russo left in a different fashion."

"How?"

"I think he swam back."

Gold couldn't hide his surprise. "He *swam*?"

"He brought a speargun. He might have brought a mask and snorkel, too."

"Clever bastard."

Ridge stood close to him, looking into his eyes. She put her arms around him and gave him a hug, her face against his chest. It felt completely natural for him to return the gesture, and he wrapped his arms around her. For a brief moment, amid all the sorrow, he felt better. She looked up into his eyes, placed the palm of her hand on his face and gently kissed him on the cheek. "You need to put this behind you. We need to keep our eyes on the prize."

Gold nodded. "What's our next move?"

"Do you have a valid passport?"

"Yeah, but it's back in New York."

"Perfect. Fly back with your mother and arrange for her to stay up north for a while. I'll contact you in a couple of days."

"Where are we going?"

"I can't say for sure, but if I were you, I'd practice my Spanish."

CHAPTER TWENTY-SEVEN

From the subway, Gold wandered along First Avenue looking for the main entrance to the Manhattan Medical Examiner's office. He wondered why Kaminski wanted to meet at this location instead of her office on John Street. He knew there was method in her madness -- there always was -- but what could it be?

It took some time, but he eventually found the right door hidden behind a row of ambulance vehicles. The building was decades old, but it still housed a mortuary, autopsy rooms, toxicology and histology labs, and X-ray and photography facilities, all crammed into a few small floors.

Kaminski was waiting for him, cooling her heels in the reception area, a drab space filled with vending machines. From a distance, she looked like a Scandinavian model, tall and blonde, dressed in a tailored blue suit that revealed a lithe, athletic figure sculpted by a daily routine of Tae Kwon Do. Light makeup dusted her prominent cheekbones, and her bright blue eyes sparkled with intelligence.

Gold could tell that she had the urge to give him a hug, but she merely shook his hand with a firm grip. The skin was smooth on the back of her hand, but her knuckles were bruised. He let his irritation show. He looked at her bruises, then at her, shaking his head. "Breaking boards again?"

"Practice makes perfect."

"I wish you'd stick to breaking hearts."

"I was in a tournament."

"I hope you won."

"I did."

"You couldn't tell."

She chuckled darkly. "You should see the other guy."

Gold looked away in exasperation, then said, "Did they bring him here?"

"No, he survived."

"Then why are we here?"

"To help the police. They need us to identify a coworker." She rubbed her hands as she began to speak, looking down a long corridor as she explained that Bill Burke had been found dead, an apparent suicide. "I didn't have the heart to tell you over the phone."

Gold blinked several times, trying to make sense of what he just heard. Then he frowned. "Jesus, that's terrible."

"The police believe that he was severely depressed. He left a note, but they wouldn't show it to me. In any case, he drank a fifth of scotch and then shot himself in the head. The neighbors called the police, but they couldn't save him. He bled to death in his apartment, surrounded by photos of his wife." She shook her head, let out a heavy breath. "Did you know Burke was a widower?"

Gold nodded slowly, his face expressionless, only his clenched fists giving away the strength of his feelings. "Bill's wife died three years ago. Ovarian cancer. After she passed, he began to fall apart, but he was still a good egg. A first class underwriter. He just got careless in his old age."

"Don't we all?"

Gold felt the beginnings of a smile. He fought against it, but he didn't win. "Some of us don't wait for old age."

"Which reminds me, I owe your friend an apology."

"My friend?"

"Agent Ridge. I thought DHS was holding Burke in protective custody, but I was wrong."

"Why did you think that?"

"Because they grabbed our files. I thought they grabbed our underwriter, too."

"I wish they had."

"You and me both."

Gold's face twisted into a look of confusion and annoyance. "How long is this going to take?"

Kaminski cleared her throat. "Not long. Do you have a lunch date or something?"

"Nothing that enjoyable."

"Well, be patient. These things take time."

Gold transferred his weight from one foot to the other. It was evident he didn't want to be there and was anxious to leave. His eyes darted from the corridor to the window as if seeking an escape route. "I have to be uptown at noon."

Kaminski glanced at her watch. "We've got plenty of time. What happened in Florida?"

"Things got complicated."

"There's a surprise."

Gold tried to explain the last few days as succinctly as possible, but he knew that Kaminski was a stickler for details. He began with his phone call to Feretti, telling her that after they spoke, he came to Florida to conduct a funeral mass for Annette Russo. "He also performed some sort of burial ceremony."

"The Rite of Committal?"

"I think so."

Kaminski's expression turned contemplative, then she frowned. "She was buried in Florida?"

"Our Lady Queen of Heaven Cemetery."

"Where's that?"

"North Lauderdale."

"Why was she buried there?"

"She was dead."

She rolled her eyes. "As opposed to New York."

"I'm not sure."

"You'd think she'd be buried beside her husband."

"Unless that meant sharing a mausoleum with the rest of the Russo family, which would include her brother-in-law, Sal Russo. If I remember right, the family purchased a mausoleum in Green-Wood Cemetery. Have you heard of that place?"

"No, I haven't."

He told her that Green-Wood was Brooklyn's most famous cemetery, a National Historic Landmark, and the final resting place of many notable Americans. Among the most prominent residents were Samuel Morse, Horace Greeley, "Boss" Tweed, and Henry Ward Beecher. The cemetery also contained the graves of Albert Anastasia and Joey Gallo, two of New York's most notorious gangsters.

"Sounds charming," she quipped.

"To each his own."

"So they say."

Gold tried a smile that mostly failed. "There's something else you should know. Lou Feretti is dead. He was murdered by Nick Russo."

Kaminski looked at him with overt disbelief. Her eyebrows lowered suspiciously. *"Murdered?"*

"Two days ago."

"Oh my God."

"The feds are holding the body. I guess they want to conduct an autopsy."

"God, I'm so sorry. I never met him, but I know he was a friend of yours."

"Yeah, we understood each other." He gave her a brief recap of the events leading up to the murder, and by the time he finished, she was holding his hand. "I have to learn to keep my mouth shut."

"I hope you don't blame yourself."

Gold tried to sound philosophical, but the news didn't lend itself much to that. "Feretti was like a bull in a china shop. Once he saw red, there was no stopping him."

"I know the type."

"Are you referring to me?"

"If the shoe fits..." The words trailed off as she spotted an Indian man waving at them. The man was about fifty-five, short, and bald, wearing a white lab coat. "Showtime," she muttered. "There's our cue."

An autopsy had revealed, unsurprisingly, that Bill Burke died from a single gunshot to the head. In real life, death was not a given but depended on what type of firearm and bullets were used. Most handguns were categorized as "low velocity," but at close range, they were highly effective. Dr. Kapoor, an assistant medical examiner, told them that survival often depended upon the laws of physics and how much damage the bullet caused. The heavier the bullet, the faster the movement and the more damage. By and large, the combination of velocity, bullet dynamics, and the area of penetration determined the odds of survival.

Strangely enough, a close-range shot often prevented a bullet from yawing, which increased the energy transfer and enlarged the cavity.

"Headshots are tricky," Kapoor said. "Just like real estate, it's all about location, location, location. Some bullets pass through the skull with relative little damage, while others destroy whatever tissue or organs are in its way."

"Luck of the draw?" Gold asked.

"Luck is the right word," Kapoor said. "If the bullet velocity is high and there is no yaw and it passes through noncritical parts of the brain, less damage occurs and survival is possible." He glanced at the cadaver in front of them, its toe tag visible from under a sheet. "Unfortunately, the deceased shot himself with a .357 magnum revolver. Needless to say, the damage was extensive." He gestured them forward and lifted the sheet, exposing a massive head wound. "As you can see, the brain was obliterated."

Gold slowly walked to the autopsy table. The smell hit him first, and he recoiled, gagging. *Dear God*, was all he could think. He shook his head and murmured, "Jesus Christ."

Kaminski's mouth went dry, and she found it hard to speak.

Dr. Kapoor pointed to a cross section of the brain, explaining that the bullet had destroyed everything it hit, from top to bottom: the skin on the scalp, the skull bone, the dura mater, and the gray matter, known as the cerebral cortex. "If it helps, he never knew what hit him."

Gold felt a tickle of sweat on his back, the faint recurring headache that had plagued him recently. He'd successfully ignored it for a while, but the throbbing had returned. "What do you need us to do?"

"Identify the deceased."

"William Burke," Kaminski said. "He was one of my employees."

"One of my coworkers," Gold added. "He worked at the Anchor Insurance Company."

"111 John Street," Kaminski said. "You can reach us there if you have any more questions." Shaken by what she had just seen, she took Gold's arm and pulled him outside. "I need some fresh air."

"You all right?" Gold asked.

"Yes, I'm fine. I'm just getting too old for this crap."

"I know what you mean."

She drew a breath, collected herself, and let the breath out. It was possible, she supposed, though doubtful, that she bore some responsibility for Burke's death. After all, she was the one who fired him. Maybe that was the straw that had broken the camel's back. Maybe she should have given him a second chance. She looked briefly at Gold and said, under her breath, "Uneasy lies the head that wears a crown."

Gold caught the look and sighed. "What a way to start the week."

She looked down at her swollen hand, closing and opening it again a couple of times. "Did Burke have any children?"

"One son, but he was killed in Afghanistan."

"Any brothers or sisters?"

"I don't think so."

"Any close friends?"

"The man was a loner."

Her next comment surprised him. "Most men lead lives of quiet desperation."

Gold looked at her, his head cocked, wearing a slight frown. “You’re starting to sound like Victor Wong, the man of a thousand quotes.”

She stared at him, struck by another thought. “By the way, the old rascal was in my office yesterday. He was looking for you, so give him a call when you get a chance.”

Gold pushed back his sleeve to check the time. “How do you want to handle the funeral arrangements?”

“I’d like you to handle them. See that he gets a first-class funeral. Spare no expense. Send the bill to my office.” There was a long moment of silence, and then she stepped closer and gave him a hug. “We take care of our own.”

CHAPTER TWENTY-EIGHT

Park Avenue residences were all pretty much the same to Gold -- solemn doormen, hushed elegance, the distinct smell of money. Joe DeCarlo's thirty-second-floor perch overlooking Central Park might have been one of the most expensive in the city, and it surely had one of the best views. The luxury condominium was inside 432 Park Avenue, the tallest residential tower in the hemisphere. The building stood 1,396 feet above ground, and its 85 floors featured 104 high-end units.

The woman who answered the door to DeCarlo's humble abode was a tall blonde in her thirties. Her smile was dazzling as she looked up at Gold through thick lashes, flirting. "I thought you'd be older," she told him. "Please come in."

Gold detected a Russian accent, and he immediately found himself distracted by her smooth, creamy skin, the beginning swell of her breasts, the curve of her neck, and the scent of her perfume. Once his eyes had retracted back into his head, he introduced himself. "I didn't catch your name."

She eyed him speculatively. "My name is Svetlana."

Gold found himself grinning manically, and he couldn't douse it out. "Nice to meet you, Svetlana."

Perhaps a little tipsy, she folded her arms across her chest and leaned slightly into him. "Joseph is waiting," she whispered, then added, "Follow me."

"Anywhere," Gold said.

Just beyond the foyer, a white marble hallway led to a spacious living room with vaulted ceilings, white crown moldings, Macassar Ebony flooring, and plenty of natural light from French doors that led to a plant-covered terrace. The chairs and couches were upholstered in rose-colored damask, and there was a black marble table in the center of the room. The walls were covered with western art, which seemed totally out of place.

Svetlana poured two generous shots of vodka. She handed one to Gold, gave him a big smile, and held up her glass. *"K vashemu zdorov'yu."*

"L'chaim," Gold said.

She started to say something, but suddenly cut it off when DeCarlo walked into the room. He maintained a show of indifference, but inside he was annoyed. He had no time for distractions today, and he needed to be alone with his guest. He walked toward Gold, scrutinizing him closely, coming closer and closer until he was just a foot away. "I'm Joe DeCarlo." He didn't offer his hand. "Thanks for coming."

"Thanks for the invitation."

"Believe me, they're few and far between."

"Should I be flattered or worried?"

"Relax. You're among friends."

Gold had been expecting a certain formality, but now that he was here, he still didn't know how to play it. He started to say something and stopped himself. Finally he said, "Nice place you got here."

"I'd offer you a drink, but I see you've got one." He smiled at Svetlana, but there was no warmth in it. Gold wasn't sure whether he was happy or disapproving. "Make yourself comfortable. You need a refill?"

"No, I'm good."

"Have any trouble finding the place?"

"You can't miss this building."

"Yeah, she's one of a kind." He snipped off the end of a cigar and lit it, puffing till it caught. "I love this baby. She's tall and sleek. Wonderful lines. She reminds me of Svetlana."

Gold nodded and tried a comforting smile on her. "You're a lucky man."

Svetlana heaved a big sigh, obviously bored, and pulled up a chair and sat down. "I tell him that all the time."

"Excuse me?" DeCarlo said rudely. "I don't remember asking you to join us. Why don't you take a walk. Go to the park. Bring your little mutt."

Svetlana, perhaps struck by the abruptness of the request, cocked her head to the side. "You want me to leave?"

"Yeah, get lost for a while. We've got some business to discuss."

She stood up, put her hands on her hips in indignation, and pouted. "Whatever you say, *bobyshka*. It was nice meeting you, Mr. Gold."

Gold risked a quick, conspiratorial I-know-why-you-hate-this-guy glance at her. "The pleasure was all mine."

She broke the hint of a smile. *"Das vadanya."*

DeCarlo poured himself a scotch, lifted the glass and took a sip, then put it down carefully. He chuckled contemptuously and jammed the cigar into a corner of his mouth. He turned and glared at Gold, then looked around to make sure they were alone. "Ah, my sweet Natasha. Great piece of ass, but dumb as a doorknob."

"I thought her name was Svetlana."

DeCarlo laughed so abruptly he choked on his scotch. After recovering his breath, he smiled at Gold. It was a small, sad smile. "A Natasha is a Russian prostitute. What we call a gold digger. They're great in the sack, but a little high-strung. In any case, she seemed to dig you."

"She seemed pissed off to me,"

"What can I say? You can't please everyone. I think my mistress is gorgeous and a great fuck. My wife hates her." Showing a hint of humor, he added, "Go figure."

Gold smiled tiredly. "You've got an eye for beauty."

"You think so?"

"I was referring to your art collection."

DeCarlo looked at him, his eyes moving slightly back and forth as he seemed to be searching his face for something, maybe the slightest hint of insincerity. "Yeah, that's my pride and joy. I love western art. Cowboys and Indians fascinate me. I grew up watching the *Lone Ranger* and *Roy Rogers*. Of course, I always rooted for the outlaws."

"Naturally."

"My favorite artist is a guy named Olaf Wieghorst. He was a painter in the vein of Frederic Remington and Charles Russell. You familiar with those guys?"

"Yes, I love their work."

"In my humble opinion, Wieghorst was better."

"I don't know much about him."

DeCarlo took the bait, apparently needing to decompress for a few minutes before turning the discussion serious. Gold was surprised to learn that the artist was from Denmark and that he'd spent most of his working career on mounted patrol with the US Cavalry. Wieghorst was actually part of the military campaign that chased Pancho Villa back across the border. Before he joined the cavalry, he was a stunt rider in a Danish circus, and in his later years he appeared in two John Wayne movies: *McLintock!* and *El Dorado.*

Gold was duly impressed and tempted to ask how much a Wieghorst painting would fetch in today's market. He decided against it, reminding himself that if you have to ask how much it costs, you can't afford it. Instead, he asked if the paintings had been appraised and were properly insured.

DeCarlo's dark eyes widened as if he considered the inquiry slightly impertinent. Then he seemed to realize that it was part of Gold's job. Shoptalk. "Don't worry," he said, breaking the silence. "I'm in good hands."

"I didn't mean to pry, but you can never have too much insurance."

"You really believe that?"

"Absolutely."

DeCarlo gave a little snort, half agreement, half amusement. He glared at Gold from under bushy eyebrows, then said, "I'm glad you feel that way, because that's why you're here. To provide some extra insurance." He rose from his chair and began to pace nervously before the French windows, glancing at the tree tops in Central Park. Then he said haltingly, "As you can see, I've surrounded myself with the finer things in life. A Russian babe. A high-end condo. A valuable art collection. These are things I intend to keep -- and you're gonna help me keep them."

When DeCarlo didn't elaborate, Gold said, "I don't understand."

DeCarlo returned to his chair and sat ramrod straight, speaking in a deep, melodious voice that conveyed his "I am a serious man" persona. "I heard about Lou Feretti. I'm sorry he got whacked. He was a stand-up guy."

Gold shifted uncomfortably in his chair at the mention of Feretti's name. "Yeah, he was a good man."

"I understand you were friends."

"That's right."

"How far did you go back?"

"I knew him when he was a cop."

"Well, you know what they say. Once a cop, always a cop. Those boys in blue stick together, and they don't take kindly to losing one of their own. Active or retired, makes no difference. Mark my words. Feretti's death will be avenged."

"How does that concern me?"

"Somebody will have to answer for killing an ex-cop, and I need to make sure that person isn't me. I had nothing to do with this shit, and I need you to get the word out. The last thing I need are a bunch of angry cops breathing down my neck. That would be bad for me, bad for my family, bad for business." He fixed Gold with a cold eye. "And bad for you if you don't cooperate. *Capisce?*"

Gold closed his eyes for a moment as if trying to shut away the vision that accompanied what they were talking about. "What makes you think they'll believe me?"

DeCarlo paused and smiled slyly. "You're a civilian. A straight arrow. A guy with the right connections. I want you to lay it out for them. Name names. You've got nothing to fear. I've got your back."

To his credit, Gold managed to keep his voice calm and even. "Mind if I ask you a question?"

"Fire away."

"What's in it for me?"

"Besides your survival?"

When DeCarlo didn't elaborate, Gold said, "In addition to that."

DeCarlo looked at him as if he couldn't quite believe what he was hearing. Anger crossed his face, but instead of getting nasty, he crushed out the remains of his cigar, lit a fresh one, and blew smoke. They looked at each other through the gray haze. Eventually he said, "What makes the world go round?"

"Money."

"I'm sure you know that the feds are looking for Nicky Russo. My sources tell me they're about to offer a sizable reward for information leading to his capture. You can be the guy who claims the reward."

Gold looked up, eyes wide with surprise. "You know where he's hiding?"

"No, but it wouldn't be hard to find him. Wiseguys stand out. All I have to do is pick up a phone and call my associates in Florida. Before the day's over, five hundred soldiers will be looking for him. How does that sound?"

Gold hesitated, thinking it over. If there was a downside, he couldn't see it. Besides, DeCarlo wasn't going to take no for an answer. He stood up and hovered near the couch for a few moments before saying, "I'll try my best, but I can't make any guarantees."

"I realize that. Just give it your best shot."

Gold smiled. *My best shot?* Poor choice of words. He wondered if DeCarlo was trying to be funny. "There's something I don't understand."

"What's that?"

"Russo's a made man. How can you throw him to the wolves?"

DeCarlo blew air out through his nose in a long sigh. He was reluctant to discuss the subject, especially with someone outside of the family. He gave it some consideration, then said, "Russo crossed the line when he killed an ex-cop. There are rules that govern this thing of ours, and when those rules are broken, you pay the price. Besides, nobody ever liked the son of a bitch. The Commission will be glad to see him go."

Gold said what he was thinking. "I know exactly how they feel."

CHAPTER TWENTY-NINE

There were hundreds of restaurants in Chinatown, and Victor Wong was determined to try them all before his cholesterol level got too high. Among his favorite haunts were the eateries on Mott Street, but he also enjoyed the ones that were located on Bayard, Canal, Catherine, and Doyers.

So many restaurants, so little time.

The diner's lament.

As president of the Chinatown Chamber of Commerce, Wong understood the historical connection between the influx of Chinese emigrants and the large number of ethnic restaurants in Lower Manhattan. Strangely enough, a xenophobic immigration law had inadvertently fueled the Chinese restaurant boom. In the early 1900s, the federal government barred Chinese laborers and made it extremely difficult for legal residents to reenter the country after visiting China. An exemption was made for Chinese business owners who were allowed to travel to China and bring back employees. In 1915, a federal court ruled that restaurant owners should also be exempt, and almost overnight, a restaurant boom began.

Gold had heard this history lecture many times, but he listened politely as Wong rambled on, referring to the immigration law as the "Lo Mein Loophole." Although he worked hard to maintain his serene unflappability, he was getting hungry and anxious to order some food. Finally he decided he had heard enough. Holding up a palm, he said, "I've heard this story before. Your countrymen were very brave. They made a long and arduous trip."

"The journey of a thousand miles begins with one step," Wong said.

Gold sighed. "Confucius?"

"Lao Tzu."

"Never heard of him."

"He's the author of the *Tao Te Ching*. The founder of Taoism."

"Would he mind if we ordered some food?"

"The superior man does not, even for the space of a single meal, act contrary to virtue."

"What does that mean?"

"I'm not sure."

Gold looked around the room, wondering why Wong had chosen to dine in a dim sum parlor. "Have you been here before?"

"No, but I love the name. Yew's Your Noodle. Very amusing."

"Why don't you order for us?"

"Don't you want to look at the menu?"

"The menu is printed in Chinese."

"You cannot open a book without learning something."

"Lao Tzu again?"

"Confucius."

Gold grimaced. "Time for Tsingtao."

Wong ignored the joke and began to study the menu, a task he clearly relished. He confessed that dim sum was dear to his heart, which was fitting since the word meant "touching the heart." Originally a Cantonese custom, dim sum was linked to the Chinese tradition of "yum cha" or drinking tea. Without being asked, a diminutive waiter placed a pot of tea on the table. Wong sniffed the tea, then shook his head. "We do not want jasmine. *Bushi molihua*."

The waiter, taken aback, said, *"Meyeh cha?"*

"Bo lay," Wond said. "Black tea."

Gold smiled at the waiter. "I'll take a beer. *Tsingtao.*"

When the waiter walked away, Wong heaved a great sigh. "Beer with dim sum? Very bourgeois."

"To paraphrase Louis Pasteur, a bottle of beer contains more philosophy than all the books in the world."

"To each his own," Wong said. "What's in the duffle bag?"

Gold had almost forgotten about the bag he'd placed on the chair beside him. "I brought your machine."

"What machine?"

"Your portable polygraph."

"*My* portable polygraph?"

"I'd like to return it."

"Why?"

"I didn't use it, and I don't need it."

"Who doesn't need a portable polygraph machine?"

"Me."

"I think you should reconsider."

"I already have a paperweight."

Wong frowned. "No refunds."

"Yeah, I remember. Store credit only."

The waiter returned with a steaming bowl of rice. He set the bowl on the table and left without a word.

Wong unzipped the duffle bag and examined the contents. He mumbled something in Chinese, then said, "What am I supposed to do with a used machine?"

"I'm sure you'll find some use for it."

"A good opportunity is seldom presented and is easily lost."

"Why not take this opportunity to order lunch?"

Wong rolled his eyes at Gold, wondering why he was always so hungry. He busied himself studying the menu, and then he ordered a wide variety of dim sum. Enough to feed a small army.

Chinese dining etiquette dictated that the oldest person at the table ate first, which meant that Gold had to wait until his host was good and ready to begin. The wait seemed interminable, but the ensuing lecture was even worse.

Gold had forgotten that there were rules and conventions relating to chopsticks.

Wong told him that it was not polite to jam his chopsticks into his food in a vertical position. Especially not into rice. "If you do that, a Chinese person will think of funerals."

Gold look mystified. "Why's that?"

"During a Chinese funeral, joss sticks –– sticks of incense –– are stuck into a pot, and the pot is placed beside a bowl of rice on the altar."

"I never knew that."

"Apparently not."

"The last time we had lunch you scolded me for waving my chopsticks in the air."

"Also bad form."

"And then there was the time I stabbed my food with them."

"Another faux pas."

"I don't know why you put up with me."

Wong let out an exasperated grunt. "If jade is not polished, it can't be made into anything."

Gold smiled with feigned regret. His patience was wearing thin, but he didn't let it show. He knew that Wong was biding his time, waiting for the right moment to tell him why he'd called. In an effort to speed things along, he mentioned that his desk was covered with mail. "The price for going out of town."

Wong got the hint and gestured for Gold to scoot a little closer. He let the silence extend another moment. Finally, in a conspiratorial whisper, he said, "Bad news travels fast."

"Another Chinese proverb?"

"The current state of affairs."

Gold played along, knowing it was part of the game. "Are you referring to Bill Burke?"

"No, but I was saddened to learn of his death."

"What are you referring to?"

"Your recent imbroglio."

"Run that by me in English."

"Your involvement with Nick Russo."

They regarded each other for some time without speaking, then Gold shook his head. "Nothing personal, but I'm not at liberty to discuss the situation."

"I didn't come here to discuss it. I thought you might like to know that I ran into him."

Gold blinked several times and said, "You ran into Russo? Where?"

"In a Florida casino. Last week. I was playing in a poker tournament. In a place called Immokalee."

"Where's that?"

"North of the Everglades. Near I-75. After the tournament I played in a cash game, and Russo was at my table. He lost a lot of money. Too much bluffing."

Gold pulled at his ear, doubting what he'd just heard, wanting to be absolutely sure he was getting it right. "Are you sure it was him?"

"He introduced himself."

"To the whole table?"

"That's right."

Gold's mouth curled into a sneer. "He's a brazen bastard. I can't believe he's been hiding in plain sight. If I were on the run, I'd keep a low profile."

"Yes, but you're not sick."

"Sick?"

"Russo's a degenerate gambler. He's hooked on the action. Addicted to the rush. I've seen it many times before, and it's difficult to treat, harder to cure."

Gold guessed that Wong was speaking from personal observation, and he was right. Gambling addictions were common in the Asian community. In fact, the Chinese had a saying: "If you don't gamble, you don't know how lucky you are." A strong belief in luck, fate, and fortune were the driving forces behind Asians and gambling. Research showed that Asian-Americans had a much higher rate of addiction than the general American population. The rate ranged between 6 percent and nearly 60 percent, depending on the specific Asian ethnicity.

Wong didn't want to dwell on the subject, but he did point out that Chinese people placed a higher regard on superstition, numerology, and the notion of "luck" than other ethnic groups. In Chinatown, good fortune was often seen as a blessing from the gods.

Gold raised the tea cup to his lips, and he watched Wong carefully as he sipped. He had just discovered Russo's weakness, an Achilles heel that might prove his undoing. "Are you sure about Russo's addiction?"

"Allow me to elaborate," Wong said. He leaned forward, elbows on the table. "The worst starting hand in Texas Hold'em is two and seven off suit. They're the two lowest cards you can have that can't make a straight. Even if they're suited, they'll make a very low flush, and if either pairs, you've still got a low hand."

Gold drew himself up in his chair, smiled a little, and sighed. "What's your point?"

"Russo stays in with the hammer."

"The hammer?"

"A two and seven off suit. Russo never folds the hand. He plays to the river all the time. Only an addict would play so foolishly."

"Yeah, you're probably right. What was the name of that Florida casino?"

"Seminole Casino Hotel."

"Indian owned?"

"One of six."

"I wonder why Russo picked that place."

"Maybe he likes the ambience. The Seminoles run a tight ship. Great service, good food, and clean accommodations."

"Where are the other casinos?"

Wong had to think about that for a while. Eventually he said, "Brighton, Coconut Creek, Hollywood, and Tampa."

"That's only five."

"There are two in Hollywood."

"Big operation."

"Profitable, too."

"I'm not surprised. A gambler never makes the same mistake twice. It's usually three or more times."

"Well said, my friend."

"I didn't mean to steal your thunder."

"I'm never at a loss for a proverb."

"I didn't think so."

Wong looked up almost whimsically toward the ceiling. "Ah, now, let me see." He thought for a moment. Put a single forefinger to his lips. "Luck always seems to be against the man who depends on it."

"Are you referring to Russo?"

"I am."

"His luck is about to run out."

"I hope so."

Gold smiled. "You can bet on it."

CHAPTER THIRTY

Gold left his house on Long Island at the crack of dawn, and as Ridge requested, he took a cab to the JetBlue terminal at JFK Airport. He still had no idea where they were going, but with Ridge calling the shots, it could be just about anywhere.

Ridge was waiting for him at the gate, tickets in hand, and she looked tired. There were dark circles under her eyes, but she smiled for the requisite few seconds, then said, "Good morning, Kemo Sabe. Ready to ride?"

"Where are we going?"

Ridge couldn't keep him in the dark forever, but she would have preferred to wait a few more minutes. Setting her apprehension aside she said, "Havana."

Gold stared hard at her and spoke slowly. "Wait a minute. We're flying down to Cuba?"

"Unless you've got a better way to get there."

They exchanged a long look, which was interrupted by a boarding announcement. Out on the tarmac, under a cloudy sky, planes were taxiing hither and thither.

Gold stood with his hands at his sides, gazing off somewhere. Then a shadow crossed his face, a flinch as though he had been slapped, and everything changed. "I don't mean to pry, but why the hell are we going to Cuba?"

"To make some new friends."

"I've got enough friends."

"Yes, but none of your friends work at the *Dirección de Inteligencia*."

"What's that?"

Ridge stifled a yawn, and then she explained that the Intelligence Directorate —— commonly known as G2 —— functioned as the main intelligence agency of the Cuban government. The agency was responsible for all foreign intelligence collection and was currently composed of six divisions, employing about fifteen thousand people.

Gold shook his head, taking no comfort in her words. "No offense, but I'd rather visit a rum factory."

"No need to worry. Our host will take good care of us."

"We've got a host?"

"Naturally."

"Who might that be?"

"General Eduardo Fernández."

"Is he the guy in charge of firing squads?"

Ridge's mouth turned upward briefly in a parody of a smile. "He's the guy in charge of the intelligence agency."

Doing a slight double take, Gold said, "Now I feel better."

"You'll be fine, but if I were you, I wouldn't mention the cigar claim."

"*Mi madre* didn't raise no fool."

There was another announcement.

"Time to board," Ridge said.

"After you, comrade."

JetBlue's nonstop flight to Havana left at 9:30 a.m., taking off under a low ceiling of clouds that soon gave way to a bright blue sky. The Airbus A320 was scheduled to land three and a half hours later at Jose Marti International Airport. During the flight, Ridge revealed that the Cuban embassy in Washington had contacted DHS requesting Russo's extradition.

"The Cubans thought we had him," Ridge said. "When they learned we didn't, they offered to help us find him."

"They offered to help?"

"That's right."

"Why?"

"We're not sure, but you know the old saying. Never look a gift horse in the mouth."

"I know another saying about horses. Beware of Greeks bearing gifts."

"I share your concern, but there's no harm in hearing what they have to say. In case you haven't noticed, we've reached a dead end."

"Not quite," Gold said. "I've been a busy bee."

"What does that mean?"

"You'd better tighten your seat belt."

"Been there, done that."

Gold told her about Bill Burke, describing the identification process in some detail, following up with his unexpected visit to

Joe DeCarlo's condo. "I have to admit, I was a little nervous. I'm glad I went, though. I met a Natasha named Svetlana, and I got to see how the other half lives –– the crooked half."

"I could've passed on both."

"Nothing ventured, nothing gained."

"What did DeCarlo want?"

"He made me an offer."

"One you couldn't refuse?"

"No, not exactly. Sort of a quid pro quo."

"This should be good."

Leaning over the armrest, Gold lowered his voice and repeated almost word for word the conversation he'd had with DeCarlo. After he described the offer, he offered his own spin. "You scratch my back, I'll scratch yours, and we'll both scratch Russo off the list."

Ridge sat back and closed her eyes. "What a lovely thought."

"I just had another thought. You could help me spread the word about DeCarlo."

"You want me to help you clear his name?"

"You know more cops than I do."

"Maybe I could take out an ad in the *New York Times*."

"Do I detect a note of sarcasm?"

Ridge opened her eyes and looked at him. "Not sarcasm. Realism. Why in the world would I want to help DeCarlo? He's just as bad as Russo. Maybe worse. He's the underboss of a ruthless mob family. A criminal enterprise that's bigger than Russo's operation."

"I realize that, but sometimes you have to dance with the devil to get invited to the party."

"I'm not sure what that means, but I can tell you one thing. You've been spending too much time with Victor Wong."

"Yeah, I know."

A troubled expression clouded her face. "Do you realize what you're asking me to do?"

"I'm asking you to run interference."

"You're asking me to vouch for a mobster."

"A mobster who didn't kill Feretti. What's the big deal?"

"You won't be risking your reputation."

Gold made a sour expression. "Look on the bright side. When you bust Russo, you'll be the toast of the town."

"Or just toast."

"Do me a favor, and give it some thought. In the meantime, I've got some other good news."

Ridge raised her hand to cut him off. "Wait a minute. I need a drink. Would you like one?"

"Why not?"

She ordered for both of them. Vodka and tonic. When Gold seemed puzzled, she said, "Vodka smells the least. We don't want to be reeking of alcohol when we land."

Gold resumed speaking, his voice low but clear. He told her that he'd recently had lunch with Victor Wong. Between proverbs, he'd heard some startling news. "Wong loves to gamble. He was down in Florida last week, playing in a poker tournament. He was at a Seminole casino in a town called Immokalee. After the tournament, he decided to play in a cash game, and you'll never guess who was sitting at his table."

She rubbed her chin thoughtfully. "Well, let's see, we can eliminate Confucius."

"You're a riot, Alice."

"Give me a hint."

Gold waited until the flight attendant finished serving them, and then he said, "The devil himself."

Ridge looked at him incredulously. *"Russo?"*

"Believe it or not, he introduced himself to the table."

She exhaled, closed her eyes tightly, and slowly shook her head. "I can't believe he'd show his face in public. He's not that stupid. I must be missing something."

"You are missing something. According to Wong, Russo's an addict."

She looked at him in bewilderment. *"An addict?"*

"He's got a gambling addiction. Apparently he gets an adrenaline rush from playing poker. He never drops out of a hand. Plays to the bitter end, all the time. He's a big bluffer and a big loser."

"The last part I knew."

"Now you know more."

Ridge bit her lip, seemingly thinking about what he'd just said. After sampling her drink, she muttered something under her breath, then said, "A gambling addiction, eh?"

"The man is full of surprises."

"Most of them bad." She took another sip of her drink. "Well, that would certainly explain his behavior."

"According to Wong, the addiction's a bitch. Difficult to treat, harder to cure."

"You're preaching to the choir."

"Excuse me?"

"My ex-husband was an addict. He was addicted to Blackjack. One of those fools who thought they could beat the house. Nobody ever does, but once you're hooked, it's all over. When you hit rock bottom, you're left with bills, bad debts, and bankruptcy." A twinge of regret seeped into her voice. "I hate to admit it, but a lot of Indians fall into that trap." She looked off into space trying to recall the numbers. They were not good. "The last time I checked, over 40 percent of Native Americans had some difficulty with gambling."

Gold almost choked on his drink. "Jesus, that's nuts."

She told him that drug abuse and alcohol abuse were the key factors. Both were rampant on reservations, and when a tribal member couldn't hold down a job, he turned to making an easy buck.

If the truth be told, the Supreme Court bore much of the blame. In 1987, the Court ruled that Native American tribes, being sovereign, could not be barred from allowing gambling. Shortly thereafter, casinos began to spring up on reservations across the country.

"They produce big bucks," Ridge said.

"How big?" Gold asked.

"Billions."

Gold's face took on a puzzled look. "Forgive my ignorance, but I don't understand something. If Indian casinos are so profitable, why is the unemployment rate so high?"

A good question, Ridge thought. She told him that the belief among whites that Indians had struck it rich by owning casinos was a myth. Of the more than 560 Indian nations, only half were involved in gaming. Many tribes were shut out of the industry due to their geographic location in rural, unpopulated areas. "Which explains why the Indian unemployment rate is 15 percent, three times higher than the general population."

Gold was digesting this, but not comfortably. "Okay, enough sociology. I'm getting depressed."

"Have another drink."

Missing the irony, Gold said, "Yeah, that should do the trick."

CHAPTER THIRTY-ONE

By the time JetBlue's flight 243 touched down at Jose Marti airport and offloaded its passengers at twenty minutes past one, Gold and Ridge were swapping war stories and feeling no pain. They deplaned at Terminal 3, the largest and most modern of the four passenger terminals. Before they reached the baggage carousel, they were intercepted by an officer from the Cuban Revolutionary Armed Forces. She introduced herself as Capitán Almonte, military intelligence.

"Pleasure to meet you," she said matter-of-factly, though her expression said something altogether different. "Welcome to the Republic of Cuba."

Thanks to the captain, the whole airport process was easy. After they pointed out their luggage, they were escorted past the duty-free shops advertising "the world's best cigars and rum." Gold had never been fast-tracked through customs so effortlessly, avoiding any semblance of a line. He almost felt guilty. Almost.

Almonte informed them that they would be staying at the Hotel Nacional de Cuba, one of the best hotels in Havana. The city was about nine miles from the airport, and along the way, they learned that Jose Marti had been a Cuban revolutionary, a national hero who had fought for independence against Spain. During his lifetime, he'd also worked as a poet, essayist, and journalist. The airport that bore his name was the largest and busiest in Cuba, and it was a great source of pride to Almonte and her compatriots.

The hotel was at the base of the famed El Malecón, the five-mile-long boulevard that stretched along Havana Harbor, passed through Centro Habana, then ended in the Vedado neighborhood. Almonte told them that the main purpose of building the seawall was to protect the city from wind and water caused by *Nortes*, but in reality, the strip was more of a nighttime promenade and a great spot to fish.

The front desk of the hotel was managed by an overweight, pasty-faced fellow who seemed bored and lazy to Gold, but he had to discount his own perceptions. The older he got and the longer he worked as an investigator, the more worthless most people seemed to him.

The manager adjusted the red handkerchief in his suit coat, which matched his tie, then consulted the guest register. A moment later, he placed a single key on the counter and said, "Royal Suite. I hope you enjoy your stay."

Ridge glanced at the key, then frowned. For a moment, she seemed ready to protest, then quickly remembered why she was there. No sense irritating her hosts. She told Almonte that they would need a few minutes to unpack and freshen up, and then they'd be ready to proceed.

Almonte saluted like it didn't matter to her, like nothing mattered. "Take all the time you need. I'll be waiting in the lobby."

Ridge momentarily toyed with the idea of returning her salute, but she decided against it.

When they entered their suite, Gold burst into laughter. The rooms were large, but they were decorated with the most gaudy and outdated furnishings he'd ever seen. Circa 1950-something. "Well, comrade, welcome to workers' paradise."

Ridge sat down dejectedly. "This is how they treat royalty?"

"You forget that the royals were executed by the Bolsheviks."

"Who told you that? Your friend Svetlana?"

"Jealousy does not become you."

Ridge exhaled deeply. She looked drained. "I need at least twenty minutes."

"Nap time?"

"I need to shower."

"So do I."

"I'll meet you downstairs."

"Sounds like a plan."

Gold went into the bathroom to shower and shave. Ten minutes later, dressed and holding a cold Cristal beer, he looked out the front window. The promenade was filled with *Habaneros* and tourists, strolling along the seawall, seemingly without a care in the world. Closer to the Morro, Havana's lighthouse, fishermen were casting for bonefish and tarpon, but nobody seemed to be having much luck.

Gold finished his beer, then went downstairs, scoping out the bars and restaurants for later in the evening. There were four restaurants and an equal number of bars. He was studying the menu of the hotel's luxury restaurant, *Comedor de Aguiar*, when Ridge stepped out of the elevator and made her grand entrance.

And grand it was.

She wore a tan skirt, a white silk blouse with the top button undone, and black high heels. Her jewelry was a single strand of pearls and turquoise earrings. Her long brown hair was pulled into a ponytail, and it bounced when she walked. All this Gold noticed in less than three seconds.

"You clean up nice," Gold said, smiling. "Very nice."

"I'm trying to make a good impression."

"Mission accomplished."

"I hope so. We don't want to face a firing squad."

"Not funny."

"Lighten up, *amigo*. The Cubans wouldn't harm an invited guest."

"They invited you, not me."

"*Au contraire, mon ami*. You were invited, too."

"I beg your pardon?"

"General Fernández requested the pleasure of your company."

"What are you talking about?"

"He asked if you would join me."

"Why?"

"They've arrested one of your friends."

Gold glanced around to see if anyone in the hallway was listening, and lowered his voice. "One of *my* friends?"

"I forgot to mention it on the plane. Too much vodka." She smiled and pointed at Captain Almonte, who gave her a thumbs-up sign. "Our chauffeur is waiting. Let's finish this conversation on the way to the prison."

"Wait a minute. We're going to a prison?"

"Villa Marista."

For a moment he didn't respond. *She has to be joking*, he thought, but her gaze was absolutely steady.

"You're pulling my leg," he finally said.

"Nope."

"Have you lost your mind? What if they don't let us out?"

"You're such a worrywart."

"I'm serious. They could lock us up and lose the key."

Ridge chuckled, genuinely amused. "If that happens, I've got the top bunk."

On the way to the prison, Ridge told him that Ricardo Paz had been arrested, but she didn't know why or when. All she knew was that Paz had mentioned Gold's name during his interrogation, and that was enough to get him invited to Cuba.

More than enough.

Villa Marista was located on the outskirts of Havana, only a fifteen-minute drive from their "luxury accommodations." They had to wind through narrow streets flanked by dilapidated buildings to find the entrance to the infamous prison. After gaining admittance, they parked in a space reserved for *Oficiales de Inteligencia Militar*, then went inside. The smell hit them first. Urine usually has a distinct odor, but under normal circumstances, the odor is relatively mild and not too noticeable. Within the confines of a hot, musty prison, the odor becomes intolerable.

"The Villa," as it is known to Cuban dissidents, was originally a Catholic seminary run by the Marist Brothers. In 1963, it became an interrogation center, the place where suspected CIA agents were brought, where purged officials repented, and where all Cubans feared to tread.

Captain Almonte escorted them through several security checkpoints, each guarded by stern-looking soldiers in olive fatigues. When they reached the first cell block, she led them to a dimly lit cell, unlocked the door, and gestured for them to step inside.

"You have five minutes," she said firmly. "Please leave the door open."

When they entered the seven-by-seven-foot cell, Paz rolled off his bed and greeted them like long-lost friends. "Jesucristo," he shouted. "You're finally here. My prayers have been answered!"

Gold ignored him, keeping his attention fixed on the door. "Be careful what you pray for. We're only passing through."

"I knew you would come. I never doubted it. God, I'm so happy I could cry."

"Hold the tears," Gold said. "We've only got a few minutes." He introduced Ridge, then looked around, appalled by the filthy, moldy walls and the raw sewage on the floor. "Damn, this place is nasty."

"The toilet is broken," Paz said. "So is the shower."

"How the hell do you bathe?"

"We don't. Prisoners get one dirty towel and one bar of soap each month."

Ridge grunted in disgust. "I'm afraid to ask about the food."

Paz smiled ruefully. "Unfit for human consumption."

Gold couldn't keep the emotion out of his voice. "You were a free man. You could have gone anywhere. Why the hell did you come to Cuba?"

Paz stood silently a few seconds, and Gold thought he looked pale and frightened. He cleared his throat several times, then said, "I received word that my mother was dying, so I came to visit her one last time. The moment I stepped off the plane, they arrested me. They won't tell me why. They won't tell me anything, but I think it has something to do with Russo."

Ridge's eyebrows went up in surprise. "Why do you say that?"

"I heard them mention his name during my interrogation. The bastards thought I'd passed out, but I was just pretending to be unconscious." He chuckled and then scanned the area to make sure that none of the guards were around. "I was tired of their stupid questions."

Gold's face showed he did not entirely agree with that strategy, but he nodded. "How did my name come up?"

"They didn't believe that I was a law abiding citizen. I needed someone to vouch for me. Someone who could get me out of this mess. You got me out of jail in Miami, so I figured you could do the same in Havana."

Gold let irritation show. He looked at Ridge, then at Paz, shaking his head. "Do I look like a public defender?"

"You're a man with connections."

"You're a man with a big problem. General Fernández doesn't know me from a hole in the wall."

"I gotta get out of here. I can't last much longer."

"You should have thought of that before you came back to Cuba."

"Look, I just want you to give it your best shot. That's all I'm asking."

"You're asking a lot," Gold said. "What do you intend to do when you get out? Go after Russo?"

"Yes, I'm going to kill that son of a bitch. Nothing will stop me."

Ridge expelled breath loudly. "Why don't you leave Russo to us?"

Paz turned furiously on her. "Never!"

"Not a smart move," she said. "You'd be jumping out of the pot and into the frying pan. You might get yourself killed."

"I'm willing to take that chance."

Gold patted Paz's shoulder solicitously and raised an eyebrow. "If you're smart, you'll listen to agent Ridge. She knows what she's talking about."

"Just get me out of here. That's the most important thing."

"But it's not the only thing," Gold said. "You need to think of your future. You're still a young man. Why throw it all away?"

Paz's anger was evident as he glared at them, his jaw set tight. "If you don't get me out, I'll bust out."

Ridge restrained an urge to whack him across the head. To knock some sense into him. "Before you do something rash, remember where you are and who you're dealing with." She reminded him that proportionately, Cuba had one of the highest prison populations in the world, with over 57,000 inmates spread across 200 facilities in a country of 11 million people. "You don't want to screw around with these folks."

"Unless you're bulletproof," Gold said.

Paz swore under his breath and sat down. "The next time you come, bring cigars."

Gold shot a sad look at Ridge, then said, "A box of Cohibas?"

"Any brand will do."

Almonte knocked on the cell door, then said, "Time to go."

Gold glanced at his watch. "I'll let you know if I make any progress." Unable to fake even a stab at levity, he simply added, "Try to behave yourself."

CHAPTER THIRTY-TWO

It was a bright, clear afternoon, although rain threatened as they walked along a gravel path, past a playground with swings and climbing equipment. A mixture of brown and black children -- the offspring of the guards -- played together while others, younger children, clung close to the day care workers.

Almonte escorted them into another drab building, a dark, two-story structure that contained more guards and an X-ray machine. They were waved through and brought to a large, private office at the end of the hallway. The receptionist was not at her desk, so Almonte pressed the intercom and said something in Spanish. The woman who answered the call wore white skinny jeans, high heels, and an off-the-shoulder top. Her long brown hair had a slight wave. She was pretty but not what Gold considered beautiful. Her toenails were painted red, which matched the polish on her fingers, and she wore lots of jewelry and plenty of perfume.

Definitely not a typist, Gold thought.

Almonte spoke to the woman in Spanish, then told them that General Fernández was in flight and would be landing momentarily. Five minutes later, the general's helicopter landed softly on a patch of grass near the playground. As the rotor blades slowed, a short flight of steps unfolded. The door of the Russian-made copter swung open, and Fernández appeared, wearing a full dress uniform that made him look like a character in a B movie. He stood at attention and returned the salute of the waiting troops, then proceeded to his office.

Almonte handled the introductions, then touched the rim of her cap and said, *"Bienvenido, General. Estaré afuera si me necesitas."*

Fernández sat in a straight-backed chair, took out a cigar, and rolled it thoughtfully between his hands. He didn't reach for a match. "Please sit down. We have much to discuss. May I offer you something to drink? Some coffee or rum?"

Ridge shook her head.

So did Gold.

General Fernández was a heavy-set man with a florid, fleshy face. His hair -- what there was left -- was pushed to one side, and he had a pencil-thin mustache that made him look like a used car salesman. He kept a meaningless smile in place as he rambled on about the virtues of Cuba's Marxist-Leninist socialist state and how it had produced the world's best coffee, rum, and cigars. "I hope you don't mind if I smoke." He lit the cigar, blew a cloud of smoke in their direction, then studied them through the haze. "So, your flight was pleasant. Sí? We are very proud of our airport. Jose Marti is the third busiest in the Caribbean region. Last year we processed over four million passengers. We expect that number to grow now that we are becoming friends with *las Estados Unidos*." He poured himself a cup of coffee from a thermos jug and sipped on it. “Speaking of friends, I’m sorry we had to arrest Señor Paz, but we had no choice. In our country, nobody is above the law.”

“Nobody should be,” Gold said. “What did Paz do?”

“He tried to sneak into Cuba.”

“Why would he have to sneak?”

“Because of his past. He was deported for insulting a government official.”

“I didn’t know that.”

“I thought you were friends.”

“Paz is more of a business acquaintance.”

Fernández lifted his shoulders in a small shrug. “In any case, the man is a troublemaker.”

“Has he been charged with a crime?”

“Not yet.”

“Does he have a lawyer?”

“These things take time.”

Gold raised a single eyebrow. “The wheels of justice turn slowly down here.”

“Sí, but we can make them turn faster. Paz is barely on my radar. To me he’s *papas pequeñas*. Small potatoes. I’ve got bigger fish to fry.” He tossed a wanted poster across the desk. “Do you recognize this man?”

Gold lowered his voice to an all-but-inaudible whisper. “Nick Russo.”

“Enemigo público numero uno.”

Ridge wasn’t sure whether that was a statement or a question, but it didn’t matter. She didn’t come to Cuba to play games or be coy. There was no time for that sort of nonsense. She spoke slowly, as if she felt that Fernandez would otherwise have difficulty understanding. "We've been after Russo for a long time, and we're grateful for your assistance. I'm just curious why you want to help us."

The smile fell from the general's face, and his entire bearing changed. "Senor Russo is a menace to society. He needs to be caught and punished. *Lo más rápido posible!*"

"Did he commit a crime in Cuba?"

Fernández reminded her that there were times when a simple question required a long and difficult answer. He began slowly, hoping his English would rise to the occasion. He told them that many years ago an infamous American gangster came to Cuba, ostensibly to enjoy the island's lovely beaches and its world-class rum. Back in the states, it was too cold to swim, and there was a nationwide constitutional ban on the production, importation, transportation, and sale of alcoholic beverages –– a prohibition that would last three more years. The gangster and his entourage left from Miami and flew south on a seaplane operated by N.Y.R.B.A. Airlines, which stood for New York, Rio, Buenos Aires.

The date was April 23, 1930.

The gangster's name was Al Capone.

When Capone and his party arrived in Havana, they registered at the Sevilla Biltmore Hotel, an elegant, Moorish-style structure located on Calle Trocadero in Old Havana. The very next day, the Cuban Secret Police, acting on orders from the American Embassy, brought Capone and his party to police headquarters for questioning. The police chief demanded to know what the *bandidos Yanquis* were doing in Cuba. Capone calmly replied that he was there to spend some money and drink some booze. The chief told him that the Cuban Government was glad to have him as a visitor, and he hoped his stay would be a pleasant one.

According to Fernández, this was Capone's second visit to Cuba. During his first visit, in 1928, he bought three Patek Philippe watches at a swanky store called Le Palais Royal in Calle Obispo. Capone kept a watch for himself and gave one to his bodyguard and one to a man named Rafael Guas Inclan, who would later become Vice President during Batista's dictatorship.

"Excuse me for interrupting," Gold said. "But 1928 was a long time ago. Almost a hundred years. How do you know that Capone was actually here?"

"We have proof," Fernández said. "Documents and photographs." He smiled condescendingly. "Would you like to see the evidence?"

"If you don't mind."

"I don't mind." He opened a thick folder and extracted a photograph of three men standing in front of the Tropical Brewery and Gardens in Havana. He identified the men as Miami lawyer "Fritz" Gordon, Al Capone, and Cuban Navy Commander Julio Morales Coello. "The photo was taken on April 23, 1930. The day that Capone arrived in Cuba."

Gold grunted skeptically. "Photos are easy to fake."

Fernández gave him a droll look. "Your government was kind enough to provide further documentation." He produced a form he'd received from the US Department of Labor. The print was faded but still legible. "This is a passenger list for a flight from Havana to Miami. Do you see the date? May 1, 1930." His voice was low and calm, but he took hard pulls on his cigar, drawing the smoke deep into his lungs and blowing it out between tightly pursed lips in a long jet. "Passenger number five is listed as male, thirty-one years of age. Take a look at his name."

Ridge's eyebrows went up as she studied the form, eventually accompanied by a smile and a slow shaking of her head. "Alphonse Capone."

Fernández answered in a smooth, indifferent voice. "I believe you call this a smoking gun."

"Fascinating," she said as an aside to Gold.

Gold stared at the list of names, his mind in a fog.

Fernández grinned at them in a not-quite-professional way. "Now that we know that Capone was here, we must ask ourselves a question. What was he doing in Cuba? What was his real purpose?" He took another drag on his cigar, and exhaling, he studied the cloud of smoke as if it held some interest. "Do you know how Capone made his money? He had many sources of income. Breweries, distilleries, gambling casinos, houses of prostitution. They say that crime doesn't pay, but in 1930, Capone's net worth exceeded $100 million." He looked at the old photograph, a smile playing across his lips. "I wonder where he kept his money. Certainly not in a bank. Not with the Treasury Department breathing down his neck. If I were a gangster, I'd look for a friendly nation close to the US mainland. A poor country where government officials could be easily bribed. A place like Havana, Cuba."

There was something condescending, Gold thought, in the way Fernández was leading them to an inescapable conclusion. Nevertheless, the conclusion was just short of incredible. "Let me get this straight," Gold said. "Are you telling us that Capone stashed his loot in Cuba?"

"Not all of it," Fernández replied. "Forty or fifty million."

Ridge gave him a quizzical look. "He only made two trips to Cuba?"

"As far as we know."

"He must have brought a lot of luggage." She did some quick calculations, then said, "One million in one hundred dollar bills weighs about twenty-two pounds. Fifty million would weigh over one thousand pounds."

Fernández contemplated this with a puff on his cigar. "I neglected to mention that Capone's family also traveled to Cuba. His brother Ralph and his wife came to Havana in November, 1930. They were here to promote a racehorse. Two months later, Capone's sister, Mafalda, came to Cuba on her honeymoon." He went silent for a moment, staring at them, his eyes distant, his look impenetrable. "The timing of these visits is rather curious. In 1931, one year later, Capone was convicted of tax evasion and sentenced to eleven years in federal prison. As I'm sure you know, he was sent to Alcatraz, and after his release, he succumbed to syphilis."

Gold stared at the general for a few moments, thinking. "So what do you think he did with the loot?"

Fernández smiled. A fake smile. Like he had a pain in his side but was trying not to let on. "We know what he did with the money. It was stored in safe deposit boxes. Under assumed names. Unfortunately, we don't know where the boxes went after the revolution. They could be anywhere in Cuba." He leaned back into his chair and let out a loud breath. "As far as I know, only two people are looking for those boxes. Nicholas Russo and me."

Ridge let this register a moment before asking the next question. "Is that why you want to help us? To eliminate the competition?"

Fernández laughed harshly. "The money doesn't belong to me. It belongs to the Republic of Cuba." He reached for his heavy desk lighter and made a ritual of refiring his cigar, inspecting the smoldering tip, and blowing smoke rings in the air. "If we work together, we can both get what we want. My country gets rid of a pest, and yours gets to make an arrest. *Suena bien, no?*"

"Yes, that sounds good."

"Do we have a deal?"

Ridge nodded. "I'll notify Washington."

Fernández contemplated a moment, then spread his hands expansively across his desk. "All right, then, I'll set the wheels in motion. Will there be anything else?"

Against her better judgment, Ridge asked about Paz. She wanted to know what the Cubans intended to do with him, and she insinuated that his welfare was important to her. "I can't divulge our plans, but we need to keep him alive and well."

"What would you like us to do with him?"

After a time, she said carefully, "Release him from prison, but don't let him leave the country. You can send him back to the states after we arrest Russo."

Fernández let out a humorless laugh. *"No problema."*

Ridge turned sideways and looked at Gold questioningly. "Can you think of anything else?"

Gold shook his head. He was pleasantly surprised, but he kept his mouth shut and his face a mask of neutrality.

Fernández rose to his feet, signaling that the meeting was over. "Captain Almonte will drive you back to your hotel." He winked at Gold. "Enjoy your stay in Cuba."

CHAPTER THIRTY-THREE

Ridge didn't have much to say on the way back to the hotel, and neither did Gold. They didn't feel like talking in front of their chauffeur, who worked for military intelligence and was probably recording whatever was said. Almonte seemed indifferent to the silence, which lasted until they reached the Plaza de la Revolución and turned onto Salvador Allende Avenue. Suddenly they became ensnarled in a traffic jam caused by Habaneros heading to one of the city's unbiquitous street festivals. The sidewalks and streets were filled with revelers, but despite the crowd, Almonte claimed it was a modest event. The real fun and games began in mid-July, with the start of the Santiago de Cuba Carnival, which lasted a full week and was the biggest *carnaval* in all of the Caribbean.

How, Gold wondered, did anybody get any work done with so many pleasant distractions? Obviously the Cubans took enormous pride in their cultural heritage, and they loved to throw a good party. During the summer months, Havana hosted parades, street parties, congo lines, fireworks, and musical celebrations.

The only hard part was getting from point A to point B.

And point C was out of the question.

Almonte was unnaturally calm about the traffic, which had come to a standstill and showed no signs of clearing any time soon. Ridge had asked to be dropped off in Old Havana instead of the hotel, but the congestion made that problematic. She had hoped to bring Gold to La Bodeguita del Medio, a storied Cuban watering hole frequented by Ernest Hemingway. The establishment claimed to be the birthplace of the Mojito cocktail, a concoction they'd been serving since 1942. When she aired her concern about the traffic, Almonte suggested a restaurant closer to their hotel.

"La Guarida would be a better choice," Almonte said. "They serve the best food in Havana, and you can walk back to your hotel along the Malecon." She turned around and winked at Gold. "Very romantic."

The moment they stepped out of the car, Almonte sped away, and Ridge punched Gold in the shoulder. "What are you trying to do?"

"Excuse me?"

"You're ruining my reputation."

"What did I do?"

"I don't know, but that was your second wink."

Gold smiled a moment, as if acknowledging the subtlety of the compliment. "Listen to the music. Love is in the air."

"Watch your step. Poop is on the ground."

"You're such a romantic."

"Shut up."

"You need a Mojito."

"Gosh, I hope I don't lose my head."

Gold placed a reassuring hand on her shoulder. "Don't worry, dear. What happens in Havana stays in Havana."

"You know, there's never a gun around when you need one."

"Nice."

She winked at him. "Dinner's on me."

In English, La Guarida meant "the lair," but there was nothing ominous or secretive about the restaurant. On the contrary. The waitstaff was warm and welcoming, and they greeted their customers like old friends. Ridge said something in Spanish, and they were given the best seat in the house, a table for two on a balcony overlooking Havana center and the Malecon.

The first order of business involved cocktails, but they both opted for something other than a Mojito. Ridge ordered the specialty of the house, a drink called "La Mansión," which was a potent mixture of Havana Club rum, sugar, lemon juice, honey, mint, and peach marmalade. Gold kept it simple and asked for a shot of Santiago de Cuba rum –– the twenty-five-year-old version.

As Ridge selected an assortment of tapas, Gold looked around them. The tables were filled with couples and foursomes, some smiling, some serious and intent, all enjoying the balmy weather. He leaned over the railing to stare down at the bay. The water was azure beneath clear skies; there were a couple of sailboats, a small armada of fishing boats, a cruise ship, and a freighter from Russia. After the waiter left, he reached for his napkin and wiped his brow. "Warm night."

Ridge seemed not to hear him. She pulled at the collar of her blouse, exposing one of her bra straps. "What's your favorite rum?"

"Ron Zacapa."

"I'm not familiar with that one."

"It's made in Guatemala. Aged in oak barrels for twenty-three years. I discovered it on a cruise when we stopped in Santo Tomas."

"Sounds interesting."

"What about you? Do you have a favorite?"

"No, I enjoy them all. My reservation frowned upon the consumption of firewater. I'm the only one in my family who drinks alcohol." Her eyes took on a furtive cast. In a quick pass, they scanned the length and breadth of the balcony, then came back to him. "I attribute that weakness to work-related stress and to spending too much time with characters like you."

"So you think I'm a bad influence?"

"If you weren't, we couldn't be friends."

After the second round, they ordered dinner and a bottle of Chilean Sauvignon Blanc. Ridge chose the grilled snapper, and Gold ordered grouper. Both dishes came with white rice, black beans, and fried plantains.

Between bites, they talked about their meeting with General Fernández, and they agreed that it went well. Better than they'd expected. Much better. Despite his reputation, the general was gracious and agreeable, and he seemed to be a genuinely patriotic fellow. He gave them everything they asked for, and they had no complaints.

Gold thought Ridge deserved most of the credit. "I'm glad you wore that outfit. I think the old boy was smitten with you."

"I couldn't tell."

"He couldn't take his eyes off of you."

"Look who's talking."

"I beg your pardon?"

"You couldn't take your eyes off of his secretary."

"I barely noticed her."

Ridge's voice grew somber, almost hesitant. "I noticed her. She has a face that's hard to forget. I've seen her before, but I can't remember where or when. It's driving me crazy."

"She was driving me crazy, too."

Ridge made no effort to disguise the fact that she was frustrated. "I know I've seen her somewhere. I never forget a face."

"It'll come to you."

"I hope so."

A frown settled on Gold's face. He looked down, looked up, looked down again. "Since we're on the subject of femme fatales, how did the Cubans know that Paz was in Havana?"

Ridge settled back in her chair and heaved a great sigh. "Morella Perez?"

"Bingo."

"I thought she was working for Russo?"

"Maybe she's playing both sides of the fence."

"Maybe, but I don't feel like talking about her tonight. Tomorrow's another day. Let's enjoy our time together."

Gold was rendered momentarily speechless. Ridge was usually all business. He took a moment to consider her words, as if he had forgotten that there was a time and place for everything. "You're right," he finally said. "Tonight should be about us."

They chose to forego coffee and dessert, opting to take a stroll along the Malecon as they made their way back to the hotel. As usual on a warm evening, the esplanade was a river of love struck locals and sweating tourists. They milled arm in arm, elbow to elbow, oblivious to the monuments of Cuban generals and the monument dedicated to the victims of the USS *Maine.* Wary of pickpockets, they walked close to the street, waving away the prostitutes and souvenir hawkers who hovered like flies.

Since they were feeling no pain, they decided to have a nightcap in the Churchill Bar at the hotel. When they asked for rum, the bartender told them that he had a bottle of *Máximo Extra Añejo*, a luxury rum that sold for over $1,000 a bottle. He explained that production was limited to 1,000 bottles per year, and that it was so good it was packaged in a hand-blown glass bottle.

Ridge ordered two glasses, straight up with ice on the side.

Gold smiled, but he wasn't thrilled about the ice. "Why water it down?"

"One cube works wonders," she said. "It opens up the rum."

"You don't say."

She began to ramble on about guaiacol, an aromatic oil that provided a smoky flavor to the rum. Adding a bit of water or ice moved the oil closer to the surface, resulting in a better smell and taste.

Gold heard her out, but he was thinking of something else. The bar's subdued lighting cast a flattering glow over Ridge, and it crossed Gold's mind as they talked that she was quite attractive. He'd always been drawn to women with dusky skin and dark hair. Maybe it was the alcohol, but he also noticed that her large eyes were almond-shaped, her lips sensually full.

They sat in silence as the bartender opened the bottle and put it down on the counter to breathe for a few moments. Gold picked up the cork, sniffed it, and nodded approvingly.

A minute later, the bartender poured two generous glasses of the rum. When he left, Gold leaned close to Ridge and thanked her for the treat. Then he said, "You look very beautiful this evening."

"You're drunk."

"No, just grateful."

"For what?"

"For your company. I'm also grateful for what you did for Paz. You didn't have to intervene on his behalf or protect him from Russo. You did those things out of the kindness of your heart."

"Not exactly. I did those things for you, not Paz." She batted her eyelashes at him. "I'd do anything for you."

"You're drunk."

"No, just grateful. You're a good friend, and you've always got my back."

"I like your back. I like your front, too."

"One more compliment and I'll have to cut you off."

"We should both be cut off." He lowered his voice, just a little. "These drinks are fifty bucks apiece."

"We're worth it."

On the way upstairs, inside the elevator, Ridge began to giggle, and she didn't stop giggling until they were inside the room. She didn't bother to explain her amusement, but she did declare that there were only four men she trusted: Jim Beam, Jack Daniels, Jose Cuervo, and Adam Gold. "You're the only one that doesn't give me a headache."

"That's quite a compliment."

"You're quite a guy."

"And you're quite a lady. Which is why I'd like to do something for you."

Ridge smiled a little, sighed, and put her head on Gold's shoulder. "What did you have in mind?"

"I'd like to give you some money."

"Money?"

"The reward for finding Russo. We've got the mafia and the Cubans looking for him, so it's only a matter of time before we nail his sorry ass. You can't collect the reward, but I can. I'd like you to have the whole enchilada."

She smiled at him with affection. "You'd do that for me?"

"In a heartbeat."

She straightened up and placed a hand on his shoulder. "Adam," she said softly, "I've got a crazy idea."

Something in her tone made Gold nervous. "I'm listening."

"I've done something nice for you, and you've done something nice for me. Why don't we do something nice together?" She kissed him lightly on the mouth. "What do you think?"

Gold gazed back at her for a few moments, then brought his hands to her cheeks and kissed her deeply. She kissed him back, less passionately, but tentatively, neither sure where this was going. He smiled disarmingly, then slowly slid his hand along her silken leg, moving up to her calf, then to the edge of her thigh. "I think we're drunk," he whispered.

She dismissed the comment with a wave of her hand. Her next move was more surprising. They began kissing again, and her inhibitions were soon abandoned. She slid out of her dress, then removed her bra and panties. Her breasts were high and firm, and her skin was the color of cream. She looked the most beautiful she had all day, Gold thought as he unzipped his pants.

She pressed her breasts against his chest, and they kissed for a while. Completely naked now, she looked at him and smiled. "Is this really happening?"

"My God, Sally, you are beautiful."

"Pretty is as pretty does."

"So they say." He suddenly picked her up and laid her down on the couch. He bent over her and kissed her neck, her breasts, and her stomach. She sighed his name and slid downward, pulling him into a long kiss. He stroked her spine until he was cupping her backside. He enjoyed the tension in her muscles. She lowered her lashes and then looked up again, coy and challenging, and he pulled her even closer. He could feel her heartbeat and the rapid catches of her breath as he held her against him. Or was that his own heart and breath? Now was hardly the time to be too analytical. His fingers threaded through her hair to cradle her head. He put his lips directly against her ear. "The first time I saw you, I wanted to kiss you. How do you feel about this?"

She turned her face toward his and rubbed her lips across his jaw. "I feel pretty."

CHAPTER THIRTY-FOUR

Morella Perez was surprised by the incompetence of the two men who were following her, and she wondered who was responsible for their poor training. There were three possibilities, and they were all American. Tweedledum and Tweedledee were either working for the CIA, the FBI, or DHS. There was no way to tell which one without a confrontation, and that was out of the question. She was running late for a meeting, and the person she was meeting did not like to be kept waiting. Best to give the feds the slip and get to where she was going.

Most spooks were trained in surveillance techniques, but the two that were tailing Perez had forgotten the general rule of following someone: If you can see them, they can see you. She spotted their black Cadillac when she glanced in her rearview mirror on US-1, and she could hardly believe that the driver, a guy in dark sunglasses, remained directly behind her. When she pulled into the parking garage in Mizner Park, they got lazy and parked in the same row, a few spaces away.

The shopping mall was an open-air venue, so it was easy to keep an eye on her company without looking back. All she had to do was use the reflective surfaces of the store windows. Instinctively, she took note of their appearance, paying close attention to their clothing and the characteristics that couldn't be easily changed -- such things as height, weight, and shoes.

On foot, it was easy to pop into a store, scoop up some clothing, and find a vacant dressing room. Moving quickly, she changed her blouse and skirt and put on a baseball cap. She paid for the items with cash, then left her old clothes on the counter and walked out with a group of teenage girls.

Tweedledum and Tweedledee didn't notice a thing, and when she glanced back, they were still waiting outside the store.

They would have a long wait.

And a lot of explaining to do.

Back on US-1, heading south, the traffic was light, and Perez reached Royal Palm Estates in less than five minutes. As instructed, she parked on the street and walked into the backyard of one of the homes. Nobody was in the pool, but the deck lights were on, and the waterfall was running. Her sharp green eyes swept the backyard, taking in every detail. A moment later, she heard the sound of footsteps on the deck and turned to see Nicholas Russo coming toward her, a cigarette dangling from his mouth.

"Jesus Christ," she said crossly. "You almost gave me a heart attack."

"Why so jumpy?"

"I don't like surprises."

Russo gave her an apologetic look. "I was afraid you might be followed."

"I had a tail, but I lost them."

"The feds?"

"Probably."

"Those bastards never give up."

"Something to keep in mind."

"I've got more important things to worry about." He told her to take a seat at the table, then joined her. "I'd offer you a drink, but I don't have the keys to the house."

"Who lives here?"

"A woman named Harriet Gold." His scowl deepened for a moment and then, suddenly, he found himself chuckling. "Adam Gold's old lady."

She felt hairs bristle on her arms and neck. "Oh my God. The place might be under surveillance."

"Calm down. Mrs. Gold went back to New York. The feds wouldn't watch an empty house."

"Jesus, I hope not. Why the hell did we have to meet here?"

"Gold's flying back from Cuba. He should be here in a couple of hours. I've got a homecoming gift for him."

"God, I hope you know what you're doing."

"You know me. I don't leave anything to chance." He broke his gaze and looked past her, as if there was something fascinating over her shoulder. He tried to smile, but it came out crooked. "I'm sure going to miss that place."

"What place?"

He pointed to the island on the other side of the canal. "Capone Island. Ever been there?"

"No, but I've heard you talk about it. Are you still looking for that treasure?"

Russo looked over, his eyes dead. "No, I had to close up shop. Too risky to dig, even at night. You'd be surprised how many people trespass." A look of mock irritation crossed his face. "Nobody has any respect for the law."

She let that one pass. "I'm surprised you gave up. You were a bit obsessed with the treasure."

Russo smiled and wiped the sweat off his forehead with the back of his hand. "Well, you know what they say. Better safe than sorry. I can live without the money, and just between you and me, there wasn't that much. Six million, tops. Of course, in 1930, that would have been worth about eighty-four million bucks."

She shook her head admiringly. "How much was Capone worth?"

"Nobody knows for sure, but at the peak of his career he was pulling in one hundred million per year."

Perez digested his answer for a moment, then shook her head again. "Damn," she said. "That's a lot of money."

"Most of it was taken to Cuba for safekeeping. I'm hoping to find it before the commies do. I've got a plan, but you know what they say about the best laid plans of mice and men. Something always goes wrong. Especially when the mice turn out to be rats." He leaned closer, and she could smell the heaviness of his cologne and the cigarette smoke on his breath. "I don't know about you, but I hate rats." He blew a long stream of smoke out but didn't say anything for a while. With a deep sigh, he slumped back in his chair and glared at her. "I knew you were a Cuban spy, but I thought you retired. I had no idea you were still on the payroll."

She floundered before coming up with a response, and it was surprisingly lame. "I don't know what you're talking about."

"Oh, Morella," he said regretfully. "This is disappointing. This is *muy* disappointing."

"Are you drunk?"

Russo tsked. "Morella, please. A little respect." He leaned even closer. "I know about you and Generalíssimo Fernández. How is the old rascal? Well, I hope."

Perez's mouth hung half open in shock, although she quickly recovered. "I barely know the man."

"Really? Who do you speak to when you call his office?" The quizzical expression remained. "I hear you call once a week. Sometimes twice." He threw his head back and grinned, obviously enjoying himself. "You're a regular Chatty Cathy."

She didn't understand the reference, but she knew it was not a compliment. "If I were you, I wouldn't pay attention to rumors."

"You're not me, and you never will be. You're just a means to an end. Nothing more than a good-looking tool."

Perez hesitated, allowing a small grin to slide across her face like a cloud passing in front of the moon. "I don't know what your problem is, but I don't like the tone of your voice." She reached into her purse and pulled out a metal nail file, brandishing it like a weapon. "Try to remember who you're talking to."

Russo's cell phone chirped, interrupting his thoughts. He snapped it open in the middle of the third ring. "Speak to me." He listened without comment, laughed harshly, then said, "*Muchas gracias.* I'll call you later." He hung up and gave Perez a withering look. "They let your boyfriend out of prison, but he's under house arrest."

"I don't have a boyfriend."

"What do you call Ricardo Paz?"

"A loser."

"People who live in glass *casas* shouldn't throw stones."

"Are we done here?"

"Don't you want to know who told me about Fernández and Paz?"

"I already know."

"You do?"

"The general's secretary. The slut that's on *your* payroll."

"Excellent guess. You're not as dumb as I thought. By the way, her name is Angela Borrego. She's half Cuban and half Italian. Born and raised in Havana. Her great-grandfather was the underboss of the Luciano family. He was one of the architects of the Havana Conference."

"Which Havana conference?"

Russo put on a sad smile. "You see, that's the problem with commies. You don't know anything about life in Cuba before the revolution. Let me tell you something. Those who don't study history are doomed to repeat it."

"I didn't come here for a lecture."

He held up a hand, silencing her. "Please, Morella. I'm trying to explain the situation. Angela's great-grandfather was a great man, a man of vision. He understood the potential of Cuba. How the Cosa Nostra could create a criminal empire outside the United States." He searched for some interest in Perez's face, found none, but continued anyway. He told her that the Havana Conference had been held during the week of December 22, 1946, at the Hotel Nacional. The attendees included such notables as Charles "Lucky" Luciano, Meyer Lansky, Frank Costello, Vito Genovese, Albert Anastasia, Joseph Bonanno, Gaetano Lucchese, and Sam Giancana. The conference dealt with mob policies, rules, and business interests. "These men had great plans for Cuba."

Perez sneered. "Those men supported Batista and his thugs."

"The guy who replaced him wasn't much better, or did you forget the last fifty years?"

"You have no idea what you're talking about."

"Look, sweetie, I don't have the time or the inclination to engage in a debate. I only mentioned the conference so you'd understand where Angela is coming from. Where her loyalties lie. She's not a communist, she's a capitalist -- part of this thing of ours."

Perez grimaced and somehow managed to smile at the same time, and she wasn't buying any of Russo's crap. "The bitch is nothing but a traitor."

"Jesus, talk about the pot calling the kettle black."

She looked at her watch. "If you're finished berating me, I'd like to leave."

"What's your hurry?"

"I need to pick my daughter up from school."

"I'll take care of that."

"Excuse me?"

"I'd be happy to pick Benita up from school. If I remember right, she goes to St. Brendan?"

Perez stared at him in icy silence, and he could feel her rage, her pent-up anger about his offer. Finally, she said, "Stay away from my daughter."

Russo looked at her, pretending to be puzzled by the angry reaction. "Why so hostile? I would never hurt your sweet little girl." He looked around nervously, biting his thumbnail. He hesitated just a fraction longer before saying, "I've got big plans for Benita. I'd like her to be my protégé."

A disgusted look settled on her features. "I'll kill you if you go near my daughter. I mean it, you bastard. I'll cut your damn heart out."

Russo calmly lit another cigarette, puffed a tiny cloud of smoke, then held it and admired it. "I was hoping you wouldn't feel that way. Now you leave me no choice." His left hand came up. A small automatic in it. A silencer on the end. He moved the thumb safety lever on the left of the slide up to the fire position. The whole process took about three seconds. "Parting is such sweet sorrow."

Perez felt her stomach twist into a wrenching knot. Seeing the cruel grin on his face, she instantly knew this was the end. For betraying him, Russo was about to kill her. Of that, she had no doubt.

Slowly, deliberately, Russo aimed the pistol at her forehead. Slowly, deliberately, he pulled the trigger. The bullet hit her right between the eyes, spraying blood, flesh, and bone on the deck. He fired two more shots, hitting her in the chest. The impact threw her backward, then she tumbled out of the chair and landed by the edge of the pool.

A hard, swift kick caused her to roll into the water.

When she sank to the bottom, Russo peered over the edge of the pool and said, “They got it wrong. Shit doesn’t float.”

CHAPTER THIRTY-FIVE

The flight from Havana to Miami should have taken one hour, but the departure was delayed due to a slow-moving thunderstorm. Most of the passengers grabbed something to eat or drink, but Gold decided to make a few phone calls. He hadn't checked in at home or at work in a couple of days, which was par for the course, but inconsiderate. Neither call went particularly well. Harriet Gold was on the warpath, driving his wife crazy, demanding that she be allowed to return to Florida. During one of her tirades, she threatened to report her son for elder abuse, and was on the verge of removing him from her will. Irene Kaminski was less hostile, but she was tired of playing telephone tag with her lead investigator. She advised him to stop moonlighting for the feds and return to his day job –– while he still had one.

Gold heard the message loud and clear, but first he had to get back to Boca Raton, which was no easy task. The delay in Cuba put them on I-95 at the start of rush hour, and by the time they reached Broward County they were in bumper-to-bumper traffic. Hillsboro Boulevard wasn't much better, but the worst part was still to come. When they turned onto Alexander Palm Road, they ran into a throng of police vehicles, and several of them were parked in his mother's driveway.

Lights and sirens were off, but it was a hell of a homecoming.

Gold felt something in his gut tighten. "What do we have here?"

Ridge seemed worried, and for good reason. Squeezed between the police cars were two ambulances and a mobile morgue trailer. A morgue unit was typically employed to a mass fatality event, but there were exceptions to that rule. Sometimes the units were requested for individual needs, primarily because they contained a MERC –– a Mortuary Enhanced Remains Cooling system.

The system that was used for cold storage of a crime victim.

Almost instinctively Ridge snapped on her ankle holster. She turned toward Gold, her voice barely a whisper. "Somebody just bought the farm."

Gold stepped out of the car and waited for Ridge to find her identification. He stretched muscles made doubly tired by hours of sitting on a plane, wondering what he was about to find at home. Whatever it was, it wasn't good. "This looks bad," he said out loud.

Ridge stepped out slowly. Little worry lines had invaded her calm image, creasing out from her mouth in rays of subsurface strain. "Never a dull moment, eh?"

"You got that right."

"Thank God you called home."

Gold nodded, knowing what she meant. "Yeah, I was just thinking about that. Is the house still under surveillance?"

"No, I pulled our people off the job."

"When?"

"The day your mother went to New York."

"Well, let's take a look."

"Follow me."

When they walked through the front gate, a small, balding man with thick black spectacles checked Ridge's ID, then waved them forward. The front door appeared to be locked, so they used the side path to reach the backyard. Yellow crime-scene tape had been stretched across the deck and stapled to palm trees surrounding the pool. The Palm Beach County Police seemed to be in charge, but they weren't the only law enforcement agency on the scene. Two FBI agents were taking notes and photographs, and a stern-looking plainclothes detective was snooping around.

A detective named Sergeant Grimes.

Grimes gave them a frosty look, then yawned. He hadn't slept all night, but he looked as if he hadn't slept for a week. He walked over and stuck his nose up next to Gold's and said in a low, mean growl, "What the hell are you doing here?"

Gold gave the rude and abrasive detective his very best, ultra-friendly smile. "I live here."

"You live here?"

"Occasionally."

"What does that mean?"

"When I come to Florida. This is my mother's house."

"Your mother's house?"

"Are you going to repeat everything I say?"

Grimes laughed aloud, a broad, full-bellied laugh that turned heads and drew curious and disapproving stares. Remembering where he was and what had happened there, he winced, then lowered his voice and said, "Jesus, that's rich. I guess they're right. Karma's a bitch."

Gold ignored the sarcasm. "What's going on?"

"Your pool service called the police."

"Why?"

"Something got stuck in your filter." He hesitated, looking Ridge over. Then he said haltingly, "A dead body."

Gold glanced at Ridge, puzzled. He wasn't sure if Grimes was serious. "God, I hope you're joking."

"I don't find murder amusing."

"Murder?"

Ridge dropped her eyes to the bottom of the pool and sadly nodded. "The body's face down, but it looks like a woman."

Grimes folded his arms across his chest and just stared at her. His face was still set in stone. "You have to wake up pretty early in the morning to fool DHS."

Ridge was as calm and composed as usual in the face of adversity, and it was reassuring, Gold thought to himself. She smiled indulgently, then said, "What happened to that woman?"

"She was shot," Grimes said. "Three times. The shell casings were found on the deck."

"Robbery?"

"Nope. Her purse was on the table. Nothing missing, but they did find a metal nail file under her chair."

"Who is she?"

Grimes was silent for a few moments, trying to get his temper under control. He did not like being questioned like a schoolboy. After a while, he said, "Her name is Morella Perez. She lived in Miami. Worked at Sun Coast Realty." He exhaled sharply and gave Gold a look that conveyed his disgust. "Ricardo Paz was her boss. You remember him, don't you, Gold? He's the guy you sprung from jail. The poor Cuban immigrant who was just trying to live the American dream." He spit on the ground. "More like a fucking nightmare."

Gold stood perfectly still, trying to absorb the situation. Every hair on the back of his neck stood straight up, and his skin actually goose-bumped for the first time in years. He cleared his throat the way people do when they want someone to shut up. "Paz didn't kill Morella Perez. They were lovers."

"Hell hath no fury like a woman scorned."

"She wasn't scorned

"How do you know?"

"I just know."

Grimes looked contemptuously at Gold, wishing he could punch him in the nose. "You're getting on my nerves."

"The feeling's mutual."

Ridge interceded. "Take it easy, boys. We don't want to cause a scene." Grimes opened his mouth to protest, but she raised her hand. "Gold is right. You're barking up the wrong tree. Paz is under house arrest in Cuba."

For a moment Grimes said nothing, just stroked his chin. “How do you know that?”

“We just flew in from Havana.”

“Did you actually see him?”

“We actually spoke with him. He just got out of prison.”

“Why did the Cubans arrest him?”

“He snuck into the country.”

“A trumped-up charge,” Gold said. “They wanted to bust his balls.”

Beads of sweat had broken out on the sergeant’s forehead. None of this was anticipated. None of this was easy to swallow. He glared at Gold, then said, “You seem pleased. I guess Paz can do no wrong.”

Gold cracked a smile. “The knucklehead can’t do anything right. But he’s not a murderer.”

Grimes remained silent. But his eyes said quite a bit.

The silence was finally broken when Ridge said, “Forgive me, sergeant. I don’t mean to be rude, but this isn’t your jurisdiction. Why are you here?”

After fishing out a cigarette and letting it dangle unlit from his mouth, Grimes said, “I’m not investigating the murder. I’m working on a related case. The victim’s daughter was kidnapped. Taken on the way home from school. The crime occurred in Miami, so they sent me.”

Gold looked at Grimes like maybe he didn’t believe him. *“Benita Perez was kidnapped?”*

“How do you know her name?”

"I just know."

"Back to that again?"

"Her mother mentioned her to me. I never met the girl."

"Unless we get lucky, you never will."

"Did the kidnapper leave a note?"

"No, there was no ransom request."

"That's odd."

"Depends on the motive –– and who's involved."

"What do you mean?"

"Human traffickers won't demand money, and if they're involved, we've got a big problem."

Ridge seemed a little confused. "I thought you worked homicide?"

"I do, but this is a special case. I've got a hunch that these crimes are connected. Mother and daughter victims. What are the odds of that?"

"Depends on the motive," Gold said. "And who's involved."

Grimes thought about that for a second, then arched his eyebrows. "Are you trying to tell me something?"

"I think you should follow your instincts."

"I intend to."

Ridge looked across the backyard and the canal beyond. The afternoon was bright and sunny, the skies clear, the temperature in the low nineties, a complete contrast to the gloom she felt inside. She took a deep, steadying breath, then said, "We'd like to help you, sergeant."

Grimes felt a surge of anger. "You don't say."

"We can point you in the right direction."

"I don't need any help from the Ricardo Paz Fan Club."

"We can save you a lot of time."

"Save your breath. I'm not interested in anything you have to say."

"Why be stubborn? We're all on the same team."

"Bullshit. If you were on my team, you wouldn't have pulled rank, and Paz would still be in jail."

"For a crime he didn't commit."

"Let me tell you something. You may be the toast of the town in Washington, but you don't know shit from Shinola. I was close to breaking Paz, and if you hadn't interfered, I would have gotten a full confession."

"Don't confuse him with facts," Gold said. "His mind is made up."

Grimes glanced at Gold, then turned his attention back to Ridge. He managed to keep his face impassive, but the skin on his cheeks started to burn. "You don't know these people like I do. You have no idea how they take advantage of our laws. Did you know that Cuban immigrants are allowed to enter the United States without visas or background checks? They come here seeking asylum, but they're allowed to return to Cuba whenever they please. When they go back, they bring money. Lots of money. Money they've stolen in our country. There are Cuban crime rings all over Miami, and they do quite well. They stage auto accidents for insurance fraud, they hijack trucks, smuggle contraband, and sell their Medicare numbers to the highest bidders." He looked at Gold. "Those are the facts, smart-ass."

Ridge took another deep breath and decided to hold her tongue. She struggled with her temper. "I'm sorry you feel that way, sergeant. I was hoping we could work together."

"Not a chance," Grimes said.

"Well, if you change your mind, you can reach me at DHS."

"Don't hold your breath."

"I won't." She glanced toward the pool, then sighed. "When I hold my breath, it makes me blue."

CHAPTER THIRTY-SIX

Gold was secretly relieved when he learned that Ridge was flying up to Tallahassee to consult with her superiors at DHS. He'd been hoping to avoid "the talk," the obligatory conversation about their last night in Cuba, and how it might affect their relationship. Some things, he thought, were better left unsaid. There'd be time to take a stroll down memory lane after they caught up with Russo –– if they were still alive.

Before she left, Ridge made a startling confession. She'd been thinking about their meeting with General Fernández, trying to recall where and when she'd seen his secretary. The answer had come to her while she was staring at the lifeless body of Morella Perez.

"Her name is Angela Borrego," Ridge said. "Her family is well known to law enforcement. They do business throughout the Caribbean. Drugs, guns, money laundering. The usual sources of income. She was on our radar for a while, but then she went underground. Last I heard, she was freelancing for one of America's most wanted –– a mobster named Nick Russo."

Gold shook his head in disbelief. "Are you sure it's her?"

"Yes, I'm sure. She cut her hair and dyed it black, but I never forget a face."

"How the hell did she get that job?"

"If I know Fernández, it had nothing to do with her typing skills."

"Just her undercover skills?"

"I don't know how she slipped through the cracks, but she's perfectly positioned to spy on the general. God only knows what they discuss in the sack."

"Do you think he told her about Morella Perez?"

"I guess so. Of course, she could have blown her cover simply by touching base. Either way, Russo got wind of what she was doing and decided to cut his losses. Why else would he kill her?"

"I can't think of any other reason."

"Neither can I."

"I had a hunch she was still a spy."

"Old habits die hard."

"So did she."

"So will Russo."

"I don't understand why he had to kill her at my mother's house."

"He wanted to send us a message."

"A message?"

"The middle finger."

Gold nodded slowly and with a tired sigh said, "What are you going to do about Angela Borrego?"

"After we catch Russo, I'll send the general a gift. A dossier on his beloved secretary. He's got a lot to lose if word gets out, so I'm sure he'll handle the problem discreetly. Knowing the Cubans, she'll have a fatal accident or commit suicide. Either way, Mata Hari is not long for this world."

Gold frowned. "I thought we were the good guys?"

"What do you mean?"

"Why do you have to throw her to the wolves?"

"If we don't, the Cubans might think that we killed Morella Perez, and that could lead to a nasty reprisal. There's an unwritten rule within the intelligence community. If the enemy hits one of your people, you hit one of theirs. It might sound harsh, but it serves as a mutual deterrence."

"Makes sense."

"I didn't make the rules, but if I were you, I wouldn't lose any sleep over Angela Borrego. Have you ever wondered why there are three hundred thousand Haitians in South Florida?"

"No, I can't say that I have."

"Allow me to explain." She threw him the look of a school principal dressing down a rowdy pupil. "The migration began in 1959, after a Haitian dictator named Francois Duvalier created a paramilitary force called the Tonton Macoute. Duvalier was known as "Papa Doc," but don't be fooled by the name. He was a ruthless dictator who nearly destroyed his country. Under his leadership, the Tonton Macoute kidnapped thousands of people and were responsible for unknown numbers of murders and rapes. They operated in broad daylight and preferred to stone their victims or burn them alive. The corpses were often hung in trees as warnings to others, and family members who tried to remove the bodies for burial often disappeared themselves. Nobody knows exactly how many people were murdered, but the number is somewhere between thirty thousand and sixty thousand Haitians."

"Jesus," Gold said. "No wonder they left the country."

"Duvalier's son, Jean-Claude, became President in 1971. He was known as "Baby Doc," and he ruled until 1986, when he was overthrown by a popular uprising. During his tenure, the Macoute continued to operate, and thousands more were murdered."

"Like father, like son."

"Unfortunately."

Gold's mouth tightened up in concentration. "I appreciate the history lesson, but what's your point?"

"During their heyday, the Macoute had twenty-five thousand members. They were a small army, equipped with the best weapons money could buy. Weapons supplied by the Borrego crime family."

"I see."

"I thought you might."

"Payback's a bitch."

"I don't usually gloat about pulling the plug on someone, but Angela Borrego is different. She's been a willing participant in the family business, and she's got blood on her hands. The blood of innocent Haitians."

Hard to argue with that, Gold thought, and he had no interest in trying. "When are you coming back?"

"Tomorrow night. I'll give you a call before I leave Tallahassee."

"I'll be here."

"Do me a favor, and stay close to home."

"I intend to."

"If you go out, bring protection."

"Protection?"

"You can never be too careful."

"About what?"

"Living." She placed her ankle holster on the table and smiled at him. "You can borrow my backup. Try not to go off half-cocked."

Later that evening, Gold decided to grab a bite to eat at his favorite Italian restaurant in Boca Raton. The place was called Casa D'Angelo, and as usual, it was packed to the rafters, so he was compelled to sit at the bar. The specialty of the house was an oversized meatball swimming in marinara sauce. The dish paired nicely with a glass or two of Brunell di Montalcino, followed by a second course of pappardelle or risotto. While Gold was deciding which to order, a large man sidled up to the bar and sat beside him.

Glancing sideways, Gold noticed that he was a giant of a man, wide neck and barrel chest. He sat stiffly in the leather bar stool, which barely enveloped his considerable bulk. He struggled for a moment to get comfortable, shifting about. *"Marone,"* he muttered, "you need a freakin' shoehorn to fit into these chairs."

Gold looked over and gave him a long, searching look. He thought the guy looked like he was wearing a Kevlar vest under his shirt, only there was no vest, just solid muscle. He had to be at least six feet, four inches tall, maybe more because he seemed to bend forward at the waist, broad shoulders slumped over the bar.

After he placed his order, Gold began to think about Morella Perez, and he realized that Sergeant Grimes had glossed over two salient points. First, the pool service had called the police, not one of the neighbors, which meant that nobody had heard any shots. Maybe Russo got lucky, or maybe he used a silencer. Second, the police had found a metal nail file on the deck, but it seemed highly unlikely that a person would be filing their nails while under duress. He concluded that it was brandished as weapon. Too bad she never got to use the damn thing.

The big man tipped up his glass of scotch, sucked in a small ice cube, chomped it, looked across at Gold. "What do you recommend?"

"Excuse me?"

"What's good here?"

"Everything."

The man flashed a quick grin, then said, "My first visit."

"There's a first time for everything."

"Yeah, that's true. Do you remember the first time we met?"

Gold cleared his throat the way people do when they feel uncomfortable. "We've met?"

"Briefly."

"I don't think so."

"Back in New York."

"I think you're mistaken."

"I think not." Then in a lower voice, he said, "I work for Mr. DeCarlo. I was the guy that frisked you in the elevator."

Shit, Gold was thinking. *How could I forget a face like that? The guy was right out of Central Casting. The real life Luca Brasi.* "I don't think I caught your name."

"Let's keep it that way."

Gold willed himself to remain calm. "What are you doing here?"

Luca Brasi laughed, dispelling the tension. "Relax, pal. I come in peace."

"What do you want?"

"I've got a message from the boss. Some good news."

"How did you know I was here?"

"I was parked outside your house. I would've knocked on your door, but I didn't want to intrude. You had a lot of company."

"What's the good news?"

"First things first. Why all the cops?"

Gold hesitated, formulating his thoughts and considering how much to tell him. He saw no reason not to tell him everything, so he gave him all the gory details, leaving nothing out. "The police are looking at the victim's boyfriend, but he didn't do it."

"How do you know?"

"He's in Cuba. Under house arrest."

"Let me get this straight. They both worked at Sun Coast Realty?"

"That's right."

"And they were lovers?"

"Yep."

"How do you like that."

"Let's get back to your message. What's up?"

"We've been beating the bushes." He wheeled around with narrowed eyes. "We found the guy you've been looking for."

"Russo?"

"No, the tooth fairy."

After nearly a minute of silence during which both men simply stared at each other, Gold said, "Where is he?"

"Close by."

"How close?"

"Big Cypress Indian Reservation."

"Where's that?"

"Somewhere between Lake Okeechobee and Alligator Alley."

"Is that a Seminole reservation?"

"How should I know? Do I look like a tour guide?" He snorted, then rolled his eyes. "Here's the story. The local yokels like to play high-stakes poker. They play on the reservation so they don't get hassled by the cops. One of the regulars is a stoolie named Roman Boychuck. He's the guy that tipped us off." He leaned closer, lowered his voice. "Tomorrow night, Russo will be at the game."

Gold could hardly concentrate on his words, for his mind was scrambling. "How reliable is your source?"

"Exact-a-fuckin-dactly."

"Huh?"

"Spot on."

"Do you know where they're playing?"

"A place called Waylon's Chickee. Some sort of beer joint. Boychuck drew us a map." He passed it to Gold under the bar. "If I were you, I'd come heavy. You need a piece?"

"No, I'm good."

"You ever whack a guy?"

"Nope."

"Let me give you some advice. Keep your mouth shut. No talking. No tough-guy routine. Just walk up behind him, and shoot him in the head. Don't forget to ditch the gun."

Gold was tempted to ask about the cannolis, but this was no time for lame humor. "Thanks for the advice, but we plan to capture Russo, not kill him."

"You'll never take him alive."

"Maybe not, but we have to give it a shot."

"Make it your best shot." He tossed a twenty dollar bill on the bar, then stood. "You may not get another one."

CHAPTER THIRTY-SEVEN

Ridge flew back to South Florida the following afternoon, anxious to hear more about Gold's meeting and to see the map he'd been given at the restaurant. Gold had called the night before, so he didn't have much to add, except for one important detail. According to Luca Brasi, Russo was going to be a tough nut to crack, and he wouldn't be taken alive.

"As long as we take him," Ridge said. "That's all that counts."

"It would be nice to rescue the girl."

"Perez's daughter?"

"She might be with him."

"Let's hope not. We don't need any distractions."

Gold cleared his throat and went into a deep frown. "She might need us."

"We'll cross that bridge when we come to it."

Gold looked at her steadily, saying nothing. Then he gave her the map. "Do you know how to get to Big Cypress Indian Reservation?"

"No, but it shouldn't be too hard to find."

"The game's at Waylon's Chickee, which is some sort of beer joint. It's circled on the map." He tapped the spot with his finger. "Funny name for a watering hole."

"You think so?"

"Don't you?"

"Not really. Many Seminoles speak Maskóki, and in that language, the word 'chickee' means house."

"I see, said the blind man."

Ridge drove, and as they left the airport, she explained that the early Seminole lived in chickees -- or stilt houses -- along marshes, river banks, and swamps. Houses were raised several feet off the ground, and they had no walls. "They were built on thick posts, and most of them had palmetto-thatched roofs." She flashed a quick grin. "When you live in South Florida, ventilation is critical."

Gold nodded as though he'd been thinking the same thing. "Necessity is the mother of invention."

"Yes, and in this case, survival was the father."

"What do you mean?"

"The chickee became popular in the early 1800s, when US troops began to pursue the Seminole Indians. The tribe needed a fast, disposable shelter while on the run, and there were plenty of cypress trees."

Gold hesitated, thinking. "Why were they being pursued?"

Ridge's face showed something like surprise. "I thought you were a history buff?"

"Buff, not expert."

Fair enough, she thought, as she answered his question, sticking to the facts. In 1821, the lives and homelands of many southern tribes were changed forever when troops under the command of Andrew Jackson invaded Florida in order to seize the state's vast riches. Nine years later, Jackson became president and pushed the Indian Removal Act through Congress, pushing many tribes west of the Mississippi River and chasing the Seminole into the Florida swamps. The tribe's departure opened up large tracts of land to white settlements and led to the Seminole Wars, which lasted forty-one years. During this period, most of the Seminole population was killed in battle, ravaged by starvation and disease, or relocated to Indian Territory in Oklahoma.

"An estimated two hundred Seminoles refused to surrender or leave, and they retreated deep into the Everglades, living on land that was unwanted by white settlers. Their main refuge was a place called Big Cypress Swamp."

Gold cocked his head to the side, unnerved by the odd coincidence. "So we're heading to sacred ground?"

"More or less."

"Wonderful."

"Did you expect them to roll out the welcome wagon?"

"No, but I was hoping for a neutral site."

"Beggars can't be choosers."

"No, I suppose not."

"We'll be fine. We just need to mind our manners."

Gold didn't like the worried tone in her voice. "How do you know so much about Seminoles?"

"The Choctaw and Seminole are cousins."

"Cousins?"

"In a sense." She smiled a little, although she didn't feel much like smiling. "The early Europeans were kind enough to lump us together. We were part of what they called the "Five Civilized Tribes." The other tribes were the Cherokee, Creek, and Chickasaw. The Europeans called us civilized because we adopted Christianity, accepted intermarriage with white Americans, and permitted slavery." Gold thought he saw a flicker of irritation in her eyes, but then it was gone, and she shrugged and said, "Red and white are no longer the important colors. Everybody loves green."

"The color of money."

"You got it."

Big Cypress Indian Reservation was located in the southeastern portion of Hendry County, sixty-five miles west of Fort Lauderdale Airport. Despite its meager population, it maintained a thriving casino, swamp safari, entertainment complex, and the twelfth-largest cattle operation in the country. Six hundred tribal members owned about six thousand head of cattle, which grazed on forty-two thousand acres of drained swampland.

Waylon's Chickee was well-hidden, squeezed between an RV park and a commercial turtle farm. Waylon was behind the bar, but there were no customers in sight. He was a fireplug of a man, short and powerfully built, with facial features and skin color more Black than Indian. Ridge stopped to regard him with a wide smile. There were a handful of Black Seminoles in Texas and Oklahoma, but until this moment, she'd never met one. Also called Seminole Maroons, they were the descendants of the free Blacks and runaway slaves who intermarried with the Native American Seminoles in Florida. Back in the day, they lived in harmony with the Indians and were celebrated for their bravery and tenacity during the Seminole Wars.

Waylon sat himself on a stool behind the bar, lit a cigarette, blew a cloud of smoke in their direction, and began without preamble. "If you're with ABT, you're wasting your time. We're on the res, so I don't have to show you jack shit." He took a solid belt of whiskey and wiped his mouth with the back of his hand. "I'm no lawyer, but I know my rights"

Ridge stopped smiling. "You don't say."

"I don't have to answer to anyone but the Tribal Council."

"That right?"

"That's right, sugar."

Not used to being spoken to rudely, Ridge narrowed her eyes and stared at Waylon for a moment before speaking. "If you were a lawyer, you'd know that the holder of a tribal license must maintain an alcohol beverage license with the state of Florida. In other words, sugar, if we yank your state license, you're out of business. *Comprende?*"

"Yeah, I understand."

"Smart lad."

Waylon's demeanor suddenly changed, and for a brief moment there was a crack in the facade, allowing a quick peek at the worried soul beneath the bravado. Switching to an offhand, almost friendly tone, he said, "What can I do you for?"

Ridge regarded him for another brief moment. "What time's the game?"

"What game?"

"The poker game."

"I don't know what you're talking about."

"If I had a nickel for every time someone said that and was telling the truth, I'd have five cents."

Waylon grabbed two beer bottles from the refrigerator, slammed them down on the bar, and then smiled at them. "Drinks are on the house."

"Answer the question, Waylon."

"Some things never change," Waylon mumbled as he twisted the tops off the bottles. He patted his paunch and tried to arrange his wild hair. "We're always being oppressed."

"You're breaking my heart."

"You got a heart?"

"What time's the game?"

Waylon poured himself another shot of whiskey and downed it in one gulp. His hands shook. He was scared. "If I get busted, I'm out of business."

Ridge was a touch confused by Waylon's tone. She had expected the man to be cool, calm, sure; instead, there was an undeniable strain in his voice. She showed him her shield and identification. "We're not from ABT, and we don't care about you or the game.

We're looking for one of the players. A guy named Russo. Do you know him?"

Waylon stopped feeling sorry for himself, sat there a moment, and thought about it. "Yeah, I know him. Bigmouth Italian. Thinks he's Al Capone. He was gonna play tonight, but he backed out of the game."

"Jesus Christ," Ridge growled. "He's not coming?"

"Nope."

She looked away in exasperation. For a moment words evaded her. Then, "Why not?"

"Car trouble. He asked me to pick him up, but I told him I couldn't leave."

Gold did a double take. "He asked you for a ride?"

"Yeah, the guy's got big balls." He barked a quick, short burst of laughter. "I run a bar, not a taxi service."

"Does he live around here?"

"He rents a hunting cabin in the Everglades."

"How far south?"

"Nine or ten miles."

"Have you been down there?"

"Once or twice."

"We need directions."

"I could draw you a map –– if you make it worth my while."

"What's your while worth?"

"Fifty bucks."

Gold smiled. "Sounds fair."

Ridge placed a fifty dollar bill in the bar's gutter, and Waylon went to work, creating a detailed map of the area. She was impressed by the man's artistic ability, but her focus turned to a row of his pen-and-ink drawings on the wall. Waylon had drawn three portraits of Osceola, the great Seminole chief, the tenacious fighter who had initiated and orchestrated the longest, most expensive, and deadliest war ever fought between the US Army and Native Americans. The chief was one of her heroes, and even though he was seldom mentioned in the same breath as Geronimo, Sitting Bull, Crazy Horse, or Cochise, he was still the most successful of all the Indians leaders.

The irony of the present situation was not lost on her. Here she was, a full-blooded Choctaw working for the federal government, protecting the homeland against all enemies, foreign and domestic.

The same homeland that had been stolen from her people.

A strange feeling crept over her, but she told herself to get over it. There was work to be done.

Waylon put the finishing touch on his map, then said, "Have you folks ever been in the glades?"

Ridge answered for both of them. "Not for any length of time."

"Well, if I were you, I'd get to the cabin before dark, and I wouldn't plan on spending the night. One wrong turn and you could find yourselves in a heap of trouble."

"Sounds like Miami," Gold joked.

Waylon didn't think that was funny. "Miami's a walk in the park. Down in the glades there are mosquitoes as big as your fist. Giant spiders and little ones that can kill a person. Wild boars, panthers, and alligators that are fifteen feet long. If you survive those critters, there are six different types of poisonous snakes and a giant monster called a Burmese python. That bad boy can swallow you whole." Another thought crossed his mind, and he smiled mischievously. "Right about now I'd be asking myself a question. What sort of man would rent a cabin in the Everglades?"

A long silence stretched between them. Nobody moved or looked away. Eventually Ridge said, "The type of man who's got a lot to hide." She reached for the map, grabbed a beer, then thanked him and said goodbye in her native tongue. *"Yakoke. Chi pisa lachike."*

Waylon was dumbstruck, but he managed a little smile.

CHAPTER THIRTY-EIGHT

The afternoon was hot and sultry, the air at body temperature and almost motionless. Lightning was playing on the horizon, accompanied by a squall that seemed to be moving in their direction. Rain was a welcome sight, and if they were lucky, a cool breeze might follow, putting a damper on the mosquitoes. They were five miles south of the reservation when it began to pour, causing them to slow to a crawl. Five minutes later, the rain ceased, and the sun peeked through the clouds, intermittently shedding an unsteady glow over the drenched landscape.

When the rain stopped, they got a bird's-eye view of the River of Grass that stretched out before them as wide as the horizon. There were sawgrass marshes, cypress swamps, and mangrove forests as far as the eye could see. The Everglades encompassed some thirteen thousand square miles of wilderness, most of it low and flat, making for poor drainage.

From their position on a narrow rise, it was hard to tell where Big Cypress Swamp ended and Everglades Park began. The terrain was nearly identical and a little intimidating. Not so long ago, in geological terms at least, the whole region was under a vast sea. When the water level dropped, limestone sinkholes formed "ponds," which were now surrounded by domes of cypress. Dry land was scarce, most of it covered by dense hardwood trees and plains of sawgrass.

Beautiful but daunting.

Before long, they found themselves on a dirt road flanked by sawgrass and the edge of a dense wood. "Jesus," Ridge muttered as the car crested another rise, then bottomed out with a thud before she could brake. "I'm glad we've got a four-wheel drive."

On impulse, hoping to relieve the tension, Gold said, "Trivia question. Name the six snakes."

Ridge glanced at him, frowning. "What?"

"The poisonous snakes that live in the Glades. Waylon said there were six different species."

"I don't feel like playing games."

"Come on. Play along."

"No thanks."

"I can name five." He ticked them off on his fingers. "Diamondback Rattlesnake, Cottonmouth, Pygmy Rattlesnake, Coral Snake, and Copperhead. I don't remember the sixth one."

"You still get a prize." She reached behind her and gave him a bulletproof vest. "Put this on. We're almost there."

"Semper paratus."

"I try to be."

"Where's your vest?"

"I won't need one."

"Why not?"

"I'm staying behind."

Gold theatrically used his finger to clean out his ear. "I'm sorry, Sally. I thought I just heard you say you're staying behind."

"You heard right."

Squeezing at his temples, Gold sighed deeply, then looked across at her. "What the hell are you talking about?"

"Our game plan." She drove a half mile further, then stopped the car and shut off the engine. "There's Russo's cabin. Off to the right at three o'clock." She looked at him squarely. "We have no chance of catching him by surprise. Not out here in this wide-open terrain. The property is probably booby trapped, so we can't circle around. We need a different approach –– something he won't expect."

Gold eyed her thoughtfully. "What did you have in mind?"

"I think you should knock on the door and ask him to step outside."

"Come again?"

"When he shows his face, I'll shoot him."

"What if he comes out shooting?"

"You'll be wearing a vest."

"What if you miss?"

"I won't miss. I'll be thirty yards away. From that distance I could hit a target with my eyes closed."

"I'd prefer you kept them open."

"I intend to –– and so should you. Try not to step on a snake."

Gold winced. "Maybe we should call for backup."

"I didn't come this far just to come this far."

"I was afraid you'd say that."

Ridge told him to walk up to the cabin slowly and stay on the road, which made him tense. Once again, he was putting his life on the line. Risking way too much for his comfort level. She seemed pretty calm for a person who was about to take down a killer.

But then, she'd been here before.

She patted Gold's shoulder solicitously and raised an eyebrow. "Ready to roll?"

Gold's palms were sweating, and he kept rubbing them on his pants. He leaned against the car door, trying to appear relaxed, but in truth he was afraid. He felt his stomach churn, as if what he wanted to do most was to run –– to get the hell out of there. "Did you bring a rifle?"

"In the trunk."

"I hope it's a good one."

"The best money can buy."

Ridge had a small arsenal in the trunk, but she only took out one weapon –– an M40 sniper rifle. The M40 was a precision bolt-action rifle used by the US Marine Corps. It was basically a highly modified Remington 700 hunting rifle, chambered to fire 51mm NATO cartridges, equipped with a custom 25-inch barrel and topped off with a Schmidt and Bender scope, capable of no more than half-an-inch deviation per 100 yards.

Frowning in concentration, she made a few adjustments to the scope. "My papa use to tell me, 'Don't bring a knife to a gunfight.' The same could be said about this situation. Why use a regular rifle when you can use an M40?" In one smooth, swift move, she pulled back the bolt and loaded a single cartridge. There was a moment of strained silence, and then a look of anxiety crossed her face. "Remember to hit the ground as soon as he comes outside."

Gold pulled himself together with a visible effort. "Remember not to miss."

"You have my word."

Gold gripped hold of his nerves, squared his shoulders, and headed toward the cabin all alone. The cabin was situated at the end of the road, in the middle of a clearing that needed more clearing. Once it might have provided decent shelter, but as a closer approach made clear, the years had not been kind to it. The roof had been replaced with sheets of rusting corrugated aluminum. Trees and bushes grew wild around the porch, blocking off the sides. Most of the windows were too dirty to see through, and many of the glass panes had been replaced with plastic, which was starting to decompose in the sun.

Halfway down the road, Gold spotted a Jeep Wrangler partially concealed by tall sawgrass. The hood was open, but he couldn't tell if the engine was running. Sensing movement, he forgot about staying on the road and went to investigate. Suddenly, he tripped. He lost his balance and fell down hard, with his elbows breaking his fall. He ignored the pain shooting up his arms, more concerned about the pond he had fallen into and the mud that was sucking him down. He pushed himself to his hands and knees, then crawled to dry land. He glanced back to see what had caused his fall. Something solid. He expected to see a fallen tree, but not more than a yard away was a small alligator, nestled in the mud and leaves.

Gold scrambled to his feet, his knees shaking, his stomach in a tight knot. When he turned toward the Jeep, he got another unpleasant surprise. Russo was staring at him from under the hood, and right beside him, propped against the grille, was a .30-30 lever-action Winchester.

Russo's jaw dropped, astonished to see Gold standing in front of him, covered in mud. He let the silence between them hang for a moment. Very gingerly, he reached for the rifle, cocking the hammer with his thumb. To Gold's surprise he began to laugh, hard and long. He had to wipe his eyes before he could speak. "What the fuck are you doing here?"

Gold's mouth opened and shut several times before anything intelligible came out. "Well, this is awkward." He closed his eyes and sighed, letting his hands dangle at his side. For a moment he looked like he was going to faint. Then he opened his eyes and smiled, breathing deeply until he had a grip on himself again. "Watch out for that first step. It's a doozy."

Russo instinctively looked over his shoulder, then scanned the road. He glared at Gold and literally spat out the words. "Dumb shit. How did you find me?"

"The usual way. There's no honor among thieves."

"Fucking rats."

Gold stood still, breathing hard, fighting down panic. "I hate to be the bearer of bad news, but you're under arrest."

Russo's lips twisted into a strange smile. "You came out here to arrest me?"

"Citizen's arrest."

"Jesus, you're a piece of work."

"We can make it official when we get to Miami."

Russo shook his head in a slow, disapproving way. "Are you a religious man, Gold?"

"Time to start praying?"

"Unless you've got a better idea."

"Actually, I do. Why don't you put down the rifle and come with me? I'd like you to meet someone."

"You're not alone?"

"Of course not."

"Let me guess. You drove out here with that Indian broad. The bitch that's been tailing me."

"Agent Ridge is anxious to meet you."

Russo grinned. "You mean anxious to shoot me."

"It doesn't have to end that way."

"I can't think of a happy ending."

"If you shoot me, she'll drop you like a sack of potatoes. She's got a sniper rifle, and it's pointed at your head."

Russo inched closer to the hood of the Jeep. "I don't think she has a clear shot. If she did, we wouldn't be talking. Why don't we continue this conversation in the cabin? Turn around, and walk over here. No tricks."

Gold did as he was told, wondering what Ridge was thinking. She was furious that he ignored her instructions, but she focused on the problem at hand. She squinted through the scope, cursing softly under her breath. She didn't have a clean shot, and now she had to deal with a hostage situation. She froze, heart pumping madly. There was nothing she could do. Nothing but wait.

Russo grabbed Gold's belt and pulled him close. Using him as a shield, he began to walk backward, toward the cabin. They were almost on the porch when the screen door flew open and Benita Perez ran out screaming. After that things happened so quickly that, in hindsight, it would be impossible to put them in sequence or to say which were causes and which effects.

Ridge fired a warning shot at Gold's feet, hoping to distract Russo and make him loosen his grip.

Gold threw his head back, butting Russo in the face.

Russo cursed, but he held onto Gold's belt.

Benita ran down the steps and charged at Russo, spewing obscenities. She was half-dressed and in a wild fury, her fists flailing at him. "You bastard!" she screamed. "You filthy bastard!" She kept coming, stabbing at him with a metal nail file -- the same type of file that her mother had dropped near Harriet Gold's pool. One of her stabs struck Russo's neck, puncturing an artery. Blood began to squirt from the wound. He spun around and tried to take ahold of her wrists, but she fought him off. Two seconds later, a bullet crashed through his skull, and he fell to the ground.

Gold's reaction was delayed a bit. It took several moments to process the scene, to realize that Russo was actually dead. Benita gave him a long and piercing look. He started to say something to comfort her but couldn't seem to find the words. From the corner of his eye he saw Ridge walking toward him, the sniper rifle flung over her shoulder. He hesitated, perhaps fearing in advance what response his question would elicit. "Did you see what happened to me?"

Ridge gave him an icy look. "I told you to stay on the road."

"I thought I saw something."

"You almost got yourself killed."

"Almost only counts in horseshoes and hand grenades."

"Spare me the humor. You're on my shit list." Scowling, she walked over to Benita and asked if she was okay. "We got here as fast as we could."

"He kidnapped me."

"I know."

"I need to call my mother."

"In a minute."

Benita's chin began to quiver, then her entire face collapsed. She sobbed into her hands. "He raped me," she whispered. "I tried to stop him, but I couldn't. He was too strong."

Ridge hugged her, then stroked her cheek, wishing with all her heart that she could say something to ease her pain. "You're a strong young woman," she said quietly. "You'll be all right."

Benita looked frightened, staring into Ridge's eyes, trying to reassure herself that she was safe. "Is he...dead?"

Ridge patted her reassuringly on the back. "You don't have to worry about him. He won't hurt you anymore."

Gold muttered something under his breath, then said, "The son of a bitch had one annoying habit. Breathing." The instant the words were out of his mouth, he cringed, mentally kicking himself. That had been a stupid thing to say under the circumstances.

It took a moment for the joke to register, but Ridge finally chuckled. She looked as though a great burden had been lifted from her shoulders. Her matter-of-fact response made the whole situation more surreal. "I guess it's true. What they say about fate. Karma never forgets an address."

Gold nodded. "I won't forget this address either."

"Neither will I," Ridge said. "Let's get the hell out of here."

"After you, Annie Oakley."

THE END.

ABOUT THE AUTHOR

Stephen G. Yanoff is a 20-year veteran of the insurance industry and an acknowledged expert in the field of high risk insurance placement. He holds a bachelor's, master's, and doctoral degree from the Texas A & M University System.

In addition to CAPONE ISLAND, he is the author of five other award-winning mystery novels, including THE GRACELAND GANG, THE PIRATE PATH, DEVIL'S COVE, RANSOM ON THE RHONE, and A RUN FOR THE MONEY.

He has also written several highly acclaimed historical non-fiction books, including THE SECOND MOURNING, TURBULENT TIMES, and GONE BEFORE GLORY. The author's history books have won numerous gold medals for "Best U.S. History Book of the Year."

A native of Long Island, New York, he currently lives in Austin, Texas, with his wife, two daughters, and an ever-growing family.

For more information about the author or his books, readers can go to: www.stephengyanoff.com